Beneath the Patchwork Moon

ALSO BY ALISON KENT

The Second Chance Café: A Hope Springs Novel

Beneath the Patchwork Moon

A Hope Springs Novel

ALISON KENT

Text copyright © 2014 Alison Kent
All rights reserved.

Published by Montlake Romance, Seattle

www.apub.com

ISBN-13: 9781477848456
ISBN-10: 1477848452

Library of Congress Control Number: 2013910016

Cover design by Anna Curtis

Printed in the United States of America.

To Walt,
for everything you went through during the writing and
rewriting and re-rewriting of this one.
I couldn't love you more.

CHAPTER ONE

Oscar Gatlin's BMW had plunged off the Edwards Plateau along the Devil's Backbone on a Sunday evening at 7:42 p.m. That day in September had been sunny and clear, the sunset a watercolor wash of pink and orange, the only sounds to be heard those of tires chewing up the uneven road and the whoosh of resistant wind as his car and the one following sliced through the late summer night.

With her eyes closed, it was all as real to Luna Meadows today as it had been ten years ago—the sights, the sounds, even the smells of cedar and juniper and pine. She'd been driving an appropriate number of car lengths behind Oscar and Sierra. Her window had been down, her elbow on the doorframe, the wind—dry and hot and fiercely cutting—whipping at her hair held wound around her hand. Her seat belt had nearly strangled her.

She'd been clinging to any hint of warmth, the pain of the trip's purpose chilling her, when ahead on a too-sharp curve, tires had squealed, and Oscar's car fishtailed, then vanished. Screaming, she'd slammed on her brakes, spinning in the loose gravel at the road's edge and crashing into a barrier of boulders, barely escaping her friends' fate. Her eyes, already closed at impact, saw all too clearly the empty space where the

BMW should've been. She remembered nothing else—except the secret Sierra had taken to her grave.

She opened her eyes onto the present, ten years since the accident, eight years since she'd set foot on the property in front of her, which she, as of this morning, now owned. She'd driven by this house—Sierra's house—plenty of times, watched the elements stake their claim, but she'd done nothing. How could she move on with her life when Oscar and Sierra never would? What right did she have to plan for the future when her friends had had theirs stolen away? But now, because of the house, she had to.

All this time it had sat forlorn, mourning the family who'd left it abandoned. Luna missed them, too—day in and day out, beneath moonlight and sunlight, from behind painful scars. She missed them with more longing than she'd felt for anything else in the whole of her twenty-eight years. She missed them as if they'd been her own. In many ways, they had been, she mused, straining to hear the voices that had once filled the rooms, picturing the four youngest Caffey children running circles around the legs of the two older, the siblings' parents laughing the loudest of all.

Leaving her car in the driveway, she walked up the pebbled path to the porch where the swing still hung from now-rusted ceiling chains, where the two big rockers and the table between had weathered to the gray of old age. The lawn, in the past always lush and verdant, was dried to straw and littered with rotting leaves and acorns. The dark wood of the structure was a victim of creeping moss and clinging mold and ground cover crawling above its station.

Key ring in hand, Luna searched out the one that fit the front door and let herself into the house. The interior was dark and stale, the living room lit only by beams of light able to cut through shade trees, through windows smeared with the dirt of time and absence. The lamps had long since gone dark. There were no bursts of illumination shining into the hallway from beneath closed bedroom doors, no glow from the kitchen as Angelo, the oldest Caffey child, stood in front of the open refrigerator searching for something to eat.

Angelo. Angel. While Sierra, a cellist, had attended the St. Thomas Preparatory School on a music scholarship, Angelo had played quarterback for the Hope Springs High School Bulldogs. Workshops and recitals often kept Sierra away, but Luna never missed a game, begging rides from her father to those across town, even those across the state during play-offs. Harry Meadows loved his football. And he'd loved pretending his daughter did, too.

With so much of her life tied to this house, Luna hadn't been able to bear the thought of it falling into a stranger's hands. She'd lost Sierra. For all intents and purposes, she'd lost Oscar, too. Once the Caffeys had left Hope Springs, the house had become her only connection to a friendship that had shaped her. Learning it was in foreclosure and would most likely be razed, she'd jumped; if the house was gone, no one in the family would have a reason to return to Hope Springs. And that had been the deciding factor.

Seeing the deterioration wrought by the years, however, she realized listening to her heart and ignoring her head might not have been particularly smart. Who bought a place the size of the Caffey homestead without a walk-through? Fortunately, the time spent waiting to close had allowed her to settle on an idea for using it, one that would honor the friends she had lost. But she couldn't move forward until she knew what she'd paid for.

Tucking her keys into her front pocket, she gathered up her hair and knotted it at her nape. She needed to know if it would be worth her time to sort through what the Caffeys had left behind, or if hiring a service to empty the rambling two-story farmhouse would save her as many broken fingernails as it would heartache.

She pulled a chair toward the refrigerator and stepped onto the seat. Opening the first of the high cabinets above, the one where Sierra had hidden things she wanted to keep out of her younger siblings' hands, Luna reached inside, finding nothing but light bulbs and sports tape and loose batteries, and wishing she'd thought to bring gloves. And a flashlight. Next time for sure, she mused, and then she went still, cocking her head at the sound of footsteps on the back porch.

She didn't need permission to be inside a building she owned, but no one knew she was here, and no one else had reason to be. She eased from the chair, her second foot touching the floor as the kitchen door opened and a man moved to fill the entrance. He stood still as he took her in, his face shadowed, his body large. Her heart thundered in her chest and her ears.

She thought she'd seen knives in the block beside the stove, but she'd never reach it before he did. She dipped her fingers into her pocket, her hand wrapping around her key ring, the keys jutting between her fingers like spikes.

The man stepped over the threshold, ducking beneath the door's facing. The light he'd been blocking followed him in, and in that moment recognition dawned, her stomach tumbling to the floor and unraveling toward him like a spool of thread.

"Angelo?"

"Hello, Luna," he said, his voice deep and sure and aged like fine wine.

Angelo Caffey wore the last eight years well. He was thirty now, to her twenty-eight, and she very much appreciated the differences wrought by his age. Though he'd left it loose and brushed away from his face, his black hair was long enough to pull back at his nape, and strands of silver shimmered in the sea of black. She wasn't surprised by the touch of gray.

Even knowing nothing of his current life, she was well aware that he'd earned those stripes. His strong jaw was darkened with several days' growth of beard, his nose blade-straight and narrow, his full lips pulled into a too familiar smirk. His body wore years of use that showed on his arms in muscles and scars. His hands were a mess of healed cuts.

"You scared me," she said, her voice a weak quaver.

"Wouldn't want that now, would we?" He closed the door, shutting out what light had been shining through. Shutting them in the room that was full of old pain, and Sierra, and that very sad silence, and moments only the two of them knew.

She wanted him to reach back and fling the door open. She wanted him not to know how nervous she was. She wanted to ask him a thousand questions. She wanted him to leave. She wanted him to stay. But most of all, she wanted to know why he was here. And if, somehow, he'd known she would be.

After eight years in the wind, Angelo Caffey, her first love, her first lover, had returned to Hope Springs. *Be careful what you wish for, Luna. Be very careful indeed.* "When did you get to town?"

"No, sweetheart," he said, stepping closer to where she stood, and smelling of sunshine and sawdust and the spicy soap she knew well. "You're in my house now. I get to ask the questions."

CHAPTER TWO

Except it isn't my house anymore, is it? Angelo thought. The five acres, the house, the woodshop and the barn, the contents of all three. The trees his siblings had climbed. The one he and Luna had, too. She'd snatched up everything his family had left behind, when he'd been waiting for the day of the razing. Now his connection would remain. The only one he had to Hope Springs.

Except that wasn't the way of things either.

Neither of them had moved, and she took him in as if daring him to challenge her right to be in this room. Here where his parents' closest friends had prepared food and washed dishes and brewed coffee and poured drinks for the dozens of others attending Sierra's wake. It had been an endless, miserable, suffocating day. He'd spent it torn between crumbling from the unbearable loss and being a rock for his siblings and folks.

Luna Meadows had spent most of it anesthetized in a hospital bed.

She looked nothing like he'd expected after all this time, yet she looked the same as when he'd last seen her. Her eyes were as expressive as ever, her hair as dark as ever. She was no more than five-foot-six to his six-foot-two, but she'd worked out, or filled out, or something. Her arms were buff, her nails short, her hand holding her keys, a clever weapon, as wrecked as his.

So, yeah. The same but totally different.

"You here to see what you spent your money on?" His upper hand warranted something pithier, but it was all he had, and since she had every right to be here . . .

She shook her head, looked down, and scuffed the toe of her shoe at the floor, as if she didn't have it in her to argue. Especially when she knew as well as he did that neither of them was going to give an inch. That was their history. Why they'd fit so well. Why in the end neither had been able to back down. Why things between them couldn't be fixed and had died.

Finally, she swallowed. Then she said, "You know what today is."

Ten years ago today his sister had lost her life in a car accident, but that didn't answer his question. "I do."

Her hands were back in her pockets when she shrugged, when she looked at him. "Then you'll understand why Sierra's on my mind."

There was a lot of that going around. "I'd tell you you're not welcome, but since you own the place . . ."

"Oh, Angelo," she said, her accompanying sigh heavy. "You made your feelings perfectly clear the day your family moved."

No. He hadn't. But he could understand why she thought so. He took in the colors in the scarf she wore, wondering what they meant to her, how bright the shades of red would look in the sun, because in the light from the windows they made him think of blood.

He nodded toward the chair and the open cabinet. "Looking for something?"

She waved one arm in an expansive gesture. "How many meals did your family sit here to eat? How many did I? I guess I thought . . . I don't know what I thought. That there wouldn't be so many personal things. So many reminders."

"I think that was the point of their leaving. They didn't want to be reminded anymore."

She seemed to let that sink in, returning the chair to the table. The left front leg caught on the same nick in the linoleum it always had, and Angelo closed his eyes.

"I could get a service to come in and clear everything away, but I don't want to throw out something your parents or your siblings . . . or you," she said, and he looked at her again, "might want. Maybe something of Sierra's?"

He'd argued with his parents that they pack up her room, that one day they'd want her school pictures, her recital trophies, the long tail of her hair still bagged for the donation she'd never managed to make. But they'd left every bit of her behind, as if doing so made it easier to forget she was gone. What a laugh.

Since the day she'd been ten and drawn a wooden spoon across the strings of their father's flamenco guitar like a bow, Sierra had been the family's Great Musical Hope, a ticket out of a life where nobody ever had enough of anything—money, time, attention, privacy. Milk. Clean clothes. Sleep. No one was going to forget.

"We all took what we needed to take." It wasn't an answer, but it was all he had, off-balance as he was, thinking about his sister today, feeling hollow. "What are you going to do with the place?"

"Actually, I've set up a nonprofit, and we're opening an arts center." She said it as if thankful for the change of subject. "It's a community-based initiative, and it'll be run by parents and educators who've recognized the need and want to fill it."

Uh-huh. "You're not a parent. You're not an educator. Why would you be involved?"

"Because I want to be."

"Giving back lets you buy your way out of a guilty conscience?"

"I don't have a guilty conscience."

"You're not bothered by telling lies? Or at least not telling the truth?"

Her chin came up. "I'm not here to get into this, Angel."

Something in his gut caught and held at hearing her use the nickname. Arguing with her was so familiar, and so strangely comfortable. He didn't want to be feeling either thing, and yet they were there, those emotions, caught in the web of all the others they'd left tangled because they'd been too young, and too hurt, to fight their way out of the knot.

They weren't so young anymore.

"Grow up, Sierra."

"Angelo—"

"You're old enough to get into trouble, you're old enough to get out of it."

Luna wrapped her fingers over the chair back and squeezed until her knuckles whitened. "You know Sierra hated it when we argued."

She was right about that, he mused, shoving his fists into his pockets. "I can't tell you how many times she stopped me from following when you stormed out of the house."

"She knew how much I liked getting in the last word with you."

Because then, like now, Luna had always wanted to win. "Is that what you're doing here? Having the last laugh on the Caffeys? Or is there something else you're trying to prove?"

She shook her head, her hair a wave of motion as it fell from its knot. "What could I possibly have to prove?"

"Then why?" he asked, walking toward her.

She waited until he stopped, as if she couldn't speak while watching him, as if she didn't trust him. Or as if she didn't trust herself. "Funding has been cut to arts and music programs across the country. The Hope Springs school district isn't exempt. And St. Thomas only offers so many scholarships. Not every child who deserves it will get the help Sierra did."

Something his family knew well. "And here I thought you needed a tax write-off for all that money you're making selling scarves to Hollywood."

She blinked once, twice. "You know what I do?"

"I know some," he said, wishing he'd kept his mouth shut. "Angel . . ."

Her voice, when she said his name, was tiny and soft, as if his keeping up with her had some meaning, when the truth of it was he was only here for the answers she'd never given him. With the house no longer in his family, this might be his last chance to get them. "I want to know what happened the night Oscar Gatlin's car went off the Devil's Backbone and down the ravine."

A shiver ran through her as her gaze fell. "You know what happened."

He waited until she'd stilled, then crooked a knuckle beneath her chin and lifted it. "No. I know what the investigators think. I know what you told me . . . before. I want to know the rest. I want the whole truth. I want to know what you saw. I want to know why you were there. Why, if you were following them, your car crashed at all. I want to know all of it."

"Angel—"

But he was on a roll, and he let her go as he looked around the kitchen and into the living room beyond, the mess of the place giving him an idea. "How long do you think it will take to clear out this house? Top to bottom? Drawers, closets, attic, barn, all of it?"

"I don't know. Five days maybe?"

"Can you get the power and water turned on today?" he asked, looking back at her.

"I should be able to," she said, nodding.

"Then let's do it. I'll stay here instead of at the hotel on the interstate. We'll clean it out. We'll hash it out." He paused. Maybe giving her an inch would help get him his mile. "I'm sure there are more than a few things you want to know from me."

She swallowed, then said, "There are, but I don't think this is the best way—"

He couldn't think of a better one. The two of them. This house. Their past. "Yes or no, Luna? Yes or no?"

CHAPTER THREE

If Luna had had the faintest clue Angelo would be at the house today, she wouldn't have come. Or maybe she would have; she'd never been given the option, so how could she know? And why—oh why, oh why, oh why—had seeing him again had to happen like this, when he was unexpected, and she was ill-prepared, and the past remained suspended between them, sharp-edged and unapproachable? But that question could wait. Others, not so much.

What was he doing in Hope Springs?

Why hadn't she asked?

How had he known she'd bought the house?

Where was her brain, saying yes instead of no?

He wanted five days of her time. Five days she'd never thought she'd have with him. Five days during which she'd have to watch every word she said, because along with her time, he wanted answers. Would the risk of his finding out about the accident weekend be worth learning how and why things between them had gone wrong? Apparently, some part of her thought so. She just wasn't sure it was the part she should be listening to.

That was the thing about having been confined to bed after the accident. Luna had learned so much as a fly on the wall, listening to her parents' friends talk—about Oscar Gatlin's condition, about how long it would take her own injuries to heal, how like this person's brother or that person's wife she might always walk with a limp. She was eighteen years old. The thought of being in physical pain for the next sixty or more had been another turn of the screw. Her body hurt, her soul ached. She missed Sierra desperately.

But the most unsettling talk she'd heard was that of the Caffey parents falling apart, leaving their four children still at home struggling. Leaving Angelo, who'd returned to Cornell after Sierra's funeral, to act as head of household, though he'd been but twenty, a college sophomore, and half a continent away. Yet not once during the next two years had he let on how bad things were.

It wasn't until the day his family moved that she found out. How his father's furniture orders had been canceled when his grief got in the way of his work. How the stitches in his mother's quilts had grown uneven; then the quilts themselves were left unfinished. With his parents' savings depleted, bills went unpaid and the collection calls started. The house went without a new roof, the car without new tires. The yard went to seed. Why his parents thought Angelo was equipped to handle all of that when his money was earmarked for school and living, his time for studies and work . . .

For so long, Mike Caffey had been a local institution, building furniture in Hope Springs longer than Luna had been alive. The coffee table in her parents' living room was Mike's, as were the matching lamp tables. Even the shelving unit still in Luna's bedroom had come from Caffey Furniture.

Whereas it now held the docking station for her iPod, her library of escapist thrillers, and framed photos of her scarves torn from the pages of entertainment magazines, it had once been stuffed with Beanie Babies, cluttered with bottles of glittery nail polish, covered with little sticky-note Polaroids of her friends.

Over the years the tiny pictures had fallen, the adhesive losing its tackiness to time. She'd picked them up when she'd found them, tossed some in the trash, taped others into her yearbooks. Only one remained in place, tied there with a ribbon she'd glued to the back. One she'd taken of Sierra climbing into the family's car in front of St. Thomas the day they'd met.

Angelo had been standing in the open driver's door, yelling across the roof for her to hurry. Sierra had turned back to Luna, rolling her eyes and sticking out her tongue, and Luna had taken the shot. Not focusing on Sierra, but on her brother, his dark hair falling over his forehead, his mouth open, his narrowed eyes hooded as he'd looked from his sister and caught Luna's gaze.

And oh the way he'd taken her in, ignoring whatever it was Sierra was saying to study her . . . her face, her hair, which was waist-length then, too, and held back with a band, her body, which he couldn't see much of at all, covered as it was by her uniform, but which responded as if he could see all of her. As if he wanted her.

Of course, none of that longing had meant love at first sight. Even after they were together, they'd fought like dogs. That history, the accompanying memories, would no doubt make the next five days epic. She wasn't sure she was up for epic. She wasn't sure, honestly, if she was ready for Angelo at all.

Once back at home, Luna went in search of her mother. She found her propped against a stack of pillows on the family room sofa, an open book facedown in her lap, a cloth on her forehead, her eyes closed. A glass of fizzy, iced Sprite and a sleeve of saltines sat on the coffee table within reach, as if she'd just settled in to fight the morning sickness that plagued her every day long past.

Julietta Meadows smiled as Luna plopped into her father's recliner, kicking off her shoes before tucking her legs beneath her. Her bare feet squeaked against the leather seat.

"How're you feeling?" Luna asked, though the answer was obvious.

"Like I should know better." Her mother shifted to sit straighter, setting her book on the floor as she looked to where Luna sat. "All the times we talked about birth control when you were growing up, you'd think I wouldn't have gotten myself knocked up at forty-six years old."

"Momma! Don't say that." As close as Luna was to her mother, and to her father, they were still her parents. She preferred not to think about the intimate side of their relationship—even if her mother's unexpected pregnancy made that intimacy more than plain.

"Well, it's the truth," she said, reaching for her drink and toying with the straw as she brought it to her mouth. "And it shouldn't have happened. But it has, and your father and I will love this little bean just as much as we love you. It'll be harder to deal with the lack of sleep this time, but that's the difference twenty-eight years makes. I've gotten used to my nine hours a night." She shifted again, took a small sip of soda, and let it settle on her stomach before speaking again. "How goes the arts center planning?"

Luna thought about sidestepping the obvious until her mother felt better, but the obvious was why she was here. "I saw Angelo today."

ALISON KENT

"Angelo Caffey?" her mother asked, her frown caught
between curiosity and disbelief.

Luna nodded. "I went by the house, and he showed up
out of the blue. I didn't see a car, so I didn't realize he was
there until it was too late."

"Until he found you in the house?"

"Yeah." There was no need to elaborate. Her mother knew
the significance of today's date; it was the same date Luna's
hip had been broken, the same date her month-long confine-
ment to bed had begun and she'd taken up weaving. But her
mother didn't know what had happened the weekend before
the accident. Or all Angelo had meant to her before walking
away for what she'd thought was good.

"Huh. Does he know you bought the property?"

She nodded. "I don't know how, but yes."

"Do you think he'll get in your way?"

The very question had plagued Luna since she'd driven
away from the house. She shrugged, curling deeper into her
father's chair, his dip in the cushions, his imagined warmth.
"I'm more worried about the Gatlins' reaction, but Angel has
it in him to cause trouble. He's still very angry."

"Angel." Her mother smiled, then sighed. "I'd forgotten
you called him that."

"I don't know why I ever started. He's not the least bit
angelic."

"Do you want him to be?"

The question surprised her. "What's that supposed to
mean?"

Her mother took another sip of her soda, returned the
glass to the table, and pulled a cracker from its sleeve. "He's
beautiful, yes, but he possesses few other angelic traits. If he

16

did, he wouldn't have been the boy you had such a crush on in high school."

Heat flushed up Luna's neck to her face, and she wondered, not for the first time, if her parents had suspected how far her relationship with Angelo had gone. "He's who he is. I'm who I am. High school was a long time ago. Though since I still have the same bedroom, it's hard to tell," she said, latching onto the change of subject and leaving Angel behind. "Seriously. Who lives with their parents until they're twenty-eight years old?"

Her mother laughed softly. "In this economy? More young people than you think."

But Luna was shaking her head. "I understand staying for economic reasons. But I don't have that excuse. I lucked into a very lucrative profession. I've just been too lazy to pack."

"I don't think your still being here has anything to do with being lazy."

But it had everything to do with Sierra and Oscar and the accident. "The baby is going to love having her own suite of rooms. If you wanted to buy her a pony, there's almost enough space to build a stall."

Her mother chuckled, then grew pensive. "It'll be strange, Skye filling those rooms with her things instead of yours being there. It'll be even stranger not to have you here to run my errands."

That made Luna smile. She'd been running them since the day she'd gotten her driver's license. "I'm happy to stay and help out. I've waited this long, and the loft isn't going anywhere. What's a few more months?"

"No, you'll go because it's time."

It had been time for years. Her mother was just too nice to say so. "You mean you don't like having your adult daughter still living at home as if she were a child?"

"Of course I love having you here," she said, closing her eyes for a moment as she drew in a slow, steady, stomach-settling breath. "You've needed to be here, and I can't imagine what it would've been like not knowing you were just down the hall. But a new baby means a new schedule, new priorities, new everything. It's a turning point in all of our lives."

Was that what Angelo's return was? What the next five days would bring? "You didn't have to get pregnant to get me to move out, you know. You could've brought in movers while I was weaving."

"Funny girl," her mother said, reaching for her soda again and bringing the straw to her mouth. "I'm glad you'll have enough space for your loom, too."

"The light in the loft is amazing. I can't wait for you to see it. I'm so used to holing up in my shed, all that sun and blue sky might distract me."

"Who knows? It might show you new ways to tell your stories."

Except she wasn't sure what was going to happen with her weaving now that she was so busy with the arts center. "Do you realize how little weaving I've done the last few weeks?"

"You've been occupied elsewhere. That's to be expected."

"Yes, but I need to be working on Patchwork Moon's winter holiday line." The boutique in Austin where her collection was sold was expecting the new items by mid-October. Labor Day had already passed, and she was nowhere near being done. "I'm so far behind."

Her mother took a sip of her drink and swallowed, her face paler than just moments ago. "Quality over quantity,

Luna. Your scarves becoming more exclusive won't hurt your reputation or, I'm quite sure, your bank account. If anything, I worry about you suffering without what weaving provides."

She'd thought about that, too, the drying up of her emotional well. "I'll have plenty to keep me busy."

"It's not about staying busy. It's about nurturing the part of you you've poured into your craft. Yes, the arts center will easily fill your hours, but you can't neglect the artist inside of you."

"I'm not so sure I've ever been an artist. The weaving . . . it gave me an outlet for the grief. Everything I was feeling, losing Sierra . . . I put all of that into the scarves. Sometimes I wonder if I'd had to find the words instead of the right color of yarn, maybe I wouldn't still be dealing with the loss years later. I'd be over it. Or at least at peace with it." And even as the words left her mouth, others rose to taunt her.

She would never be at peace as long as she was living a lie.

"There are some things in life we never get over, or make peace with," her mother was saying. "They're just there, a part of us. They make us who we are. Your accident changed everything. You became a celebrity in your own right because of it. Don't ever regret that, or feel guilty about it. You survived. And you've dealt with it positively. So many others wouldn't have had your strength or coping ability."

"Any strength I have is due to you and Daddy. You're the best parents I could imagine having."

Her mother chuckled. "I seem to recall more than a few times in high school you holding a different view."

"It was high school. What does anyone know in high school?" She left her father's chair and moved to sit on the floor at her mother's side, holding her hand, damp from the cloth and cool from the glass of iced soda, lacing their fingers, pressing their palms together. "Skye's going to be so lucky. Not only will she have the best parents in the world, she'll have me."

"That's the part that worries me," her mother said, working hard to keep a straight face.

"I promise to never let her wear a tiara. And only the best in scarves."

"Speaking of accessorizing, I still can't find the necklace your father's mother gave me. I have no idea what I did with it. I hadn't even thought about it until recently. I gave you the one from my mother, and I'd like to give Skye the one from his."

"The gold cross with the five opals? I wore it to Sierra's last spring recital, but I'm sure I gave it back to you."

"I'm sure you did, too. And I'm sure I would've put it back in my jewelry box, but I can't find it."

"Maybe it'll turn up when I start packing . . . meaning I should probably get on that."

Her mother brought their joined hands to her mouth and kissed Luna's knuckles. "Are you leaving soon? It's getting late."

Luna nodded, waiting to hear the offer her mother made every year, ready to respond the way she always did. This was something she had to do alone, no matter how much she longed to have her mother's arms around her while there.

But her mother didn't say what she'd said on this date for the last nine years, suggesting they go together, mourn together, remember. Another turning point. A significant one. The first step in drawing the veil between the present and the past. Luna didn't know if she was ready. What she did know was that it was time.

"I do need to go," she said, pulling her hand from her mother's, getting to her feet, and then leaning down to kiss her mother's forehead. "I love you."

"I love you, too, my firstborn girl," her mother replied, cupping her cheek with her palm, her eyes as misty as Luna's. "I could never love you more."

CHAPTER FOUR

It was 7:42 p.m., and Luna shivered as she placed the bouquet of white calla lilies atop Sierra's headstone. As hard as it was to believe, today's commemorative visit was the tenth she'd made, mourning Sierra even longer than she'd had the girl in her life. She thought at times it wasn't natural, her attachment to her friend. Thought, too, her guilt at surviving her own accident wouldn't have lingered as long were it not for the truth of what they'd done that weekend.

When Angelo had accused her earlier of not being honest, it had taken all the willpower she had not to blurt out every detail she'd stoppered up like a genie in a bottle, fearing the havoc the truth could wreak. It was the first time since the accident she'd been tempted to tell all. She had no idea why, unless it was the combination of the date and Angel's appearance, and the recent urging from her conscience to come clean. And that was the hardest thing to understand.

Why, after all this time, was the genie knocking?

The sound of a car purring to a stop, the engine going silent before the door opened and closed, brought her back to the words on the simple granite marker. *Sierra Gracia Caffey. Our pride. Our joy. Our daughter.* So simple, but nothing else needed to be said—though every time she read the inscription, Luna added the words *my friend*.

Tracing the engraved name with a fingertip, she found herself smiling. Oh, how Sierra had hated her middle name. She'd said it might as well have been *gracious* for all the people who got it wrong, or *gracias* for all those who thought she was thanking them for asking when she said it.

Bringing her fingers to her lips for a kiss she then placed on the headstone, Luna mouthed a private good-bye, her heart heavy. Tomorrow she'd return to the present and think more about the future that had started to feel very real: moving into her own place, starting work on the Caffey-Gatlin Academy. Both terrified and excited her as, she supposed, did all leaps of faith. And then there were the next five days she'd promised to Angelo, a promise she hoped she wouldn't regret. But next year she'd be back here again, because so much of her life had been defined in the very moment her best friend had lost hers.

Turning to go, she looked up, stopping almost as soon as she'd taken a step, and wishing for another path to her car. Hers was blocked, the man standing there with his hands shoved in his pockets obviously waiting for her. She'd known she wasn't alone, having heard the car's arrival, but to find Oliver Gatlin on the tree-lined path from the parking lot that wound through the grounds . . .

She couldn't think of anyone she wanted to see less, except, as always, he was hard to look away from, making her uncomfortable as she approached. While Oscar had been a teen heartthrob, deep dimples and smiling green eyes and a shock of dark hair always falling forward, Oliver was something else.

Male model something else, all sharp cheekbones and elegant nose. A mouth with a natural smirk. Eyes to match Oscar's beneath a hooded brow. Feathered lashes like a chimney sweep's brush.

"Excuse me," she said, rather than ignoring him the way she wanted to as she walked by. Why had he come here today of all days to leave his mark on her private communion with her friend? Really, though. It spoke to who he was—entitled, selfish, uncaring . . . the opposite of everything his brother had been.

He turned and followed as she made her way to her car. "I heard you bought the Caffey place."

It was hardly a secret. She stopped, glanced back. "And that brought you here why?"

"I like knowing that family's connection to Hope Springs is severed for good. Except for that," he said, nodding toward Sierra's grave. "Too bad they had to leave her here."

"You're a jerk, Oliver," she said, the urge to strike out rising as she started walking again.

His footsteps sounded close behind. "And your good friend wasn't? The friend who ruined my brother's life?"

She spun, jabbed her finger toward him. "Have you ever thought you might have it all wrong? That Oscar cost Sierra hers? He was the one driving, after all. Or have you forgotten about that?"

His brow lifted. The corner of his mouth followed. He looked from her finger to her face, his hands at his hips, the tails of his blazer flaring. "You're the only one who would know, aren't you, since you're the only one who saw what happened?"

Why was he questioning who'd been behind the wheel? She couldn't fathom. "You're right. I am. So you'll just have to take my word for it, won't you?"

"I heard Angelo's in town."

"He is, yes," she said, her keys now in her hand, this conversation ridiculous, Oliver keeping pace at her side where the path widened.

"Not for long, I hope."

"He'll be here as long as he needs to be for what he's doing," she said, walking faster, wishing she could run and escape his long stride. "And before you ask, no, I don't know how long that is, and it's not your business anyway."

"Unless I make it my business."

"Good-bye, Oliver. I'd say it was nice to see you again, but it never is."

"I drove out to the crash site this morning," he said, and Luna's steps slowed, her feet moving on their own, her mind whirring. "Have you been back there since the accident?"

She shook her head, unable to imagine a reason to return, or one he would have, and rushing now, desperately needing the safety of her car. The locks clicked and the lights flashed as she hit the button on her key fob. But she wasn't fast enough.

Oliver reached the Audi the same time she did, blocking her with his hip from opening her door. "Someone's put up a new cross. I thought it might've been you. The original was on its last legs when I was through there this summer. I was hoping that would be the end of it, but I guess your girl here had other friends."

She hadn't known there was a cross at all, though she knew the custom and shouldn't have been surprised. What surprised her was hearing about it from Oliver. Why hadn't anyone else told her? "Move, please, so I can get in."

He moved, but only to lean against the car. "There were a couple of bouquets and stuffed bears when I got there around eight, I guess it was, but there were a dozen or more, a whole furry zoo, by the time I climbed out of the ravine."

Her stomach tumbled, and it took her several seconds to catch her breath. "What?"

"There were a couple of bouquets—"

"No." Her heart was beating so hard she was certain he could see the movement in her chest. "What did you say about the ravine?"

"I climbed into it. Then I climbed out of it."

"Why?" She couldn't even . . . What was he saying?

He crossed his arms, looked toward Sierra's grave. "Ten years, and I'd never seen where the car landed. Where Oscar landed."

"And you wanted to? Because . . . you thought it would be a nice way to memorialize the date?" Was he insane? She couldn't breathe. *She couldn't breathe.* "Will you move? Please? It's late. I need to go."

No dice. In typical Gatlin fashion, Oliver stayed where he was, waiting for what he wanted. Doing whatever he had to do to get it. Determined to win. "Hard to believe anything from the accident would still be down there to find. Or that anything would've survived the elements. But that's the thing about a convertible. No top. Stuff goes everywhere. Falling into places no one thought to look."

Was he saying he found something? "Oliver, just spit it out."

"Who is Beth Johnson?"

"I have no idea."

"Let me try this again." He pushed away from the car to loom over her. "Have you ever heard of an attorney named Beth Johnson?"

An attorney. *Oh, boy.* "Honestly, Oliver," she said, gripping her keys harder. "I have no idea what you're getting at."

"I found a plastic document file. Worse for wear, obviously, after ten years, but still mostly sealed. The papers inside had some water damage, but it had been wedged in a crevice beneath a rocky outcrop. Lots of the words were pretty clear."

"Okay. I care about this why?"

"You're going to pretend this folder didn't come from the accident? From Oscar's car?"

She didn't know what to say. She didn't know how she was still standing. She could barely feel her fingers when she reached for the handle and pulled open the door. "Ten years, Oliver. I can't imagine that it did."

"The one date I could make out was September. Ten years ago. So maybe you'd better start imagining."

Then he slapped his hand to the roof of her car and walked to his, leaving her there to wonder how soon her bottled-up past would crack open. And what the genie would do with all of her secrets once it was free.

∾

After her visit to the cemetery, Luna was emotionally wiped out, but she was also too tired to sleep, and that sent her to her weaving shed. She'd return tomorrow to the house on Three Wishes Road. She wasn't up to seeing Angelo again. Not yet. Not until she'd digested what Oliver Gatlin had told her.

Oscar and Sierra hadn't shared with her any of the details of the arrangements they'd made. Their attorney's name had never come up. But Oliver finding the document file in the ravine and being able to make out the words he had worried her. She was worried most of all by the date. That made it hard to believe the paperwork had belonged to anyone else.

She wondered if he'd researched Beth Johnson before coming to the cemetery. If he knew who the woman was and had been fishing for a reaction, or a confirmation of his suspicions.

Whatever he'd been up to, Luna didn't think she'd ever been more grateful to Sierra and Oscar for keeping her out of the legal loop. She only hoped what she didn't know couldn't hurt her with Oliver, because if she wasn't careful, what she did know was going to cause her grief with Angelo.

As always happened, once she closed herself inside her weaving shed, the outside world fell away. She loved her weaving shed, loved that it had once been used to store the tools her father used in his trade. When he'd built his larger shearing barn, he'd converted the building for her, finishing the inside with a hardwood floor, adding insulation, installing the lighting and climate controls she needed.

Throwing the shuttle of weft yarn through the shed of the warp, she thought back to her first conversation with Kaylie Flynn, who'd so quickly become such a close friend after they'd met earlier this year. The other woman, having returned to Hope Springs to open a café, had asked Luna why she wove scarves and not larger items. Her answer rose now to mock her. A short attention span. Instant gratification. With the right yarn and design inspiration, a scarf took almost no time at all.

But for the Caffey-Gatlin Academy's fund-raising auction, she'd committed to five larger pieces sized for use as throws or shawls. She was hoping to trade on the success and reputation of her Patchwork Moon label and bring in some serious cash. Every bit of the work would be worth it, every cent raised vital, but she would be treating herself to a serious massage and a vacation once all was said and done.

It had been a while since she'd sat at her loom for any length of time. She would feel it later, in her back and her shoulders, her hands and the muscles of her arms. For now all she felt was the work, the colors in this piece taking her back to the day she'd met Sierra, the black and pine green plaid of their school uniforms, the flecks of gold in Sierra's brown eyes. The deep emerald of the lawn fronting the St. Thomas Preparatory School. The acorns dropped by the oaks scattered across the grounds like tiny sorrel umbrellas.

Tonight she had Luigi Boccherini's cello concertos playing, the music a soothing background noise while she worked. She'd heard both Oscar and Sierra play from Boccherini dozens of times, and the familiarity of the melodies made the birth of her friendship with the other girl an easy story to weave. The music, however, was not loud enough to drown out the sound of the door opening, or her father's soft footsteps on the hardwood floor.

She smiled to herself as she pulled the beater toward her to tighten the yarn, then set the shuttle aside and spun around on her stool. "If you're trying to be sneaky and quiet, it's not working."

Harry Meadows stopped walking midstep, like a kid caught in the act of being mischievous. He was tall and limber and

29

had yet to go gray. Even the scruff on his face remained dark. Just not as dark as Angelo's. Though why her every thought had to turn to Angelo . . .

"I didn't want to disturb you," her father said, shoving his long-fingered hands into the pockets of his khakis.

She loved her father to death, but this one thing he'd never understood: It took almost nothing to disturb her, and then it took forever for her to get back on track. Working the loom was an easy, repetitive motion. It was seeing the story in the pattern and colors that demanded her focus.

But since he rarely came to find her unless he had something on his mind, she gave him a welcoming smile as she stretched her arms overhead and her torso side to side. "I love you. You never disturb me."

"I believe the first," he said, returning her smile and coming closer, pulling up a stool matching hers to sit. "But we both know the second is a big fat lie."

She held up her thumb and index finger. "Maybe a little bit of one."

"You've been out here quite a while," he said, his brown eyes sharp as he took her in. A father's concern and miss-nothing gaze. "Do you need anything? You skipped supper. Tea? Something stronger?"

His good manners had him offering the obvious, though he knew she never ate or drank more than water when working. The habit had gotten her into trouble more than once, when she suddenly found herself dizzy and on the verge of collapse. "I'll come in for a bite in a bit. I'd like to make some progress on this piece if I can."

His mouth quirked ruefully. "If you can find your groove again, you mean."

She leaned forward to wrap her arms around him, breathing in Ivory soap and sun-dried chambray. "I'll find it. But I won't ever again have this moment with you, so tell me what's on your mind. It's not like you to come out just to check on me."

"I'm that transparent, huh?" His smile was soft, his humor good.

Her sister was going to be *so* lucky. Just as she had been. Just as she was. "Or predictable, anyway."

"Guess I can live with that."

"So . . ." She watched as he pulled his mouth to one side the way he did when he had something he didn't really want to say. "Spit it out."

"Your mom tells me you saw Angelo Caffey today."

Ah, that, she mused, and nodded. She'd seen him, she'd argued with him, she'd made a deal with him. But there was no reason her father needed to know about that. Not tonight, anyway. He most definitely did not need to know any of the whys. She wasn't quite yet settled with the whys.

He took in her nod, asked, "Does he know about the academy?"

"That there will be one? Yes. That it will be named after Sierra and Oscar?" She shook her head. "I'll tell him. But we've got some other things to work out first."

"Oh?" Her father crossed his arms and swiveled on his stool. "Such as?"

Honesty being the best policy . . . "Things I should've said to him a long time ago."

"About the accident? Or about Sierra?"

"Are those my only two choices?"

"They're the ones that make the most sense. They're the two things you and Angelo have in common. You didn't attend the same school or share the same circle of friends. He was older than you, a boy . . ." He let the sentence trail, as if struck with thoughts he hated to voice. "Unless there was something between the two of you I never knew about."

"Besides my crush?" she asked, grinning and hoping her father would forgive her the little white lie should he ever learn the truth.

"Yeah," he said, his grin more reluctant. "I did know about that."

She let that settle into the mess of upset she'd been fighting since Oliver Gatlin's revelation, the pressure behind her breastbone creating an incredible ache. "I saw Oliver Gatlin earlier. At the cemetery."

Her father grew pensive, focused, his eyes narrowing. "Yeah? What did he want?"

She picked at a chip in her nail, took a deep breath. "He told me about a new memorial cross at the accident site. He'd been out there this morning."

"Paying his respects?"

"More like digging for information."

"Information about what?"

If she got through this without throwing up . . . "That weekend . . . Everyone knows, has known for years, that Oscar wasn't at his music workshop, and Sierra and I played hooky from art camp."

Her father nodded sagely. "And everyone has always wondered what you three were really doing."

That same "everyone," realizing she wasn't going to answer and wanting to spare her the hurt, had eventually stopped asking. "I know. But I promised Sierra I would never tell anyone."

Frowning, her father ran one hand back and forth over his short-cropped hair. "What do you mean?"

"I want to tell you," she said, her throat closing around the words. "But it's so big, and so many people are involved, and it's going to cause so much hurt. And I promised Sierra."

"And you think Oliver's going to find something and beat you to it."

He was quiet for several moments after she nodded, several long moments during which Luna's body was stiff with nerves. It was so unfair for her to mention this to him. She knew that. But she needed his advice, and he would understand that, even without her putting her plea into words.

"Sierra's been dead for ten years, Luna," he finally said, then hands on his knees, he pushed down as he used the leverage to gain his feet. "You're the only one holding yourself to the promise."

"Oh, Daddy," she said, sorrow nearly drowning her. But he was halfway to the door, and then he was walking through, letting it close softly on its own instead of slamming it.

But she heard the slam in her mind, because she knew he'd stopped himself only so as not to disturb her further. That was the man he was, thoughtful of others even when wounded. She hadn't been thoughtful at all. And these latest wounds, they were on her.

Every single one of them.

CHAPTER FIVE

The next morning, Luna left the farm early, using the private entrance to her suite rather than stopping in the kitchen for breakfast. She wasn't in the habit of telling her parents how she'd be spending her days, but with Angelo in town, and her mother and father both aware, she couldn't imagine not caving under their scrutiny.

Oh, they wouldn't come out and ask, but they'd know. Just like her mother always knew not to accompany her to the cemetery. Just like her father always knew she needed to hear his plain truth.

And now she had Oliver Gatlin's revelation to deal with. Unbelievable that he'd found detritus from the accident, but it made sense Oscar and Sierra would've had the paperwork with them. If the plastic of the folder hadn't torn enough to damage the papers inside . . . She didn't want to think about what his discovery would've meant if the contents were fully legible.

First Angelo demanding answers, and now Oliver finding clues to the truth. Was her father right that she was the only one holding herself to the promise she'd made Sierra? Or had her friend's death severed that bond, leaving her free to share the secrets? And how was she supposed to do that exactly? Bring everyone together for a slide show? A PowerPoint presentation?

Yeah, that would be a fun time for all. Especially after seeing the anger neither Oliver nor Angelo had been able to let go. She didn't understand the destructive emotion lingering. The pain, yes. But obviously neither man had processed his grief. Both were still looking for someone to blame, and she filled the bill.

She was the one who'd walked away from the accident. Or crawled away, rather, dragging her broken body from her own car. But her injuries didn't seem to matter to either man. All they knew was that she was the sole survivor—though her living in her parents' home all this time spoke volumes about that particular truth.

Her mother was right: it was time for her to get on with her life, time to cut the ties binding her to the past and the tragedy stored there. Unfortunately, she mused, pulling into the Caffeys' long driveway, shutting off her car, and watching the front door open as if Angelo had been waiting at the window for her to return, that would also mean losing her connection to the boy, the man, who took up a very large place in her heart. Sierra she would always have with her, but Angelo, her Angel . . .

He wore scuffed work boots, worn jeans that rode low on his hips, and a gray athletic T-shirt washed to nothing but threads. If she held it to the sun, she'd be able to see right through it. What she saw now was the outline of muscles, a thatch of dark chest hair, absolutely no fat, and biceps she had never imagined when picturing him all grown-up and his own man. Though hadn't he always been his own man? Just not aged as he was now, beautiful and so richly seasoned.

35

She pushed away the thoughts. What good would they do her, making her long for . . . something, she wasn't sure what, that she couldn't have? He didn't want to be her friend. He certainly wouldn't want to resume their previous intimacy. Admiring him with more than a quick glance would only leave her frustrated. And since the next five days would have them both inside the house, the proximity close, the tension high, she didn't want to be fighting an attraction she feared would give Angel any sort of edge.

Nope. Best not even go there, no matter how tempting he was.

"I was beginning to wonder if you'd changed your mind," he called as she opened her door and set one foot on the ground. Saying nothing, she swung her other leg from the car and stood, pocketing her keys after hitting the lock on the fob. Still silent, she made her way up the sidewalk to the porch, where he leaned against a support beam, arms crossed.

Funny how after the lecture she'd just given herself, she still wanted to grab his shirt in both hands, hold it to her face, and breathe deeply of who he was now. Instead, she said, "Not a chance."

He took her in. Head to toe. And a second time, lingering. Her boots were suede. Her sweater cashmere. Her scarf, well, a Patchwork Moon exclusive. "You don't exactly look dressed for work."

That was the thing . . . "About the five days—"

"Uh-uh." He pushed off the beam. "No reneging."

"I'm not reneging. But I do have a life. Commitments. Professional and personal." She was so behind on her weaving she feared her winter holiday collection would suffer, and she'd barely begun thinking about her spring. Then there were all the plans for the center she'd set in motion before knowing she'd have Angelo to deal with. And one of these days, she really did need to pack. "I know what we agreed on—"

The corner of his mouth pulled into a smirk. "But you want out of the deal."

"No, though I need at least four hours a day for me. My business. And everything I've got going on with the center. Plus, I've just bought a loft—"

He cut her off with a huff, the corner of his mouth tugging upward. "Got tired of all the sheep jokes, did you?"

He'd teased her as often as anyone, and she just stopped herself from rolling her eyes. "You live on a sheep farm, you live with the sheep jokes. Not much to be done about it."

"I guess not," he said, though she could tell he was having a hard time not laughing, and that surprised her. Humor was the last emotion she'd expected from him today.

She took advantage, using the break in the tension between them to ask, "You never told me what you're doing here. In Hope Springs."

He stuffed his hands in his pockets and shrugged. "Figured I'd better come see what I might want before you got rid of it."

"What happened to taking everything you wanted when you left?" she asked, because she couldn't imagine that was the whole truth.

"You didn't own the house then," he said, as if the name on the deed made a difference.

Why it would, especially to him . . . She thought back to yesterday, when he'd mentioned her selling scarves, and wondered what else he might know. "How did you find out?"

"I hear things," he said, after a long moment spent weighing his response.

She hadn't heard from him in eight years. She didn't even know where he lived. "But apparently not that your family had stopped paying the mortgage?"

Something she couldn't identify flickered in his eyes. "We don't talk."

That wasn't an answer. At least not to the question she'd asked. "If you'd known about the foreclosure, would you have stepped in to keep it from happening?"

This time his shrug was a lot less sarcastic and more a gesture of having no answer.

"You don't know if you would've saved the house, and yet you want to make sure I don't destroy anything you might want." His logic made her head hurt. "You can't have it both ways."

"Yet here I am and here you are."

Because that had been his plan? She broke the hold of his impenetrable gaze, squinting through the front window as if she could actually see inside. What she saw instead was his reflection. It was just as striking. Just as stirring.

Her heart ached in ways—and for things—she wasn't sure she understood. "Did you start going through the rooms last night? Or did you decide to wait for me?"

"I worked in the shop," he said, giving a jerk of his head that direction. "There are some tools out there I could use. I'll buy them from you."

So he still did woodworking? Did he build furniture like his father had? Had he finished his architecture degree? "You don't have to buy them," she said, turning to face him again. "Anything you want, it's yours."

"It's business, Luna. Don't be sentimental. You could sell them to a local carpenter and put the money back into your center."

"Does that mean you're a carpenter?"

He huffed. "Are you fishing?"

She had been, but now that he'd called her on it, she changed her mind and the subject. "I haven't told you, but we're calling the center the Caffey-Gatlin Academy."

He leaned his head to one side, popped his neck, leaned it to the other, and did the same. "Yeah? Are you telling me now because you want to know how I feel about it?"

"No. I'm telling you to tell you. If I wanted to know how you felt, I'd ask." But she did want to know. She wanted that fiercely.

"You tell Merrilee and Orville Gatlin yet? See what Oliver thinks about having his family's name connected to mine?"

"I don't care what he thinks. And I really don't care what you think either. I just wanted you to hear it from me, rather than anyone else who'll be around."

A deep frown creased his forehead. "What do you mean? Who'll be around?"

Oh, that's right . . . "I bought the place before I had the idea for the arts center. I couldn't bear losing the connection to Sierra. But since we'll need more room than the house provides, I've hired a contractor to look into putting up something that will better suit our needs."

"So all three buildings . . . You're taking them down?"

Why did that seem to bother him? "I'm thinking about it. But we're just in the initial discussion stage. Nothing's been decided."

He nodded as if relieved, and again she wondered, what she was missing? After what had happened between them, after the way he'd left—her, his family, Hope Springs—surely he had no lingering attachment to the place.

And yet something had brought him here. "Having looked around since yesterday, do you think we'll need more than five days? Because if that's not enough to get you finished and back to . . ."

"More fishing?" he arched a brow to ask.

She arched one, too. "Isn't that what we're doing here?"

"Touché," he said, then added without her having to pull on her line, "Vermont. I'd be getting back to Vermont."

Now she was even more confused. If he lived in Vermont, how did he know about the foreclosure or her scarves? "And that's where you'd be using the tools?"

"I work for a furniture builder, so yes," he said, nodding. "It's where I'd be using the tools."

She bit her tongue against mentioning anything about his following in his father's footsteps. She didn't want to burn a bridge they'd only just started to cross. "Okay then. I'll be back tomorrow. I promise. If waiting a day to get started messes up your schedule, we can work through the night or something."

"Don't worry about it. I didn't really expect to get five days out of you."

"Then why did you ask for them?"

"Good question."

As aggravating as always, wasn't he? "You'll get your five days." If she had to rework her week's appointments, she would. She headed across the porch for the steps, then stopped. "Oh, and if you happen to run across a necklace you don't recognize, please let me know."

"I won't recognize any necklace, so if I find one I'll set it aside."

"Thank you. I've lost one. Apparently years ago," she said, and waved a hand. "It belonged to my grandmother. She gave it to my mother. I borrowed it for one of Sierra's recitals and haven't seen it since."

He considered her as he stacked his hands behind him and leaned against the porch beam again. "And you want to give it to your daughter one day?"

Smiling, she shook her head. "Actually, my mother wants to give it to my sister when she's born. Her name's Skye."

His tone was taken aback when he asked, "Your mother's expecting?"

Luna nodded. "Unexpectedly so. I'll be old enough to be my sister's mother."

"Huh. And after being an only child all this time."

She didn't think she'd ever feel like anything else. "Both of us, Skye and I, will have been raised that way, if you think about it. Neither of us will have what you had, all the running and screaming and laughing with your siblings."

"Yeah, well, that was a lifetime ago," he said, bumping his head against the beam, contemplative.

"I loved coming here because of that," she said into the peace that seemed to be settling between them. "It was so quiet at home."

"I could've used some of that quiet," he said, his tone almost regretful but still tinged with what sounded like anger.

"The grass is often greener."

"Or you don't know what you've got till it's gone."

"Sounds like you miss them."

"I miss . . . normal," he said, pushing off the beam to look across the yard. "Not cringing when the phone rings, expecting bad news. Not wondering how much I can afford to keep out of my own paycheck. Not waiting every day for another shoe to drop. Not hoping there are no more shoes."

She hated that his family's demands had been so hard on him. "I wondered if things between you had changed after . . ."

"After they disowned me?" He shook his head.

That made her sad. "I never meant for that to happen."

"Neither did I."

"They must hate me so much," she said, and took a deep breath. "Sierra. Then you."

His heavy-lidded gaze found hers. "'First you will come to the Sirens, who enchant all who come near them.'"

Angelo Caffey quoting Homer. Her world was upside down. She cocked her head, considered him. "Is that what you think I am? A Siren?"

The grin that pulled at his mouth spoke of knowing her well. "You always were, Ms. Meadows. You always were."

Day One

TUESDAY

Perhaps even these things, one day,
will be pleasing to remember.
—Virgil

CHAPTER SIX

Tuesday morning, Luna started work in the kitchen, picking up where she'd left off the day Angelo had found her. While she'd looked through cabinets and drawers, he'd brought a stack of moving boxes inside, dropped them on the kitchen table, and silently set about assembling them, taping the bottoms, lining them up along the wall.

She'd asked him about some of the things she'd found: the coffee cup his father had never been without, white with black musical notes scattered about and the size of a pint glass, the teapot his mother had used every morning at breakfast with Darjeeling, every evening at the Caffey family hour with chamomile. He hadn't been interested in either, or in any of the pots or pans or small appliances or gadgets or even the knives.

She'd filled two garbage cans, which Angelo had carried out to the Dumpster. It had arrived shortly after her, not long past seven. Sadly, there wasn't much worth donating. Time had taken its toll. Bugs and mice and, judging by their leavings, larger varmints had used the abandoned house for shelter. She'd yet to run into any that might cause her to scream, but then she'd been raised on a farm. She wasn't much of a screamer.

After two hours in the kitchen, she was beginning to doubt five days would be enough for just this one room. An exaggeration, of course, but not by much. The house was filled with nooks and crannies, and the Caffey family had put all of them to use. Who needed five bottle openers? Five packs of five hundred wooden skewers? Five cabinets filled with empty spaghetti sauce jars? Who did everything in fives? Certainly not her, because three more hours of this and she'd be on the phone to a cleaning service, forget Angelo and his five days.

Stepping off the back porch into the beautiful September morning, she breathed deeply of the warming air and lifted her face to the sun. She wasn't an outdoors nut—she had no trouble sitting in her weaving shed for hours at a time—but seeing all that clutter had her thinking about hiking boots and hiking trails and, well, hiking. Instead, she took off around the house, looking at the siding and the gutters and the window frames. She didn't know enough about construction to tell what was in good shape, but she could definitely tell what was bad. As sad as she'd be to see the house go, it was probably for the best.

A quarter of the way around it, she reached the window she knew best, the one Sierra had used to escape her first-floor bedroom more times than Luna could count. And she only knew of the times when she'd escaped, too, or stayed behind and waited up to let Sierra back in. Who knew how often Sierra and Oscar had arranged to meet past her curfew? How far down Three Wishes Road she'd had to walk to climb into his car?

How quiet they must've been, maybe rolling his convertible until they were far enough from the house to start it without being heard. Or perhaps they hadn't used his car at all, but had sneaked off into the woods surrounding the property, climbed into the Caffey children's tree house, and lain together until dawn, planning their future, talking of music, sharing their dreams, becoming one.

Luna had never had a real boyfriend. She'd flirted, been flirted with, gone out for fast food with groups of both male and female friends, done the same with concerts and movies and swimming trips to Barton Springs. But no boy had ever found a place in her heart the way Oscar had in Sierra's. No boy except for Angelo, and their relationship, at least during her sophomore year of high school, couldn't really be called one. They were both full of lust and curiosity and insatiable desperation, too young to know if they were doing anything right.

It was only later, after he'd graduated and left for Cornell, that they'd talked. Really talked. Epic phone calls she'd paid for with long-distance calling cards, buying several at a time with money her daddy thought he'd given her to spend on new shoes. Hearing Angelo's voice when she'd picked up the private line in her room, or when he'd picked up from nearly two thousand miles away, had been the best parts of her days.

Once she'd graduated, started weaving, and had the time and money to meet him halfway for an occasional weekend in Louisville, Kentucky, or Nashville, Tennessee, she'd been desperate for each first glimpse of him, desolate after the last. But boyfriend had never been the right word to encompass what Angelo Caffey had been to her.

She wanted that feeling again; it had been so long, and she missed it—the giddiness, the intoxication, the thrill. Sierra had felt it for Oscar, and Luna was a complete believer in its existence. She'd witnessed the love shared by her friends

Tennessee Keller and Kaylie Flynn. She knew well that time's joys and hardships had only strengthened the love between her parents.

She'd seen the look in Mike Caffey's eyes when he'd gazed upon his lovely Carlita. As young as Luna had been in those days, listening as Sierra's father played his guitar, watching his face while he'd watched his wife's, she'd been moved by the couple's emotional bond, swearing if she reached into the air she could grab the feeling and hold it. It had been that palpable. That defined.

Even now from beneath Sierra's window, she could almost hear Mike's flamenco guitar, though he would never have left it behind. What he had left were memories. As much as Luna had loved watching Sierra's mother with her needle and thread, doing so was made even better when accompanied by music . . . whether Mike's guitar, Isidora's ukulele, Emilio's mandolin, or Sierra's cello.

Slowing her steps, Luna returned to the present, realizing she wasn't imagining the guitar at all. The sounds, plaintive and somber, yet full of something harsh, were coming from inside the house. There was only one person who could be making them. And she hadn't even known he played.

Quietly, she returned to the back porch. The kitchen door creaked when she pushed it open, but Angelo continued to pluck and strum the strings, to strike the heel of his hand against the wooden body for emphasis—an emphasis she wasn't sure how to take.

She found him in his parents' bedroom, one hip cocked on the edge of the window seat, the guitar on his thigh, the other foot on the floor. His eyes were closed, his head moving as he played, a dip of his chin, and a darkly narrowed frown when, judging by the change in the song's tenor, he must have felt something brutal and sharp.

What she felt was indescribable as she recognized his pain, the sensation slicing through her like a garrote. Her chest clutched, reaching for air, for blood, for all the things she needed to stay alive. And yet listening to him play, seeing him entranced by the work . . . It made her swoon. And ache. For him. Because of him . . .

A sob caught in her throat, and she gasped with it. His fingers stilled; his eyes opened. He kept his gaze cast down, and she heard an audible click as he ground his jaw.

Stupid. She was so stupid. She should've left him alone. "Why didn't I know that you played?"

"There are a lot of things you don't know about me," he said, setting the guitar on end in the window seat. Then he looked up. "There are a lot of things I don't want you to know. A lot you never will."

His words shouldn't have hurt. Or at least they shouldn't have caused more than a twinge of reaction. But to hear him put them out there with such bluntness was like being punched in the midsection by a fist.

His striking out was driven by Sierra's death and Luna's survival and the ten-year anniversary reminding him of both. She knew that as sure as she was standing here near tears, aching from the inside out, hurt by his indifference when her feelings for him were . . . No. Her feelings for him were nothing. She had to believe that.

He made it easy when he stood and turned to face the window, his hands shoved into his pockets, his shoulders slumped.

He didn't care about her memories, or what his family had meant to her—and not just Sierra, but his parents, his younger siblings. How much she'd loved them all. How much she'd loved him, past tense, because she'd known him only then. And this man was not that one. He was so different, angry and mean, and so much more, with the things hiding behind his eyes.

She didn't know what to say to him, if anything at all, because she didn't know what he wanted, or needed, or what he was going through. What coming back here had done to him, was doing even now. And so she turned to go, helplessness like a scythe cutting her in half, one part unable to leave, one part unable to stay.

As she reached the door, her footsteps slowed, then faltered, then stopped completely. She shook her head, closing her eyes and seeing again the picture of his silhouette framed against the bare window. He was alone, and lonely, bereft. How could she leave him? How could she continue to be so selfish, thinking of her loss, expecting him to think of hers, too, when his was so much greater?

Knowing she could very well be making a huge mistake, she retraced her steps, continuing to where he stood, waiting long enough for him to know she was there, then placing her palm on his back. He didn't flinch. In fact, a shudder ran through him, and he flexed as if doing so would keep her near.

Except she didn't know if it was her he wanted, or just . . . someone. She didn't need to. All the things that had brought him here were things she was aware of, for the most part understood, in many cases shared. But touching him without his rejecting her, learning the man he was now, gave her such incredible pleasure that she pushed aside the issue of his wanting her there. It was where she wanted to be.

She slipped both arms around him, laid her cheek against his back, and stacked her hands over his belly. His muscles there contracted as she did. He was warm and solid, and she loved the feel of him, and she didn't want to let him go, and oh, how had she forgotten what he felt like? It had been so long, and she shouldn't have missed this so much but she had, and she hated that she had. Hated, too, that she was giving too much meaning to the moment. He would shake off the melancholia soon enough, then shake her off for bearing witness to the weakness.

But he surprised her, covering her hands with his instead, turning in her arms, breaking her hold. She looked up, and he looked down, and whatever he saw in her eyes decided him. So many emotions, like vapor trails, or wisps of smoke, manifested and then vanished, nothing clear or defined, even to her. She was wrapped up in the short years they'd had together, and a decade of deception, and Angel's arms. Only the last remained as he lowered his head, and through his reluctance, his mouth found hers.

He was warm, and he tasted of anger and goodness and incredible need as much as incredible hurt. She wanted to give to him, and take from him, and fill herself with him, and pour over him as if she were a warm spring rain. This wasn't a kiss she knew what to do with, or how to respond to, or one she understood. This was Angelo Caffey all grown up, and she'd wanted to kiss him forever. To let her body melt into his.

He angled his head, moving one hand from her biceps to her back, and lower, bringing her body into his, pushing, pressing. They were as close as one, yet many, many things kept them from being together, clothes the simplest to get rid of but a barrier too risky to remove. And yet a part of her wanted that very thing.

She slid her palms from his waist up his back, his shoulder blades sharp beneath her palms, his body lean and dangerously hungry. She wished she knew how to feed him, but she didn't know more than how to follow his lead. They'd been together, but they'd never been here. This was new, untested, and yet he was a perfect fit, as if fine-tuned by the years between them.

He kissed her hard, and he kissed her with purpose, and he kissed her with his lips and his teeth and his tongue. His mouth was harsh, but his hands were gentle, even while the pressure he used to hold her to him would not easily give. When he pushed his tongue deep to find hers, she met him, and stroked, and played, and when he pulled his tongue free to tug at her lower lip, she tugged back, shivering, tightening, sizzling in her fingertips, curling her toes in her boots.

All too soon, the sound of a text message hitting her phone punched a hole in the moment. She could've stood here in this room with him for hours, but he released first her mouth, then moved his hands from her back to her shoulders, before letting her go completely and stepping away.

She pushed her hair from her face, then pushed her fists into her pockets, ignoring her phone, which she hated so much right now. Her hands were shaking, but not as much as her knees, and her mouth was bruised and tingling.

Now that they'd done this, however, they needed to get past it or what was left of their five days would be disastrous. She wasn't sure how to make that happen, so she reached for the first thing that came to mind. "I was thinking of going to Malina's for something to eat. I skipped breakfast, and I'm pretty much starving, and he doesn't close for an hour."

Angelo's gaze darkened as it held hers, but she saw a flash, as if he appreciated what she was doing. As if he were no more ready than she was to talk about what they'd done, and what it might mean, if anything. "Malina's Diner? You eat there?"

"Of course I eat there," she said with a shrug. "Everyone in Hope Springs eats there. It's still the only place in town to get breakfast and supper."

"But not lunch."

She shrugged again, trying to look away but unable to, and still tasting him, and wishing things between them were different so she could taste more. "You know Max. Serving breakfast and supper has worked for him all these years." And then she wondered if talking about the diner was Angelo's way of letting her down easy. "If you don't want to go, that's fine."

His mouth, red and swollen, quirked. "I don't remember getting an invitation."

She thought back over what she'd just said, then smiled. "I'm pretty much starving, and wondered if you'd like to go, too."

"I could eat."

"Separate cars? Separate checks?"

He laughed, the sound withering and sarcastic and putting them back on an even keel. "Close quarters getting to be too much?"

"Maybe a little breathing room wouldn't hurt."

This time his laughter was more resigned, and more genuine. "Yeah. You being here is definitely making it hard for me to breathe."

She didn't know what to do with that. She didn't know at all. "I'll see you there in a few then?"

He nodded, but several long seconds passed before she heard his footsteps following her to the door.

CHAPTER SEVEN

Angelo pulled his rental car onto Three Wishes Road behind Luna's Audi, letting her take the lead for the drive, and not closing the distance put between them by her heavy foot and her car's many horses. He knew his way to Malina's. He didn't need to keep her in sight. And breathing room was definitely a good idea. He just wasn't sure the five miles he had to travel before sitting down across from her was going to be enough.

Why had he agreed to come with her? Why hadn't he just let her go?

The easy answer was that he wanted more of her. And that was the truth. But it wasn't the whole truth, or the part of the truth giving him grief. He'd been the one to break the kiss when her phone had buzzed, butting into his good time to remind him whose hands were roaming with clever possessiveness over his back, whose mouth was on his, hot and wet and hungry. Whose body was aligned with his, leaving no room for common sense to pass between.

Why had he agreed to come with her? Why hadn't he just let her go?

The hard answer was that he wanted more of her. And wanting her to any degree was going to cause him the sort of trouble he didn't need. He couldn't have her. *He could not have her.* He should never have let her touch him. He should've moved her hands, stepped out of her embrace, given the memories time to fade. He should have set her away, not turned and fallen into her as if she were there to save his life.

Why had he agreed to come with her? Why hadn't he just let her go?

He parked his car in the space behind hers, watching as she opened her door and stepped out, her body tight, her movements lithe, her bearing confident, her hair like an unraveled rope. He wanted to wrap the mass around his wrist and bind her. He'd dreamed for eight years of doing so again, hoping she hadn't cut it because he'd complained it got in the way.

Their past was why he'd agreed to come with her. And he hadn't let her go because eight years of longing meant the roots of his desire ran almost as deep as his anger.

"Ready?" she asked, once he'd closed his door on the strangling thoughts.

"Do you know how many times I ate here in high school? After football games?" He fell into step beside her as they crossed the asphalt parking lot.

She shook her head. "I went to a different school, remember?"

Right. Even though she'd been at all of his games. "You St. Thomas kids had squat for a football program."

"St. Thomas wasn't much for athletics," she said, stopping at the entrance and lifting her gaze to meet his. "Unless you count tennis. And fencing."

"I don't," he said, and reached around her to pull open the door. She stepped through, her shoulder brushing his arm, her hair catching on the sleeve of his forearm and cling-ing. He left the strands there as she searched out an empty booth and led the way. "You weren't on scholarship, right? Your parents paid the tuition?"

"They did. And it wasn't cheap. But I was an only child, and my dad wasn't a fan of public schools." She slid into her seat, then smiled as he slid into his. "Funny. I *was* an only child. For twenty-eight years. It's hard to realize that's about to come to an end."

He pulled the laminated menu from the prongs of the condiment caddy and stared at the clip art of the daily spe-cial. "That's gotta be strange, the idea of being a sister after all these years."

"You were what, twelve when Felix was born?" she asked, the question returning him to his recent thoughts of his family falling apart, of his impotence at its happening.

He tried to keep the anger from his voice, but doing so made room for regret, guilt. Emotions he hated. It was so much easier just to stay mad, to be brusque, abrupt. "Yep. There were two years between me and Sierra, then Isidora came along four years later. Then Emilio, then Teresa, then Felix all within six years. The house smelled like sun-dried cloth diapers until I was fifteen."

"Better than smelling like dirty ones," she said, and after a moment he chuckled.

Their waitress arrived then, her uniform the same red, yel-low, and orange of the neon sign spelling out *Malina's* above the diner's front door. Luna ordered coffee, tomato juice, bacon, and biscuits. Angelo chose the platter with the most pancakes and eggs, wishing for a beer to dull the sharp edge of his mood, having coffee instead. He had to remember the

things he needed—information, the truth, Sierra's secrets—
and forget the taste of Luna's mouth.

Once they were alone, she stacked their menus, returning
them to the circular prongs as she picked up their conversation. "Why the gap after Sierra, I wonder?"

"No clue," he said, as amused by as he was curious about
her interest. It wasn't like they were intimates anymore, discussing family issues. Except Luna knew almost as much as
he did about life in the Caffey household. At least, life before
the gaping hole where Sierra had been. Though she didn't
know everything, the bad parts, the damage. He ran his right
thumb over a scar on the knuckle of the left. "Sometimes I've
wondered if my mother lost a child."

"You don't know?"

He shrugged. "If my parents had planned to add to the
family every two years, I would've only been four when she
did, since Isidora came along two years after that. I don't
remember knowing she was expecting."

Their waitress returned then with their drinks. Angelo
reached for his mug, preferring the bite of black coffee, watching as Luna tore open a sweetener packet and poured the
contents into hers, then added enough cream to make a cow
cry. Stirring, her eyes downcast, she asked him, "Do you miss
them? The kids? Your parents?"

He hadn't seen them in eight years, but then, they *had*
disowned him. "Yeah. I miss them, but I guess the move to
Mexico helped them get their lives back on track. Though I
am kinda surprised they stayed."

"So they're still there?"

He nodded. "I get a card from Felix every once in a while."

"But you haven't gone to see them?"

"Trust me. They don't want me there." His brother's notes, though short, always ended with the suggestion that he not visit. "I'm the one who called my mother's family for help eight years ago, remember? It's just that I thought they'd send money. Or come visit for a while. Not pack them up and take them back with them."

Luna toyed with her spoon, no longer stirring, but still staring downward. "I'm not so sure your contacting your mother's family didn't make the inevitable easier."

"How so?" he asked, because none of it had made much sense.

Not their walking away from the work they'd loved. Not their abandoning their home and their friends, turning their backs on church and school. Yes, he'd been the one to set things in motion, but he'd never expected his parents to give up so easily. Except hadn't they done just that the day Sierra died?

Frowning, Luna shook her head. "I shouldn't have said anything. I only heard the rumors. I didn't get out much the first couple of years after the accident."

Though after graduation she'd come to see him, visits that for both of them were an escape. "What rumors?"

"That the Gatlins had a lot to do with how bad things got," she said, and finally, *finally* looked up.

Now he was the one frowning, her words like a bullet in his head, ricocheting and refusing to settle. Damaging. Their food arrived then, the smells of bacon and eggs and pancakes rising in smoky wisps between them. Angelo leaned forward, his wrists against the table's edge. "Oscar was the one driving. Why would they go after my family?"

Luna unrolled the paper napkin holding her knife and fork. "Sierra was a scholarship student. She didn't come from the same social set or tax bracket as the majority of the kids at school. Rumor has it, and Angel, this *is* just rumor, that the Gatlins blamed Sierra for what happened to Oscar because she didn't belong at St. Thomas. If she hadn't been there, she and Oscar would never have met."

"That's crap," he said, fumbling with his utensils, the steam from the food nothing compared to that rolling out of his ears. Sierra had earned her place at St. Thomas. She had more right to be there than those who'd paid their way with cash instead of talent. That the Gatlins, that anyone would think otherwise, would blame her when she'd been a passenger, a victim, when she'd been the one who had died . . .

"Of course it's crap," Luna said, the bite of her words tearing into his musings. "But sometimes grieving families can't accept what happened as an accident. They have to point the finger at someone."

"You pick up this psychobabble in therapy?" he asked, stabbing his short stack. "A support group? Some self-help book?"

She shook her head, using her fork to split a biscuit and butter it. "When I was in the hospital, and even after I was home and confined to bed, I had a lot of visitors. And did a lot of listening. I guess people would think I was sleeping, or too drugged up to hear their whispers, or even too young to understand the subtext of their conversations."

"But you weren't any of those things." She'd always been bright, observant, and she knew people. Knew how to read them, how to manage them. Look what she'd done to him since he'd arrived. Here he was, still wanting to be angry with her, yet sharing a meal, having a conversation. Sounding a lot like they were on the same side. Like eight years of silence didn't exist between them. That kiss . . .

ALISON KENT

"I don't know," she said, dragging a bite of biscuit through a syrup pool. "I slept a lot."

He looked up, watched her smile as she pulled her fork from her mouth. She continued to smile as she chewed, and he shook his head, returning his gaze to his food, but not before it caught on her hand, where she held her fork. He grabbed for the distraction, because her smile was getting in the way of this being breakfast and nothing more.

Nodding toward her knuckles, he asked, "What's with the scars? Those aren't from the accident, are they?"

Having set down her fork, she held her hands in front of her, turned them palms up, then palms down, rubbing at a ribbon of red skin over the knuckle of her index finger with the thumb of her other hand. "They're from my weaving."

"They look more like they came from a brawl."

Her smile softened, as if her thoughts pleased her. "If you mean have I done my share of brawling with scissors and thread and my occasionally recalcitrant loom, then yes. That's exactly what they are."

"I wouldn't have thought working with yarn was as dangerous as working with power tools." He flexed his own hands, watched the healed strips of his own skin tighten.

"I don't think it is. I'm just . . ." She returned one hand to her lap, picked up her fork with the other. "Careless isn't exactly the right word, but I sometimes get so wrapped up in what I'm doing that I totally zone out. I know that sounds dumb. But weaving for me isn't the mindless repetitive motion you might think."

"What is it?" he asked, though he would never have applied the word *mindless* to anything she did. She was too *mindful* of everything.

60

"Promise not to laugh."

"Of course not," he said, earning himself a roll of her eyes.

"My scarves . . . I don't know if it's like this for everyone, but I can't work until I know what I want them to say." She paused, and when he didn't respond, she seemed to grow self-conscious, picking uncomfortably at her food. "It's hard to explain."

"Try," he said, his chest tight with wanting to know more about this part of her.

She breathed deeply and lifted her gaze to his, holding his, as if she needed to know he was fully present before she shared this part of herself. As if she didn't share it often. Or as if this bit of who she was wasn't always taken seriously. Paid attention to.

He set down his fork, wiped his mouth, and placed his napkin next to his plate, silent, attentive. Almost like old times, when she'd talked and he'd listened.

"Earlier," she began, "when I was outside and heard you on the guitar, I remembered listening to your father play. I loved when he did. It was one of the best parts of being at your house. The flamenco music, the fire and the passion. It makes me think of a deep pink, nearly red, rich and lush and full. Like a flower in a dancer's hair. Or her lipstick. But it's never red. And it's not magenta, or a bright neon.

"So pink, and gold. Like the fires that burned in the living room fireplace. Long tongues of gold. The gold of pollen in the center of a hibiscus. A vibrant, living gold. Like that of a spiced peach. To go with the pink. And then I see black. Like a dancer's shoes. Shiny patent leather. But there's always a yearning in the songs, so I see indigo, I think. Or a violet-blue. So close to purple, but never purple. And yearning isn't all

61

of it. There's happiness. I'm happy hearing the music. Your father is happy playing. That's pure orange.

"When I have the whole story in my head, the song, the laughter, the dancer's skirts flying and the intensity I see on her face, when I have all those colors, I look at the yarn I have to choose from. You should *see* all the yarn I have to choose from. I'll have to show you. . . ." The sentence trailed, and she found another path back to her tale. "I lay out the skeins, decide which color is the theme. The color the rest have to support and complement without overwhelming.

"Then I start. And I play music while I work. And I forget everything else but telling the story. I see the dancer and hear the guitar and know just when to switch threads. And I reach for the scissors and forget I moved them and manage to slide my knuckle along the blade. And that is why my hands look like they do, and why weaving the Luna Meadows way is to be avoided at all costs." And that was it. The end. She reached for her juice, took a long swallow, sat back, and sighed.

He didn't know what to say. The way she felt about her work, her art . . . He'd never felt any of that zeal, that involvement, that sort of attachment to what he created. She was an artist. He was a craftsman, and until now he'd been fine with that. It had served his father well. He'd thought all this time he'd been served, too. And maybe he had been. But something inside of him wondered what it meant to be consumed the way Luna was consumed. To live and breathe and know nothing else.

That sort of passion . . . "How does the kiss play into that?"

Frowning, she picked up her fork, avoiding his gaze as she asked, "The kiss?"

She was trying to play it cool. She was doing a terrible job. Color darkened the skin over her cheekbones, bloomed in the hollow of her throat.

"You heard the music. You came inside. You kissed me." He finished off his coffee, shrugged. "I figure that's part of the story." Because it wouldn't make sense for it to be anything else. He didn't want it to be anything else. Anything else would get in the way, and so he waited, needing her to slip a knife through the cord choking him and set him free.

She looked down at her plate, her hands still, her hair a dark canvas behind her shoulders and neck. "I hated seeing you looking so sad. I know this can't be easy, being here, all the memories. I wanted to give you what comfort I could."

"So it wasn't about the story," he said, struggling to breathe. "You just wanted to kiss me."

"Yes, okay." Her head snapped up. "I wanted to kiss you. And it was equally clear that you wanted to kiss me."

He shifted in his seat, braced his forearms against the table, and leaned forward, his voice low, his words fiery. "I've wanted to kiss you since I walked into the kitchen and found you climbing down from the chair."

"What?" The word came out husky, almost a whisper, disbelieving and uncertain.

"I've wanted to kiss you since I walked into the kitchen—"

"I heard you," she said, shoving at her plate and knocking it against her coffee cup, grabbing that before it spilled, her hand shaking.

He gave her a moment, savoring it. He wanted her off balance, wanted to jar loose the secrets she held. Then he came back with, "What? You're not going to admit that you've wanted to kiss me just as long?"

Her chest rose and fell, the color on her face deepening. "What good would it do either of us for me to tell you that?"

So he had it right. "It might get us back to doing it again. Or at least get us back to doing it sooner, because we both know that's where we're going to end up."

She set her fork and her knife on her plate, cleaned her mouth with her napkin, and added it on top. Then she reached for her purse on the banquette seat at her hip, pulling several bills from her wallet and placing them in the center of the table. "Here's my share of the tab. If you wouldn't mind taking care of this, I'm going to make a stop in the ladies' room, and then I'm going back to the house."

"That's it?" he asked, as she scooted out of her seat and stood.

"No. There's one more thing," she said, hitching the strap of her bag up her shoulder. "Don't assume you know where we're going to end up. Don't assume you know me anymore."

"I don't have to assume anything, Luna. I do know you." He reached for his wallet, opened it, and tossed his cash to the table before he looked up. "Probably better than you know yourself."

CHAPTER EIGHT

Luna parked in the driveway behind Angelo's rental car but didn't get out, staying instead behind the wheel to gather her wits. After finding the calm she'd needed to leave Malina's ladies' room, and finding Angelo gone once she had, she'd thought about going home. Then she'd thought about going to visit Kaylie. Then about going to Austin to see who was playing in what bar on Sixth Street.

What she'd tried not to think about were Angelo's parting words. His voice, when he'd said them, had left her unnerved; the look in his eyes had perplexed her. It was as if their nearly four years together hadn't existed at all, when she knew very well that they had.

She'd been sixteen the night she'd sneaked upstairs to his bed. Too emotionally young, too mentally immature, physically just right. Granted, they hadn't really dated before he left for Cornell, but that year and the ones that followed *had* happened. She'd still gone out with her friends. He'd still gone out with his.

They'd each met a need in the other. She'd given him an escape from the pressure that came with being the oldest of six and a natural athlete with no desire to play college ball. He'd wanted to study architecture, to be Frank Lloyd Wright the same way Sierra wanted to be Yo-Yo Ma. Luna got that. Sierra got that. No one else did.

And Angelo had gotten her. Even if he'd had a car of his own, he would never have used it to impress her. He had used his star quarterback status, but she couldn't blame him; that even impressed her father. He'd read the same books she did because she did, and listened to her rant about plots gone wrong. She'd ranted about the movie versions of her favorites sucking. He'd listened then, too. He'd listened to everything.

And now that they'd kissed . . . yes, she'd wanted it; after their history, how could she not? But she was old enough to know getting what she wanted was not necessarily a good thing. She wanted ice cream. Daily. Rocky road or vanilla bean. She wanted pizza. Greek pizza, with spinach and red onions and Kalamata olives and feta cheese. She wanted salted caramel apple cupcakes from Butters Bakery. And really. There were more things she wanted than food. And food shouldn't even be on her mind after all she'd ordered at Malina's.

It was that kiss, making her hungry, making her want more of him. Making her ache to end up exactly where he'd said they would. She'd wanted to slap him for suggesting such intimacy was inevitable. As if she hadn't gained any self-restraint. As if she hadn't learned to say no. Please. She was over him. Completely over him. And she had been for eight years. That kiss meant nothing. She refused to let it.

Pushing open her door, she forced herself out, pocketing her keys as she heard another vehicle brake to a stop on Three Wishes Road's gravel shoulder. Praying it wasn't Oliver Gatlin again, she turned, and was genuinely surprised—and pleased—to see Will Bowman climbing from his big Keller Construction pickup. He headed toward her, the sun casting a funhouse shadow of his tall, lanky body down the driveway and onto her car.

Welcoming the distraction, she walked away from the house—where Angelo waited—to meet him. "Will! What are you doing here?"

His smile was coy, the light glinting off strands of his blue-black hair. "Wanted to see where you've been spending all your time."

The implication being that she wasn't spending it with him? Or was she reading more into the one dinner he'd cooked for her months ago? "I've been busy, which working for Ten you should know. And from what I hear, Kaylie's house has been keeping you busy, too."

He nodded, shoved his fists into the pockets of his skinny black jeans. "Who knew the short-term gig for the café would turn into a long-term gig after the fire? Though a lot of the delay goes to the insurance company for dicking around so long."

"I'm just glad the house was salvageable. I haven't driven by in weeks. I'm anxious to see how it looks."

"It looks a lot like it did a hundred years ago. Or it will once the exterior's painted. Though I have a feeling the particular shade of blue Kaylie chose is completely anachronistic."

Luna laughed. "I imagine Kaylie is less concerned about being period authentic than she is being able to live there. She loves that house."

"You're preaching to the choir, sweetheart," Will was saying as Angelo walked up, his scowl no doubt spawned by Will's casual familiarity. Will scowled, too, his upward chin jerk and the resulting flip of his ironically emo hair equally—and unnecessarily—territorial.

Men. Such ridiculous posturing. As if either one of them had laid claim to her. As if she'd let either one of them do such a thing. "Angelo Caffey, Will Bowman. Angelo's sister was my best friend in high school, and this was their house. And I met Will a few months ago while he was working on Two Owls Café."

"On what?" Angelo asked, continuing to take in the other man.

Instead of throttling him, Luna explained. "Do you remember Winton and May Wise? They lived in the big blue Victorian on the corner of Second and Chances? A friend of mine bought the place and converted the first floor into a café. Or was in the process of doing so when a fire broke out on the third floor."

Will offered Angelo his hand. The two men shook, each sizing up the other before Will spoke. "We've just about finished rebuilding the turret, and Kaylie's thinking she'll be open by November."

"That's great," Luna said. "I know she hated the delay."

"Pretty sure she hated more the idea of losing the house."

"Oh, of course," she said to Will, then said to Angelo, "Will works with Tennessee Keller. Keller Construction is going to be building the arts center."

Angelo only nodded, leaving Luna to ignore him and ask Will, "What do you think of the plans?"

Will looked over Luna's head, beyond Angelo's shoulder. "Seeing the place in this light, we may have gotten it wrong, thinking we'd have to raze the house."

And here, after saving it, she'd come to terms with losing it for the cause. "I thought you decided there wouldn't be enough room for the center otherwise."

"That's because we're thinking about the plans as they are," Will said. "Not as they could be."

"You want to keep talking in circles? Or maybe you could spell things out straight," Angelo said.

Luna rolled her eyes, but Will wasn't fazed. Not surprising. In the months she'd known him, she had yet to see him ruffled, even when working on a ladder three stories high replacing Kaylie's shutters.

"Ditch the utilitarian schoolhouse look. Keep the homestead, farmhouse vibe. Build the center around it, and use the rooms already here for administration, or whatever."

Luna glanced from Will to Angelo, got a *don't look at me—it's your house now* expression in response.

"It's an interesting concept," she said, turning her back on the grump to respond to Will. "What do you mean, utilitarian schoolhouse look?"

His arched brow said she'd missed the obvious. "You're building an arts center. Don't you think putting some *art* into the *center* would help your cause?"

He had a point. Still . . . "I don't want to buy frills when the money would be better spent on the supplies. And the instructors."

"Thinking of aesthetics as frills is your first problem. You're an artist. Why would you do that?"

"I just told you why. It's a *nonprofit*. We're not made of money here."

"I'll do you up a new design gratis. And I'll toss in my hours with Ten for free."

"Why would *you* do *that?*"

"Because I *am* made of money," he said, taking off on a tour around the house.

Luna wasn't sure whether to follow, or to let him do whatever he was doing on his own. She'd wondered in the past about his roots, especially after the first time they'd met, when he'd told her he'd been raised by wolves. And the night he'd cooked for her she'd been made well aware that he wasn't hurting financially. But this?

"What do you know about him?" Angelo asked, cutting into her musings.

"Just what I told you," she said, keeping her thoughts to herself. "I met him a few months ago, the morning he came to work for Ten."

"Did you date him?"

Not *Is he from here* or *Does he have family nearby* or *What's with the haircut?* "I had dinner with him one night."

"Did you sleep with him?"

And, of course. "That's not any of your business."

"Embarrassed to admit that you did? Or that you didn't?"

"I'm not embarrassed about anything," she said, crossing her arms as she looked up at him. "Except you being rude to and dismissive of Will."

He snorted. "My being rude is hardly anything new."

Nice to see he recognized that about himself. "No, but for some reason I keep forgetting."

"Because you want to civilize me?"

"I'm no Saint Jude," she said, and waited for another smart comeback.

What she got instead was a confused frown, and after an uncomfortably long moment, "You think I'm a lost cause?" just as Will finished his tour and returned.

"Well?" Luna asked, happy for the distraction. She wasn't ready to analyze the emotion she'd seen on Angelo's face.

Will was nodding. "I think it's doable."

"How much more is it going to cost me?" She wasn't totally naive. Adding on to the house and the current structure would not come as cheap as the utilitarian concept Will eschewed, even with his throwing in the design and his hours for free. And especially since the house itself would make up such a small portion of the finished center.

"That part's up to Ten. I'm just the idea man."

"Didn't take you long to come up with that one," Angelo said.

A shrug. A hair flip. A wolfish grin. "It's what I do, figuring things out. Figuring people out."

"Oh?" Angelo asked.

His tone, a ridiculous display of machismo, had Luna rolling her eyes. Then Will made a big mistake, opening his mouth and giving Angelo more ammunition along with more of the wolf: "I had a lot of quiet time to learn how during the three years I was in prison."

"You were in prison?" Angelo asked, advancing.

"Come on," she said to Will, grabbing his upper arm and turning her back on the raging bull snorting behind her. This was one drama she did not need in her life. "I'll walk you to your truck."

"While I've got your attention and you've got my arm, have you thought more about snatching up one of the textile warehouse lofts? Those things are going fast, and there aren't that many to be had."

"Not only have I thought more about it," she said, pausing before the punch line. "I pick up my keys tomorrow."

"Seriously?" He opened his door and dug for his key ring, bobbing his head as if he approved. "All right. Neighbors. We'll have to grill a crate of corn or something. Celebrate."

"Sure. If you're still there by the time I'm all moved in."

"I like Hope Springs. I like working with Ten. I might stick around awhile. It'll be good to have you close," he said, his dimples digging crescents in his cheeks when he grinned. "You know. If I need to borrow a scarf or something."

"Uh-huh." She'd decided months ago this one was too clever for her. She was pretty sure she'd decided right. "I'd thought about renting a house in town, or an apartment, but with the lofts being snapped up . . . And there's enough space for my loom. I really like the idea of working from home."

"The way you do now?"

"Except it would be out of my own home. Not my parents'."

"Hey, you've got a good thing going. You sure you want to mess it up?"

Wasn't he just urging her not to let the lofts get away? "It's less about messing it up than it is getting on with my life and letting my parents get back to theirs."

"And that guy up there?" Will canted his head to indicate Angelo, who was no doubt still glaring. "Is he part of getting on with your life?"

If he was, she certainly wasn't going to admit it to Will. "He's part of getting on with the arts center. That's all."

"Right." The corner of his mouth lifted wickedly. "You may think that's why he's here, but he's got other things on his mind."

Why was she giving him an explanation . . . ? "We have a history. I've known him forever. And most of that time we've been at each other's throats."

"I'm going to say the rest of the time you were at each other in bed."

"It's not like that with me and Angelo." Not anymore, though when it had been . . . She took a deep breath, blowing away the thought as she exhaled.

"Maybe not for you. It is for him."

Luna found herself frowning. Was he right? Or was he just being his usual frustrating self? Then she remembered the kiss, and Angelo's need. She glanced toward the porch, and lust made itself known, tingling in places heated by Angelo's narrowed gaze.

"You just met him," she said, turning back to Will and knotting her hands at her waist. "You don't know anything about him."

"I know this," he said, the dark brow not hidden by his hair arching deliberately. "I don't need to be his pal to know this."

Pal? "You won't mind if I don't take your word for it."

"Don't mind at all. You *should* find it out for yourself," he said, and tossed back his hair. "I think you'd have a really good time doing so. And he obviously needs to have a good time."

Enough. She held up one hand. "Listen, wolf boy, just because you're all about sex—"

"Don't be naive, Luna. All men are all about sex. Whether we get it or not is another thing entirely."

She bit her tongue before asking who he'd been sleeping with. "Thanks for the idea about keeping the house intact. I'll talk to Ten and the nonprofit board and see what everyone thinks."

"It worked for Kaylie. And something tells me your man up there is not as indifferent to this place as he wants you to believe. Might be you need to figure out why."

She didn't need to figure out why. She knew exactly. And then it hit her. She was sitting, as it were, on a gold mine of an architectural degree. Why wasn't she involving Angelo in the building plans?

At that, Will leaned in and brushed his lips over her cheek, then climbed into his seat. She backed away, and as he started the truck, Angelo moved into her peripheral vision. "He's a frustrating little prick."

"Funny. I was thinking the same about you," she said, heading back inside and ignoring the shiver sliding down her spine at the sound of his deep, rolling laugh following her.

～

"So what do you think?" Luna asked a few minutes later as Angelo joined her.

He'd found her on the floor in the kitchen again, as if she couldn't move to another room until she'd finished with this one. As if for some reason she had to handle every dish, every utensil, every small appliance, every long-expired coupon before letting it go. And she hadn't even been the one who'd lived here. Which had him wondering, why the OCD?

"What do I think about what?"

"Will's suggestion."

He shrugged. He was trying not to think about Will. "I don't think anything."

"You're a carpenter," she said, and sat back on her knees, winding her hair and dropping it down inside her shirt. "Or if I don't miss my guess, a degreed architect, since that's where you were headed, last I knew."

There she went, fishing again.

"I don't believe for a minute that your mind wasn't spinning while he talked."

His spinning mind hadn't been thinking about construction. His spinning mind had been wondering about her relationship with the other man, and for no reason that made any sense. "He's right. And he's wrong."

"What's that supposed to mean?" she asked, frowning.

"Using the house . . ." He came farther into the kitchen, pulled one of the chairs from beneath the table, and sat, leaning forward, elbows on his knees. "I get what he's saying. I just don't know if the house is usable. I don't even know if *we* should be using it. Rats could've taken a liking to the wiring."

"That's what happened to Kaylie's house. Or so the fire inspector thinks. Rats or squirrels and wires in the attic." She glanced upward and frowned. "Maybe I should get an electrician out here to look things over."

"I'm sure your boy Will knows someone."

She glared at him, her mouth twisting. "You really need to stop doing that. You don't even know Will."

"I know how he was looking at you."

"Oh, good grief," she said, getting to her feet. "He was looking at me like a friend making sure the man sizing *him* up wasn't a threat to me."

"When have I ever been a threat to you?" he asked, lacing his hands behind his head as he leaned back. He knew the answer was never, but he was curious to hear what she'd say.

Shrugging, she avoided his gaze, pulling a trash can close as she opened another drawer. "I guess that depends on what you mean by threat. But Will doesn't know our history."

That wasn't much of an answer, he mused, pushing to his feet and heading for the back door. He stood there, a hand braced overhead on the frame as he tried not to dwell on their past. He wasn't ready to go there yet, though he'd known coming here meant he'd eventually have to.

"The barn might work just as well." He felt her gaze when she looked up, waited while she connected the dots.

"Built out for classrooms, you mean?"

"That, or if you need it, living quarters. A house. Maybe studio apartments for your faculty. Whatever." He added the last because he really didn't care.

"Are you ever going to tell me how you knew I'd bought the house?"

But he was back thinking about their history again. Even though he'd told himself not to. "When we were together," he said, glancing over, "you never talked much about how it was for you after the accident. I mean physically. Being confined to bed for so long—"

"I missed you," she said, as if the words had been hanging there, waiting.

He wondered if she'd meant to say it. Or planned to say it. Or if it had just slipped out. If she'd missed anyone, he would've thought it was Sierra.

He'd missed seeing her, too, but he doubted their missing had been for the same reasons. He'd been eighteen when they'd hooked up, a high school senior, caught up in football and the approaching freedom graduation would bring. And the money he didn't have for homecoming or the prom. And dodging the endless recruiters who refused to understand he'd fallen into football without meaning to. That his parents had pushed him, hoping like with Sierra that his abilities would benefit the family as a whole.

Seeing Luna had been about getting away from all that. About being someone else. "We saw each other later. We saw each other for two more years."

"Until moving day," she said, her voice sad and soft but lacking the tone of accusation he'd expected. The tone he deserved.

"Yeah," he said, but that was all he had. She hadn't been the one to disown him. His parents had done that. So why had he walked away from her, too . . . ? "I shouldn't have let that happen. Any of what they said to you. And I shouldn't have gotten out of your car at the airport without looking back."

"I think the problem started when you got *in* my car. Me being the taxi driver who brought you to the house." She picked up an ivory-handled carving knife he remembered seeing his father slam point-down into their table. "That didn't go over so well."

His parents hadn't known about his relationship with Luna. Showing up with her the way he had . . . "I don't know what I was thinking. I guess that having you there would make things easier."

He'd been the bad guy that day, the one who'd forced his parents' hand by calling his mother's family. He couldn't deal anymore with the way they were living—or weren't living— since losing Sierra. He'd had a big hole in his life, too, but all they'd seemed to care about was that he was sending them away—their words, their interpretation, their idea of the truth.

Luna tossed the knife into the trash and slammed the drawer. "But it didn't."

He shook his head, let the subject drop, and then pushed through the screen and left her without a word. Just like he'd done at the airport on moving day.

Day Two

WEDNESDAY

*If you would one day renovate yourself,
do so from day to day.*
—Confucius

CHAPTER NINE

"Knock, knock," Luna called, pulling open the back door into the kitchen at Two Owls Café the next morning. "Kaylie? Are you here?"

The other woman, Luna's closest friend, had been the one to text and interrupt the kiss with Angelo. She'd asked Luna to stop by the next time she found herself in the neighborhood. Kaylie didn't have to know that Luna's being in the neighborhood so soon after was by design.

"In here," Kaylie called, and Luna followed the other woman's voice to the largest of the connected dining areas that used four of the three-story Victorian's original ground-level rooms. Kaylie lived with her fiancé, Ten Keller, on the second floor, and would take over the third as well once the construction was finished. Her living and working in the same place had done a lot to tempt Luna into moving the contents of her weaving shed when she moved herself. "Hey, you."

"Hey yourself." Kaylie stood on a step stool, straightening one after the next in a row of black-and-white photographs, matted and framed in the same alternating colors, and hanging against a wall painted the brick-red of autumn leaves. "Does this one look straight to you? Every time I stand across the room, this one is crooked."

Luna's gaze traveled from one end of the row to the other. "It's fine. I think it looks crooked because of the angled lines in the photo. They're throwing you off."

"Hmm. You're probably right. Thanks." She backed down off the stool. "And thanks for stopping by."

"I almost came by last night," Luna said, walking closer, "but figured it would be too late."

"You should have," Kaylie said, turning from Luna back to the photos while she talked. "Ten was stuck in San Marcos on a job, and it was just me and Magoo."

Luna glanced back the way she'd come. "Where is Magoo anyway? He usually shows up at the door before you do."

Kaylie gave up on the photos and joined her . "He's been extra vigilant since the fire. He likes to roam and make sure everything's as it should be. These days he's most interested in the fall garden. Things are stirring to life, and the wildlife has noticed. He patrols the plot like an embassy marine."

"Bet he loves having a job."

"The best dogs do," Kaylie said with a laugh, and Luna smiled.

She missed having a dog since losing her beloved Maya to a very old age. "Will said you're hoping to open by November."

"I should be able to. We've got a few more things needing to fall into place, and one of those"—she lifted an index finger—"is why I wanted you to stop by."

"Sounds ominous," Luna said, widening her eyes dramatically. "Or sounds like you need something from me."

"I don't *need* it." Kaylie grinned, her ponytail swinging as she cocked her head to the side. "But I'd like it."

"I'm listening."

"I want to pay you to weave something for me. And before you tell me you don't take orders, I know that you don't take orders. I also know you're up to your ears with the demands of the nonprofit, and even if you did take orders, you wouldn't have time for a while—"

"But you want to place one anyway," Luna said, cutting in when the other woman stopped to take a breath.

Kaylie nodded. "I'm hoping you're at least curious enough to ask me what I want."

"Because I know you as well as I do, I'm going to guess it's something for the café. Even though you know I only weave scarves."

"I know that's all you've done in the past, but I also know you're doing some bigger projects for the nonprofit's auction."

"Did Mitch tell you that?"

"He did," she said, moving to Luna's side and staring, then frowning, at the row of framed photos and shaking her head. "He also said you weren't advertising that fact yet, so don't be mad at him."

Even before Luna was born, Mitch Pepper had been her father's best friend, and Luna had played a large part in reuniting him with Kaylie, his daughter. Doing so would probably stay with her forever as one of the most satisfying moments of her life. "I could never be mad at him."

Kaylie reached for Luna's arm and squeezed. "Have I told you what an amazing father he is? And how much I owe you for what you did?"

"Even though I lied through my teeth while doing it?"

"I would've done the same thing," Kaylie said, squeezing again before letting her go.

"Yeah, well, lying's not all it's cracked up to be. Especially lying to people you love. Even telling yourself it's for the best, that you're protecting them, that what you're keeping from them wouldn't change anything, and might even hurt them . . ." She stopped, shuddered, and took a deep breath. "It sucks. With you and Mitch it wasn't so bad. Everything was going to come to light soon enough."

"But you're not talking about me and Mitch."

Luna shook her head and wandered into the hallway. Kaylie followed, and both women made their way to the staircase, Luna sitting on the third step, Kaylie sitting beside her.

"You told me a few months ago that you'd lost your best friend in an accident, but never told anyone everything that happened. I'm guessing this has something to do with that?"

Luna swallowed, wondering how much of the story she wanted to share. "I missed the first two months of my senior year with a broken hip. My car slammed into a boulder, but the car I was traveling with . . ." She closed her eyes, opened them, thought about Oliver Gatlin climbing down into the ravine. "The same accident killed my best friend, and might as well have killed her boyfriend. He's been in a permanent vegetative state ever since."

Kaylie pulled in an audible breath. "Luna, sweetie, I had no idea."

"I don't talk about it. And since we all went to St. Thomas rather than Hope Springs High, fewer people in town knew about it when it happened, but it's pretty much common knowledge now." She cast a knowing glance toward Kaylie. "Especially since the boy involved was Oscar Gatlin."

"Merrilee Gatlin's son?" Kaylie asked, and Luna nodded. "Wow. I'd heard she and her husband had a child in the rehab facility, but I had no idea of the details. I'm so sorry this happened to you."

"Nothing really happened to me. Except the break—"

"Luna," Kaylie said, and wrapped an arm around her. "You lost a friend. You lost two friends. And knowing what I do of Merrilee Gatlin, I can't imagine she did anything to help you with your suffering."

An understatement if ever there was one. "According to Merrilee Gatlin, her family was the only one who did suffer. I was alive, so my parents couldn't know what she and her husband were going through. And the Caffeys buried their daughter, so they got closure. As if that was supposed to be some kind of consolation." Even now, thinking about that family's grief had her chest tightening. "Oscar was the one driving the car, and yet the Gatlins made life so miserable afterward for Sierra's family they eventually packed up and left town."

"That's the property where you're building the arts center, right? Where their home was?"

"The house is still there, and still filled with all their things. They only took clothes and keepsakes, and even then they left a lot." She thought of the personal items she'd found. How Sierra's room appeared to be untouched, though she hadn't been inside to check carefully. "They just up and started over."

"Where did they go?"

"To Mexico. Angelo, he's the oldest son, called their mother's family, and they came to help." She breathed in, breathed out. "He's here now. Angelo. He came to go through the house before it's torn down. If we do tear it down. Will's going to talk to Ten and see if maybe we can save it."

But Kaylie ignored all talk of the house to hone in on what was important. "You must've known him pretty well. Angelo. Being close to his sister. It's got to be good to see him again."

Oh, where did she even begin to describe what it was like seeing Angelo Caffey? "It is, except . . ."

"You've got a history with this man," Kaylie said, reading between the lines.

Luna laced her hands together, pressed them between her knees. "We spent a lot of time together in the past."

"And where exactly did you spend all this time?"

Luna felt her face coloring. "That, missy, is none of your business."

"I knew it!" Kaylie slapped her hands against her thighs, her feet against the stair. "You have a sordid past!"

Luna sputtered, then bent over laughing until she couldn't laugh anymore. "I do not! At least no more sordid than any other sixteen-year-old girl whose best friend's brother is a god."

"Oh, so now he's a god."

"Was a god. Was. It was a long time ago."

"Hmm."

"What's that supposed to mean?"

"I don't believe you."

"Why not?"

"Because of what I see on your face when you talk about him."

"If you see anything, it's exasperation that I'm having to put up with him at all."

"I know you better than that."

Luna was ready to explode with all the things she was feeling for Angelo, but she had to work them out for herself before she said anything about them to Kaylie. "Tell me about this order you want to place."

"Are you sure?"

"Sure that I want to hear about it? Or sure that I don't want to talk about Angelo?"

"Either. Or." Kaylie reached over and tucked back Luna's hair. "Both."

"Yes, I'm sure. Now . . ."

"I want holiday napkins. Linen. I'd like holiday place mats, but since I'm already pressing my luck, I'll settle for the napkins. Then I'll buy place mats to match."

Luna smiled. "I could do napkins. I could do place mats, too. Linen's tricky. I'll probably need a different loom. And the thread requires special handling. Let me do more research. And I need to know how many you want of each, and what sort of story you want to tell."

"I'd like to tell the story of the house, my history here, the Wises and all they did for me. And the brownies, of course. I'm not sure how to do that, but thankfully that's for you to figure out. As far as how many . . ." Kaylie screwed up her face. "You know my layout, how many seats I have. But since I haven't opened yet, I honestly don't know what the lunch turnover will be. Maybe we could just plan this for next year? Asking you to take this on now is just way too much. I shouldn't have mentioned it. I—"

"Kaylie, stop. Please," Luna said, laughing. "Yes, I'm busy with the auction items, and my Patchwork Moon collection, and I honestly don't know if I can fit this in for this holiday season, but let me think about it, okay? I might need more time just to decide how to tell your story, much less do the weaving. Especially now that I'm moving."

"You close today?"

"I get the keys this afternoon."

"You've got to be so excited."

"I'm not sure excited covers all of what I'm feeling," she admitted.

"Is it going to be strange leaving the only home you've ever known?"

"Is the better question, How strange has it been to live with my parents for twenty-eight years?"

"That doesn't bother you, does it?" Kaylie asked. "I thought you loved living there."

"I do. I have." The years had been nothing less than wonderful. "But, yes. I should've been out on my own long before now."

"You support yourself. I think that counts."

She helped with the expenses at home, too. But the reasons she'd stayed so long had nothing to do with money and everything to do with the security and comfort of having her family close. The ten-year anniversary of Sierra's death, her mother's unexpected pregnancy, and the weight of the deception she'd borne so long had finally brought her to this realization. Angelo's arrival had intensified the desire to make the change she'd put off too long. Her family would always be close. He'd gone on with his life without his.

"Maybe it does, but I feel like I've hit a no-turning-back point in my life. I have to move forward. And I also need to be going," she said, getting to her feet and giving the other woman a hug when she did the same.

"I'm here," Kaylie said, tucking Luna's hair back again. "Anytime you need to talk."

"I know. And I appreciate it. And I'll let you know soon if I think I can fit in your napkins and place mats. Just know they won't be cheap."

Kaylie laughed. "I never thought they would be."

~

Talking to Kaylie helped. By the time Luna arrived at the house, she wasn't feeling as overwhelmed as she had been. Crazy, she knew, considering Kaylie had asked her to take on more work, but talking to the other woman always leveled her out. If Kaylie could deal with everything she'd had on her plate over the years, and especially the last few months, Luna could deal with Angelo Caffey.

Because that was what was going on here. That's what this was about. It wasn't the arts center, or her moving, or the arrival of her baby sister, or even Oliver Gatlin adding to the stress she felt. It was seeing Angelo. Kissing Angelo. Feeling a rush of emotions both familiar and new, an amalgam of her young crush and her later lusty cravings and her current confused state of wanting less of him and wanting him more.

And though he'd only just arrived in town, she'd been thinking about him leaving again. What it would be like to have him walk out of her life a second time when she'd never expected him to return at all. She hadn't been ready for him, had been frightened, then speechless, then their sniping had found its way into the room and things had settled into a comfortable familiarity.

She laughed to herself at that, the idea that arguing and one-upmanship was normal, and continued to dig through the built-in drawers that took up the lower half of an entire living-room wall. The upper half of the wall was devoted to shelves. Books, and dozens of school portraits in hinged frames with family snapshots, and trophies. Lots of trophies. Emilio's for soccer and Angelo's football, Teresa's for piano and Sierra's cello.

This room was as ridiculously clutter-filled as the kitchen, which she hadn't yet finished. There were drawers of sheet music, and others filled with spools of thread. Years of report cards. Tiny tools and extra screws and found buttons and twist ties and pencils with broken leads. Anything she could have needed in a pinch was in one of those drawers, but apparently no one ever had.

Angelo walked into the living room then, his steps having pounded overhead all morning as he packed the room Isidora and Teresa had shared. Familiar footsteps, though different, heavier. He was heavier now, filled out, grown up. But his impatience was what she remembered, demanding. His restlessness. She'd always wondered about that. What he had wanted. Why what he had wasn't enough.

She wanted to know. Before he left, she wanted to discover what drove him, because surely it would help her understand her continued fascination when she hadn't seen him, even heard from him, for more than eight years. She looked up from where she sat on her knees, a deep drawer open in front of her. He'd stopped at the end of the couch, resting the box he held against the back.

He wore blue jeans, scuffed work boots, another T-shirt, an old favorite she recognized that was too small for him now and washed too often for her not to stare. This one was gray, with a red, white, and green map of Italy down the center, the toe of the boot ending just above his fly. She returned her attention to the drawer, reaching for the first distraction she could, and holding up his third-grade report card.

"An unsatisfactory in conduct? So you've always been a hard case?"

He shook his head, snorted. "I had a sister in first grade, another who was two, and a newborn brother at home. Shades of things to come for the next four years, but I was eight and overwhelmed."

Interesting, she mused, looking down as she slid the card back into its slot. A real card. Printed on what felt like a manila folder. Handwritten grades and notes and signatures.

Angelo went on. "My parents wanted me to play pee wee football, but my bike was a piece of crap and barely got me to school. Practices were across town, and I was worn out when I got there."

"But you couldn't take out your frustration on Sierra or Isidora or Emilio, so you took it out on third grade."

"Mostly I took it out on fifth grade. I just happened to be in third."

That made her smile. "A scrapper, huh?"

"I knew better than to whale on smaller kids." He shrugged. "Older kids were fair game. At least to my eight-year-old way of thinking. Not so much to my dad's, though you can see his opinion didn't do a whole lot to stop me. Putting a hammer in my hand finally did." At that, he hefted up the box and headed for the front porch.

They'd been stacking things out there, one end for trash, one end for donations. A truck was due tomorrow afternoon to pick up the latter; it was the third load of giveaways, and they'd have at least one more. The trash was waiting for the arrival of a second Dumpster.

"I thought I'd run out to one of the burger joints on the interstate and grab some lunch," he said, stepping back inside and leaving the front door open. "Want something?"

"A cheeseburger would be great, thanks."

"You prefer one place over any other?"

"Any one of them's fine. Add bacon and jalapeños. No fries. A chocolate milk shake." She got to her feet. "My purse is in the car. Let me get you some money."

He waved off her offer. "I got it. You can buy tomorrow."

As if there was no question that she'd be here to eat with him. "Is that what we're going to do now? Take turns?"

"Seems fair," he said, shrugging carelessly. "Until I run out of cash. But we should finish up before I hit bottom."

And once they finished up, he'd be gone. "What would happen if you extended your time away? Would you get fired?"

"Five days not enough for you?" he asked, his expression suggestive.

"Just answer the question," she said, and tried not to roll her eyes.

"Why would I want to do that?"

The better question was, why was she asking him to? "I thought it might be nice to have someone from Sierra's family involved in putting the center together."

He waited for the full jolt of what she'd said to settle, then: "That would mean staying on. In Hope Springs."

"For a while, yes." This time she shrugged, but without pulling off careless as well as he had. "Or for as long as you wanted to."

He came farther into the room, cocked a hip, and sat on the couch arm. "And are you asking someone from Oscar's family to be involved, too?"

"I can't imagine them being interested." Because this was Luna's community-based project. And Luna came from the wrong community. And then there was Oliver's digging into the accident. She couldn't ask them because of that. And she couldn't tell Angelo why she couldn't ask them. "They never were big fans of Sierra."

He studied her fiercely, frowning. "Did she know?"

"That they didn't want Oscar dating her?" She nodded. "She never told you?"

"She may have. I don't remember." He reached up, rubbed at the bridge of his nose. "I wasn't exactly a model big brother."

"Sierra thought you were," she said, wanting to soften the blow of the things he was feeling.

"Maybe then." He shook his head, scuffed his boot against the dry hardwood floor. "I doubt she did later."

"Later?"

"When I was at school. When I was away."

Oh, he had it wrong. "Distance wouldn't have changed her mind—"

"Sierra was pregnant." Three words dropped like bricks on the surface of a still lake, the circle of the impact widening, widening . . .

"What?" Her voice broke on the word, her whole world crumbling. He'd known? All this time, and he'd known?

When she blinked him into focus, he was nodding. "She called me not long after spring break and told me. She asked me to come home and hold her hand while she told our parents."

The tips of her fingers had gone cold. They burned like icicles when she pressed them to her mouth. "I had no idea. I knew about the pregnancy, of course. But not about her calling you. Or that she'd planned to give your parents the news."

And why hadn't she known? Sierra had told her the rest. She'd told her everything. So why not this? It didn't make any sense . . . unless Sierra hadn't wanted her to think badly of Angelo for not coming. Except that wouldn't have mattered unless Sierra had known Luna and Angelo were together. She hadn't . . . had she?

"I wondered if you knew. I mean, not that she was pregnant, that was a given, but about her calling me."

They'd shared everything else. Why not this? And why hadn't Angelo mentioned knowing before now? "What did she say? I know it's not my business—"

"There's not a lot to tell." He reached up and raked back his hair. "She told me she was pregnant, and she wanted to tell our folks but didn't want to do it alone. She wanted me to fly home for the weekend and have her back while she did."

Not long after spring break, he'd said. Did that mean he didn't know the rest? "What did you say to her?"

"I told her she was old enough to get herself into trouble, she was old enough to face the music."

But she never had, and Luna wondered why, when doing so might've changed everything—for their families and their friends and a tiny life who would never know what she'd lost.

Angelo went on. "The medical examiner didn't say anything about her being pregnant at the time of her death. At least as far as I know. I assumed she'd lost it. Maybe even in the accident. Or gotten rid of it. It was half Gatlin. I didn't figure Oscar would want to be tied down."

This was what made her so sad, made telling the truth so hard. Neither Sierra's family nor Oscar's knew what the two had shared. Luna was the only one. And she didn't know whether she had the words to make anyone else, even Angelo, understand.

"She would never have gotten rid of it. She and Oscar . . ." She let the sentence trail, thought better of telling him everything the couple had done.

"She and Oscar were stupid."

"Don't say that," she said, a sharp hitch grabbing at her chest. "They were happy. They were . . . happy."

"So what happened? To the baby? How far along was she when she called me?"

"If it was after spring break, then four months. She got pregnant in December."

"Four months?" He pushed off the couch arm, paced to the front door and back, his steps hard. "I thought when she called me she'd just found out."

"No," she said and bowed her head. "She'd known awhile."

"Was she sick?"

"Oh yeah. I always had crackers with me in case she needed them."

"How did she hide being pregnant from our parents all that time? How did she hide it from her teachers?"

"I helped," she said, leaning against the closed drawers and pulling her knees to her chest. "We bought her new uniforms. They fit well enough that she just looked like she was getting fat. It was easier over the summer. She only had music classes three days a week. The other days we holed up in the tree house, though she had no business climbing up there. Or we hung out in her room. Out of sight, out of mind. And she almost didn't show through the whole pregnancy."

"If she was still pregnant during the summer, then in September . . ." He stopped, stepped away, his mind obviously whirring.

Luna swallowed. "She had the baby the Friday before the accident."

"And?" he asked, as slowly he turned back, his chest heaving, his eyes both fiery and dark. "Where's the baby now?"

Luna had no idea. And that was the gospel truth. Though if Oliver Gatlin had gone digging . . . "She gave it up for adoption."

CHAPTER TEN

Shock rooted Angelo in place. Shock and disbelief and a frightening amount of rage. Nothing here made sense. Not a single thing Luna was saying. He had to have it wrong.

He took one step closer, then another, stopping when his shin bumped the coffee table. "She had the baby? And she gave it up for adoption?"

Luna nodded, her gaze on the drawer she'd just pulled open, a barrier between them, a shield.

Dear God. He scrubbed both hands down his face, breathing hard, finally jamming his hands onto his hips. "And you didn't think her family might want to know? Might have a right to know? Might care that a piece of the daughter, the sister they'd lost, still lived in her child?"

"Of course I thought about that." The drawer shook from the pressure of her hands curled around the edge. "I've thought about that every day for ten years. But Sierra asked me to keep her secret. She didn't want anyone to know until she and Oscar told them."

"Screw what she wanted. She was a kid."

"She was an adult." She yelled the words, her hair flying as she whipped her head around to face him. "She'd turned eighteen earlier that summer. Oscar, too. They didn't need their parents' consent for anything. They were both legal adults when the adoption process was started."

He thought back to when his sister had called him, calculated the dates. She hadn't been eighteen then. "I guess she had a C-section? Or was induced? Unless someone waved a magic wand to have her go into labor the weekend you two were away at art camp."

"She was induced, yes."

"Of course. The postmortem would've shown an incision, and I can't imagine a reputable hospital releasing her so soon after surgery. But it should've been just as obvious to the coroner that she'd recently given birth."

"Unless there was no postmortem," Luna offered. "It's not like the cause of her death was in question."

He didn't know. He barely remembered those days. He'd heard nothing from his parents about what had happened with Sierra's body. Even thinking about it now . . . "What was it? The baby? A boy or a girl?"

"A girl."

He sank onto the sofa, buried his face in his hands. It was bad enough that he'd kept the secret of his sister's pregnancy from their parents . . . but this? How was he ever going to live with this? Because if he'd said something about Sierra expecting . . . "So I have a niece out there somewhere. My parents have a granddaughter."

Luna was slow to answer. "Biologically, yes, but none of you have any claim on the child. Sierra was the only one in your family with rights. And she signed those away."

He shook his head. "There's got to be some recourse. I'll need to talk to an attorney—"

"Why?"

"Why?" He looked at her, but didn't really see her. All he could see was red. "What kind of stupid question is that?"

"You're not thinking straight."

"Of course I'm not thinking straight." He yelled the words, gestured wildly. "You just told me my dead sister had a daughter."

"Angelo, listen," she said, closing the drawer, moving closer, the coffee table still between them. "The child is ten years old. She legally belongs with the family who adopted her. She may not even know she's adopted. Are you really going to charge in like a bull trying to get your way? Because, what? You didn't come home when Sierra called you, so ruining her daughter's life is going to make up for that somehow?"

"How is giving her the truth of her heritage going to ruin her life?"

"How is giving her the truth of her heritage going to make the life she has any better? She's a child, Angelo. A little girl. She may have other siblings, and no doubt friends at school, at church. She might be in dance class, or in Girl Scouts, or taking cello lessons. Telling her where she came from, what happened to Sierra and Oscar . . . Don't you see how that truth could turn her world upside down? Even if you could get access to the records, could you really do that to a ten-year-old girl?"

He didn't have an answer. He wanted to tell her that the child wasn't the only one in the picture, the only one with stakes in the game. He wanted to tell her that he and his parents and siblings were the girl's blood relatives, so of course knowing them would make her life better. But that was such a crock he couldn't believe he was thinking it. He was gripping, reaching for anything to kill the pain. He was trying to make himself feel better over failing his sister before she'd died.

If he'd come home when she'd called him that spring, if he'd stood with her while she talked to their parents, if he'd been the brother he should've been, the brother she'd needed, not the selfish ass who was too busy with his own life to care about hers . . . If he'd done any of that, she wouldn't have had a reason to be in that car with Oscar Gatlin, traveling the Devil's Backbone, returning to Hope Springs from giving birth to a child no one had known she'd had.

No one but Luna Meadows. Everything kept coming back to Luna Meadows.

He looked at her, wondering what else she knew. "Why would she have told you to keep her secret? She called me because she was going to tell our parents. Doesn't sound to me like she was trying to hide it."

"I don't know."

"Did the Gatlins talk them in to giving up the baby?"

"The Gatlins didn't know she was pregnant. They didn't tell Oscar's family either."

"So I knew, and you knew, and they knew, and the attorney and couple who took the baby knew, and that was it?"

"The couple didn't *take* the baby. They took care of Sierra. Once the adoption process was under way, she received incredible prenatal care, probably better than she would've been able to provide for herself."

He scrubbed a hand over his jaw, the guilt that had been there all these years eating away at the wall he'd built to contain it. "You don't know why she changed her mind? About telling our parents?"

Luna stayed silent, stacking old magazines from under the table in piles on the floor.

"Luna?"

"No. I don't." She reached up, rubbed at her temple. "I only knew about the adoption. And I promised Sierra—"

He surged forward, shoved at the magazine stack with one foot, scattering them, tearing them. "I don't give a crap about a promise you made a decade ago. Things have changed—"

"What exactly has changed? She was pregnant. She died. The only thing different is now you know she gave birth. Your knowing that doesn't negate the promise I made to your sister. Don't put me in this position. Not now. Not . . . yet."

"What does that mean, not yet?"

"I loved Sierra," she said, on her hands and knees, gathering the magazines again and fixing the mess he'd made. "I probably loved her as much as Oscar, just not in the same way. Keeping her secrets hasn't been easy, but I've done it because I told her I would. It's just that . . . I'm starting to wonder if I did the right thing. And if I did it for the right reason."

"The right reason? Would that be keeping yourself out of hot water?"

"Actually, no. It wasn't about me. It wasn't even about protecting Sierra."

"Then what?" he asked, waiting as she sat back on her knees.

"I didn't want the Gatlins to cause trouble for the baby's family."

He took a deep breath, letting that settle. "And you thought they could find out who they were?"

"I was eighteen. I was grieving. I was in a lot of physical pain. I wasn't thinking straight, but even if I had been, I didn't know anything about sealed adoptions or client confidentiality. What I did know was that the Gatlins always got what they wanted. I couldn't see this being any different."

"Did Sierra know the couple?"

Luna shook her head. "They did everything through the attorney Oscar contacted. She wanted the break to be complete."

"But you still thought the Gatlins could find a way around the legalities."

"Don't they always? And there had already been so much heartbreak, for Oscar's family, for your family. I didn't want to add to that by coming clean."

"You should've come clean."

Her hands on her thighs, she narrowed her gaze as she looked at him. "Why me and not you?"

"What?"

"Did you tell your parents she called you? Did you tell them she was pregnant with Oscar's child?"

"No, because I didn't talk to them all that summer." Admitting it now shamed him, but it had been wonderful not having to pick up the phone and hear that something else had gone wrong and he needed to fix it. "I was in Rome, and I thought she'd gone ahead and told them even though I didn't come home. Next thing I knew, she was gone."

"I'm sorry. I didn't know."

"Now you do. Just like now I know you have been lying all this time. And a lie of omission is still a lie. So what else haven't you said?"

She got to her feet, dusting off the knees of her jeans, then her seat, never looking at him as she pushed by on her way to the front door and walked out. He didn't turn, or try to stop her, but let her go, staying where he was, swearing to himself he would get to the bottom of the secrets she was keeping.

Five days, five weeks, five months. He didn't care how long it took.

He wasn't leaving Hope Springs till he did.

∼

His appetite gone, Angelo left the house in the other direction and made his way to his father's woodshop. His parents had brought him to this house from the hospital. Until he'd left for college, this was the only home he'd ever known. Just like the one Sierra's daughter had been living in her whole life was hers. Even if she'd moved a dozen times in ten years, she had her parents, and possibly siblings, and maybe cousins. Hopefully books she loved, and a favorite pair of shoes or boots, and a beloved plush toy she told her secrets to, and friends.

Luna was right, he mused, closing the door of his father's woodshop behind him. He couldn't turn the girl's life upside down because giving his parents a piece of what they'd lost would make him feel better. And that was all it would be, a face-saving effort because he'd been too wrapped up in himself to come home when Sierra had asked. His last words to her still haunted him, those more than never getting to say good-bye.

"Please, Angelo. I really need you."

"You got yourself into this mess. You can get yourself out."

Luna had been right about something else, too. His lie of omission was just as much of a lie as hers. He didn't know why he'd never told his parents about Sierra's pregnancy, except it wouldn't have done anyone any good. It wasn't, he told himself, because he didn't want to explain how he, living nearly eighteen hundred miles away, had known when they, living with Sierra, hadn't.

Something had happened after her phone call that had kept her from revealing her condition. Something more than his refusal to come home—he was sure of it—had changed her mind, had gotten in the way of her plans. Something he didn't know, but he was sure Luna did. One more thing he was going to have to get her to spill.

He had a niece. God, he had a niece. A piece of his sister still lived. He wondered what she looked like, if their mother's Hispanic genes had made themselves known and caused the couple to tell the girl the truth of her heritage. Or perhaps the couple themselves were Hispanic, or dark-haired and dark-eyed. He wanted to see her. He wanted to know her name, to hear her voice, to watch her tumble across a gym mat, or dribble a soccer ball down the field. To see her eyes sparkle when she laughed.

He had a niece. He had a niece. He picked up a ball-peen hammer, rubbed his thumb over the rounded striking head, and then slammed that same surface into the table littered with the detritus of his father's abandoned work. The contact reverberated up his arm, and he slammed it again, and again, and again, leaving quarter-size dents in the pine, each strike firing off nerves in his elbow, his shoulder, his neck, and his back. He couldn't swing hard enough, hit hard enough—

The workshop door opened, and he flung the hammer across the table, stirring up dust that danced in the shaft of light slicing into the darkness. Luna, of course. Finding him beating his father's hammer into his father's table, the same way she'd found him working out his frustrations on his father's guitar. Yeah. Nothing subtle here about his issues with his family.

Then again, they'd disowned him, not the other way around.

"What are you doing out here?" she asked, the door squeaking shut behind her, bouncing once, twice.

"Nothing," he said. Barked, really. Because he didn't want her thinking she was welcome. Or that he was in need of her comfort. Or wanted her.

"Sounded like you were beating something to death," she said, coming closer anyway.

"It wasn't that loud," he said, ignoring her arched brow.

She moved to the table, picking up a block of wood, a scrap, garbage. "It was loud enough that I heard it on the way to the barn."

"The barn?"

"I was thinking more about Will's suggestion," she said, as if the conversation they'd had in the living room had been thirty years and not thirty minutes ago. As if she were giving both of them an out, calling a truce, allowing him time to breathe. "And about what you said. Wondering if the center could use the barn, too." She canted her head to one side as she studied him, her hair falling in that direction, like a curtain blocking his view.

He reached for the distraction, nodding toward her. "When's the last time you cut your hair?"

"I get the ends trimmed every month," she said, her expression confused.

"Not trimmed. Cut. I'm pretty sure it was as long as it is now back in high school."

"I've had it this long most of my life. Why?"

"You're pretty fashionable. I'm definitely not, but I don't think hair that length's much in style."

"I don't wear it long for style's sake."

"Then why?"

"Because I want to."

"Yeah, but . . . It's gotta be a lot of work. Why would you want to?"

"I just do," she said.

He didn't believe her for a second. "I remember you having it in a braid the day of the funeral. I don't think I'd ever seen it anything but loose before."

"I was still immobile then. My mother braided it to keep it from getting tangled in bed."

"You never braided it when you slept with me."

Her cheeks colored, and she dropped her gaze. "Being in traction isn't quite the same as sleeping."

She knew as well as he did that sleeping wasn't what they'd done in bed. "You were in a wheelchair that day. I was surprised your doctor released you to come."

"I went right back. It was an afternoon pass." She stopped, studied him. "I can't believe you're admitting that you saw me there. You certainly didn't acknowledge me. None of you did. Unless ignoring me, walking off the path where I was sitting so you didn't have to speak to me, counts. I mean, it wasn't like we were *involved* or anything. Oh, wait. As far as anyone else knew, we weren't."

But she knew. And he knew. "It was that kind of day." Yeah. He shouldn't have brushed by her the way he did.

"I didn't get treated much better the day your family moved."

"Things with my parents moving . . ." He shook his head. He hated thinking about it. He sure didn't want to talk about it. "That was rough. They walked from room to room like they didn't even know where they were."

"They knew who I was. That was very obvious."

He'd been there. He remembered every word they'd spoken. "Like I said. Things were rough."

She reached for the hammer he'd abandoned, popped it against the table, though with less force than he had. "I came very close both of those times to telling your parents about the baby."

Interesting that she'd use the information as a weapon. Because that's what it sounded like she was saying. "Even though you had an obligation to Sierra."

"I'm human, Angelo. Your family felt like an extension of mine. To be treated like I didn't exist, like I hadn't lost Sierra, too, well, it hurt. A lot. And, yes. I thought about striking back. But it was a childish response, and I knew I'd regret it if I did."

He let that settle, wishing—and for not the first time—that he could take back that day. His parents, who for years had assumed he'd handle what they couldn't, or what they wouldn't, had seen him arrive with Luna and ordered him gone. He'd stayed and helped anyway, until there was nothing more to do, then watched his mother and father, his brothers and sisters pile into their car and leave.

Only ten-year-old Felix, on his knees in the back seat, had waved good-bye, his cupped fingers moving in the smallest of motions. That picture had stuck with Angelo more than anything else from that day. That and Luna's dry eyes as she'd dropped him at the airport in Austin for his trip back to New York.

After a long silent moment, she asked, "Do you think they still hate me? For surviving?"

"You think that's why they hate you?"

"I can't think of anything else. They didn't know about the pregnancy or the adoption."

"They knew you and Sierra were supposed to have been at art camp. That Oscar was supposed to have been at a music workshop. They knew the three of you had no reason to be driving the Devil's Backbone," he said, and watched her face blanch. "Did I hit a nerve?"

"Just the one attached to the memory."

He didn't believe her, but he watched her gaze fall, watched her hand flex around the hammer's handle.

"Do you still hate me?"

He was pretty sure what he hated was being unable to change the fact that right now, more than anything in the world, he wanted to kiss her again.

"I don't know what I feel anymore, Luna. For you, for this place. I don't know what I feel."

She returned the hammer to the table and shoved her empty hands in her pockets. "Does that mean you don't want to stay and be a part of the center?"

"I haven't decided. But whether I do or don't, I'm going to get my answers."

CHAPTER ELEVEN

Luna was just stepping onto the porch, carrying a box of clothing from the closet shared by the two youngest Caffey boys, when Oliver Gatlin's BMW rolled to a stop on Three Wishes Road, blocking the driveway. She was still dealing with the revelation of Angelo knowing about Sierra's pregnancy, and Sierra not sharing her plans to tell her parents about the baby. Her emotions felt as if they were sitting on the surface of her skin, burning. She had no desire to see Oscar's brother. But it seemed she was doomed, so she set the box on the edge of the porch with the others designated for donation.

He exited the car, all fluid motion, nothing wasted, effortless, and headed toward her, his eyes hidden behind expensive shades, his shoulders draped in cream-colored cashmere, the sweater incongruous with Texas's autumn temps. His jeans no doubt bore an expensive designer label. The word fit him: *expensive*. His clothes and car. The cut of his hair. His attitude. His expectations.

She walked down the porch steps and met him in the yard. "You need to move your car. I've got a truck coming to pick up these things."

"I won't be long." He pulled off his glasses, hooked the earpiece over the sweater's neckband. "Just thought I'd swing by."

Right. "Can't wait to see what I do with the place?"

"Can't wait to see this place gone."

Little did he know he might not be getting his wish after all. "It wasn't enough that your family drove this one from town?"

He gave a shake of his head and a huff of a laugh. "Yeah, it took me a while to figure out why my mother was so obsessed with Mike Caffey's furniture business."

So she'd been right thinking Merrilee Gatlin had something to do with the downturn in Mike's orders. "What? She needed to exact some sort of twisted revenge on Sierra's family because her son couldn't control his car? The Caffeys didn't have anything to do with Oscar's driving."

"No, but it was their daughter who had him out driving somewhere he had no business being." He shoved his hands in his pockets and looked away, a vein in his temple throbbing. "I found an attorney in Kerrville who specializes in private adoptions. Guess what her name is?" he asked, his gaze coming back to catch hers.

"I don't care what her name is." She turned for the house, hoping she could reach the porch before her legs gave out. If he learned the truth about the adoption, how long before he learned the rest? *Breathe, Luna. Breathe.*

"Wait."

It was a plea. Not a demand. One at odds with everything she knew about Oliver Gatlin. Against her better judgment, she stopped. "What?"

"I have something for you," he said as she slowly came back.

This time her better judgment, well, knew better. "I can't imagine what that might be."

"This," he said, and reached into his pocket, pulling out a check he held by the edges. It was signed. It was made out to her. It nearly bubbled with zeroes.

Her heart bubbled, too, but she knew better than to start shopping. "What's this?"

"A donation."

"Don't make me laugh."

Frowning, he turned the check around and looked at it, then looked back at her. "Even I wouldn't laugh at this kind of money."

"And you're just going to give it to me. For the center."

"I'm not a fool, Luna," he said, adding a sarcastic huff. "I'm buying, not giving."

"Buying what?"

"The truth. You tell me where Oscar was that weekend, what he was doing, and the money's yours."

No mention of Sierra. Or of her. Hardly surprising. The Gatlins were interested only in the Gatlins. "I don't think so," she said, reversing course. Again.

"I'll double it."

She stopped. Again. Looked back. Oh, the things she could do with a donation that size. "You may be buying, but I'm not for sale."

He ground his jaw, folded the check, stepped toward her, and pushed it into her pocket, the familiarity as unexpected as it was strangely desperate. "Keep it. Think about it. As soon as I get what I want, I'll release the funds and the money's yours. Books, paints, computers, cellos. Whatever you need."

She didn't want it. She certainly didn't want to touch it. To hold it. To have it in her hands. Arms crossed, she held his gaze a long, tortured moment—her torture she knew, but his?—before he broke the contact and walked away, never looking back, not even when he stood beside his car to shove his sunglasses in place.

"What did he want?" Angelo asked, snagging Luna's attention. She hadn't even heard him approach.

She looked down the long driveway to where the other man was climbing back into his car, shifted, and felt the crinkle of the check in her pocket. "Nothing good."

"What all does he know?"

More than he needs to, she wanted to say, but instead said, "Not as much as you do."

"Does he know about the adoption?"

"He doesn't even know about the pregnancy. At least, I don't think he does. He hasn't mentioned it anyway."

"Just now, you mean?"

"Now, or at the cemetery."

"You saw him at the cemetery?"

"He came by the other evening when I was there."

"Why?"

"I don't know." She shrugged. She didn't want to be having this conversation. "To cause trouble, I guess."

"What kind of trouble?"

"Whatever kind he can stir up. He's a Gatlin. Isn't that what they do?" she asked, though what she'd seen in Oliver's eyes told her it was more.

"Has he been bothering you like this all these years?" Angelo asked, frowning as he watched Oliver's car disappear down Three Wishes Road.

"I can't even tell you the last time I saw him."

"And now you've seen him twice in a couple of weeks. Something's gotta be going on with him."

Something was going on. But it wasn't a something she was going to share. Though even as she had the thought, she realized Angelo could be an ally. He knew about the pregnancy. He knew about the adoption. But he didn't know everything, and for some reason that kept her from telling him what Oliver had found.

"Can we not talk about Oliver Gatlin? Or anyone in that family? Please?"

"What about Oscar?"

"What about him?"

"Do you ever see him?"

"No," she said, the admission shaming her.

"Why not?"

"I don't know." She shook her head. "I guess because seeing him would only be for me, and I don't need to see him for what I would want to say. I can say it all to myself."

"What would you say?"

Things I can't tell you. "That I'm sorry I haven't visited him, but that he's never far from my mind. That I wish things hadn't happened the way they did."

"Would you tell him about Sierra? Do you think he knows?"

"I have no idea what he knows, if he's had any awareness at all since the accident, or if it ended his life, too, just in a different way than it did Sierra's." She lifted a hand to shade her eyes, needing a better look at Angelo's expression. "Why are you so curious about Oscar?"

"Because I'm trying to decide what his brother wants, turning up all of a sudden."

"The way you turned up all of a sudden?"

"That's different."

"Why have you never come back before?"

"No reason," he said, and she tried not to flinch. "I didn't stay in touch with anyone but you after I left for school."

"Not even any of the guys you played football with?"

His mouth pulled into a smirk. "I played football for the girls."

"Sierra hated that, you know. The girls calling, driving by and honking. Hanging panties on the mailbox. But I'll bet you loved it."

"The parents weren't thrilled about the panties, but the rest of it was a lot of fun."

"Uh-huh."

"Did you ever hang a pair?" he asked, lifting a brow.

"Of panties? Are you kidding?"

"You didn't have to, did you? You spent the night with my sister and eventually got everything all the panty-hangers wanted."

"I didn't spend the night with Sierra just so I could hook up with you." Good grief. "And why are we talking about this?"

But he answered with his own question. "Did you turn down boys from St. Thomas?"

"I went out with two or three. Before you. Why?"

"So being with me cost you what? Homecoming? Prom?"

Really? "I couldn't have cared less about homecoming or prom."

A soft smile passed over his face. "We could've gone together, you know. If we'd told everyone—"

"If we'd told everyone, I wouldn't have been allowed to spend the night with Sierra." And even then she'd only sneaked up to Angelo's room when Sierra had sneaked out with Oscar. "Where is this coming from?"

He shrugged, a boyish gesture. "Just wondering if those four years were worth it."

She'd loved him, as much as anyone could love someone else as a teen. "I can't even believe we're having this discussion."

"So they *were* worth it," he said, glancing at her from the side.

The man was going to drive her insane. "You're awfully full of yourself."

"It's the football player in me," he said.

"I might believe that if you'd gone on to play college ball."

He walked back to the porch and sat on the steps. "Never had any interest. Besides, as it turned out, I wouldn't have had time. I had to work to pay for school and expenses. Mine and a lot of my family's, since my parents took my working as some kind of signal that they didn't have to as much. Kinda took the fun out of leaving home."

Wow. This she hadn't known. "It wasn't all bad, was it?"

"No. Before Sierra called it was actually pretty good. Even after she called. That summer anyway. But that's when I went to Rome."

"Tell me more about Rome. What did you do?"

"I did everything," he said, smiling. "If it wasn't included in the Cornell in Rome program, I did it on my own."

"Is the Sistine Chapel as amazing as it looks in pictures?"

"You wouldn't believe."

The way his eyes lit up as he talked, telling her things about the trip he'd omitted in the past . . .

"I've never been out of the country," she said as she sat beside him. "I haven't even been out of Texas but once to go to LA, and once to go to New York, both times for work."

"I would've expected the Luna Meadows I knew to be more adventurous."

She had been adventurous with him. "Seeing your two best friends go down a ravine in a convertible tends to be sobering."

"Is that why you still live at home?"

"Part of it, I guess. I feel safe there. My parents have made it easy for me."

"Easy to stay? Or easy to not have to get on with your life?"

"Easy to get on with it at my own pace. It took me a while to get back on my feet, if you'll remember. And I mean that literally. I didn't even get to go to school until the second semester of my senior year."

He braced his elbows on the step above the one where he sat and leaned back. "I'm sorry you had to go through that."

"Thank you." The words were automatic.

"I mean it, Luna. I am sorry."

"I don't know why," she said, uncomfortable for some reason with his being so nice. "I had a senior year. Sierra didn't. Oscar didn't. What I went through, the physical pain, the emotional suffering, for myself as well as my friends, it was nothing. I was here, alive. Going to school. Doing homework. Passing my exams. Graduating."

"You never told me why you didn't go to college."

She shook her head. "I hadn't decided yet what I wanted to do, where I wanted to go. I wasn't a musician, so I wouldn't be going away like Sierra and Oscar. And then later, weaving took up most of my time. I stayed busy. I stayed safe. My parents saw to that, building out the house so I'd have my own suite of rooms. Enabling me because it made things less worrisome for them."

"Wait a minute." He pushed up to sit straight, then stood and hovered over her, his hands at his hips. "Sierra was going away? Did she get a scholarship? Or a grant? Because I know she didn't have money for college. And I can't imagine her working her way through school with all the practice her music required."

"I just meant . . ." She paused, searching for something to say to get her out of this mess. "I assumed she'd continue studying music. I chose my words poorly."

"Or you told the truth. That Sierra and Oscar had plans to go away together. And you were the only other person who knew."

~

Luna could backtrack all she wanted, Angelo mused, shouldering open the front door, but she'd said what she'd said before walking away, and her explanation didn't hold water. Sierra had been planning to go away with Oscar, which sounded a whole lot like she'd never planned to be a mother to her child at all. But that made no sense in light of the rest of the things Luna had told him. If his sister had no money for college, and no scholarship, what was she expecting to do? Tag along while Oscar went to class? Play on street corners for tips? Be the little woman at home?

He straightened from stacking on the porch yet another box of crap he didn't recognize. Things he'd found in the room Felix and Emilio had shared. Bits and pieces of toys he couldn't remember them playing with. Proof of life in the Caffey house going on without him. He'd missed so much of their growing up, and all because he'd chosen to stay with Luna after the accident, to not blame Luna as his parents had done.

At least until the day his parents disowned him.

It was pretty clear he hadn't known Sierra as well as he'd thought. Just as it was pretty clear Luna had known her intimately. He and Sierra had attended different schools, so they had no gossip to snark on, teachers to rag on, assemblies to bitch about, campus shortcuts to figure out. She had her music, and he had his sports. Most of their bonding had been as the oldest two of six siblings. Still, he'd been closer to Sierra than to any of his brothers or sisters, or as close as their lack of shared interests and sixteen years under the same roof allowed.

"I'm so sick of Isidora's idea of washing dishes. I have to scrub them again when I rinse."

"Try sharing a toilet with four- and eight-year-old boys. I'll take doing the dishes any day."

"At least they don't play with your makeup without asking."

"Makeup, no. Stereo, yes. You should see the sticky fingerprints all over my CDs."

"I'm looking for Luna Meadows."

Angelo looked up and stepped off the porch to meet the man he hadn't heard arrive. "And you are?"

His visitor held out his hand, a big, broad hand as scarred up as Angelo's own. "Tennessee Keller. I'm the building contractor working with Luna on the arts center."

"Something going on?" Angelo asked, shaking it.

Tennessee frowned. "Can't say. She asked me to meet her, so here I am."

Angelo canted his head toward the porch. "She's inside."

Just then, the front door opened and Luna walked out with a big bag of trash. She tossed it on top of the growing mountain waiting for the second Dumpster to arrive. "Ten, hey. I thought I heard your voice. I see you met Angelo."

"Not really," Ten said, glancing from Luna to Angelo again.

He gave a nod of apology. "Angelo Caffey. This was my family's place. I'm just back to see what's still here before Luna tears it down." Though that wasn't the reason he'd come back at all.

"That's why I asked Ten to stop by," Luna said. "I've been thinking about not tearing it down."

"What?" Ten asked.

"Will came by the other day," Luna said. "He asked if we'd thought about keeping the house and building the center around it. Like you did with Kaylie's house and the café."

"Will seemed to think the house could be saved," Angelo said.

"Not just saved, used." Luna looked from one man to the other. "Basically, why go boxy and utilitarian when we could design something that would complement the house and be an extension of it? The rooms here could be used for administration and faculty offices, and the new structure would house the classrooms."

"By *we* designing something," Angelo said, "I'm pretty sure she means you."

"Well, yes," Luna replied. "Ten's the contractor. But you *are* an architect. This is something we could work on together."

Even though she knew he had no plans to stay. Even though she'd asked him about doing so. "And that *we* means . . ."

"Me. You. Ten. Maybe Will."

Ten rubbed a hand over his nape. "What does the non-profit think? About starting from scratch so late in the game?

Because you're asking for a lot here with all the subcontractors' schedules."

"How long would it take to change things up? And would something less . . . square take more time?"

"There's also the money to consider," Angelo said before Keller could answer.

"I'll cover any overage," Luna said, dismissing his concern.

"You will?" both men asked at once.

"It's not a big deal," she said, her hand going into her pocket. "And Will said he'd do up the blueprints and throw in his time for free."

"Don't say it's not a big deal," Tennessee said. "You haven't seen *my* quote yet."

"It doesn't matter. This is about Sierra and Oscar. And I'm so glad Will made the suggestion. Saving the house where she lived will make the center that much more of a memorial to her."

Ten took a minute to consider the option. "I've got all the specs on the house at the office. Give me a few days and I'll see what I can come up with. Not saying I'll be able to come up with anything, and not saying it's a bad idea, but I'm going to have to think about it. And I'll have to get an inspector out here to take a look at the house."

"Talk to Will," Luna said. "See if you can make sense of what he was saying."

"Yeah." Tennessee huffed. "Making sense of anything Will says can try a man in a whole lot of ways."

Funny, but after a few minutes in Will's company, Angelo understood exactly what Ten was saying. Then he thought about the other things he shared with the contractor, and motioned over his shoulder toward the buildings out back.

"You know, all of my father's woodworking tools are still in his shop. I'm going to keep some, but if there's anything that would make your life easier, you're welcome to it. If Luna doesn't mind."

"Not at all," she said, regarding him curiously.

"Thanks. I'd love to take a look. A man can never have too many tools," Ten said in response, causing Luna to roll her eyes. "What? It's true."

"I'm going to have to side with Ten on this one," Angelo said.

"Hey, I'm not arguing," Luna said. "I'm thinking about the pegboard in my father's shearing barn."

"If it's as jam-packed as the pegboard in your weaving shed," Ten said, "I bow to the man."

"You have tools in your weaving shed?" Angelo asked, not quite sure why she would.

But she shook her head. "No, just skeins of yarn. They hang on a pegboard."

"Wait," Angelo said. "You weave in a shed?"

"You haven't seen it?" Ten asked. "You really need to see it. It's less shed, more studio, but very, very cool."

Luna looked from Ten to Angelo, smiling. "My father converted it for me when he built his new barn a few years ago. But I'll be moving soon, so the weaving will be moving with me."

"That's right," Ten said. "Kaylie mentioned you were moving."

"Did she say it was about time?" Luna laughed as she asked. "That I'm too old to still be living at home with my parents?"

"Kaylie wouldn't say anything like that. But if I don't get going," Ten said, tapping the face of his watch, "she will tell me I'm late. I'm taking her to Gruene for lunch. It's Mitch's birthday. She wanted to surprise him."

"Oh, that's right. He and Dolly are having dinner tonight with my parents."

"How's your mom feeling?"

"Not great, but she's a trooper."

"Tell her hello."

"And the plans for the center?" Luna asked.

"Give me till after the weekend. Call me Monday if you haven't heard from me."

"Thanks, Ten."

"Nice to meet you, man," he said to Angelo.

"Likewise," Angelo responded with a wave.

His gaze on Ten Keller's truck as it backed out of the drive, Angelo asked, "So if the house is a memorial to Sierra, what about Oscar?"

Luna took a deep breath. "I don't have access to anything of Oscar's. I'm not sure how to personalize the center for him."

Because he couldn't help himself . . . "Next time his brother stops by, ask."

"Yeah. That's not going to happen. But I do need to figure out something." She gathered up her hair, knotted it at her nape, and held it there for a long moment before letting go. "I think I should go see him. Maybe that would help."

Because of their earlier conversation? He couldn't believe he was going to ask her this, but . . . "Do you want me to go with you?"

She turned to him, a question in her eyes. "Would you do that?"

"For the center. For Sierra." *For you*, he added silently, not sure why he couldn't give voice to the words. Especially with

121

the lies she continued to tell. All he knew was the closer he kept her, the more he earned her trust, the easier it would be for her to slip up the way she had when she'd admitted Sierra and Oscar had planned to go away.

"Thank you for offering, but I need to do it alone. Turns out I've got more things to say to him than I'd thought."

"Even if he can't hear you?"

"Sadly, that makes it easier to say them."

"You know Oscar never set foot in this house," Angelo said.

"I know."

"It's weird to think about that, how he and Sierra shared everything else, but she wouldn't bring him here."

"Did your parents never meet him?"

"At concerts, sure. Other school functions. Most related to the music program. But his parents were usually there, too, and making sure our young lovers didn't get too close." Because that had worked out so well. "Too late with that, weren't they?"

She pressed her lips together, anger a flash in her eyes. "They hated that. Hated sneaking around. They wanted their families to share in their joy. Instead . . ." She left the thought unfinished, shaking her head as she made her way back to the house, and leaving Angelo to wonder about all the things she hadn't said.

CHAPTER TWELVE

On the outside, the Hope Springs Rehab Institute looked less like a hospital and more like a complex of business suites. Pebbled walkways wound from the asphalt parking lot through the landscaped grounds. The one-story building, shaped like a capital *E*, had two long patient wings, a shorter center facilities annex, and a long main corridor housing offices for administrative and medical personnel.

As the automatic doors whooshed closed behind her, Luna removed her sunglasses and stood for a moment in the foyer, getting her bearings before locating reception. Her conversation with Angelo had left her unnerved and driven to make this visit. She'd gone home, checked on her mother, showered off the grit of day two spent at work in the house, and come here before she could change her mind.

The thought that she might have done so shamed her. Her failure to make this visit before now shamed her even more; what was wrong with her? Oscar had been her friend. He'd been the most important part of Sierra's life outside of her cello, and Luna could very well be mistaken about that. Seeing them get out of his car at the hospital that day . . . Sierra in a gorgeous red dress that emphasized her baby bump, her eyes almost as red from crying. Oscar's just as damp, but not all of his tears from sorrow. Luna had known that because of the way he'd smiled.

Shaking off the memory, she made her way to the window and signed in, then spoke to the young woman who opened the frosted partition: "I'd like to see Oscar Gatlin. Last I knew, he was unresponsive, but I'd still like to visit if I can."

"I don't believe he's restricted, but let me check his file."

Luna listened to the click of the keyboard as she took in the clusters of wingback and club chairs spaced along the long hallway and looking much like the seating areas in any Starbucks. What was missing was the aroma of coffee, the indie music, the hipsters with their dark-framed glasses, MacBooks, and smugness.

She shook off the thoughts; what was wrong with her? She loved Starbucks. And indie music. It had to be the truth of why she was here making her bitter. Oscar Gatlin would never again enjoy a pumpkin latte or compose music with any Mac software suite.

"Mr. Gatlin is in room two-forty-two," the receptionist was saying, bringing Luna back to the reason she was here. The other woman stood, leaning forward to point. "Down the hall to my right, it's the second door. Hit the access button, and I'll buzz you in. His door will be the second on your left down the corridor."

"Thank you," Luna said, taking a deep breath as she turned, walking lightly to keep her footsteps from echoing, even though she was the only person in the hall. At the door, she took another deep breath because she had no idea what to expect once she pushed through.

But she did push through, this corridor broadcasting the facility's purpose with its bright lights and disinfectant smell and staff outfitted in matching blue scrubs. Seconds later, she was at room 242, fearing that if she stopped to think about what she was doing she wouldn't be brave enough to go through with it, and shamed terribly by the idea.

Soft orchestral music that she thought might be Brahms played into the room from overhead speakers, and it was accompanied by soft beeps and wheezes of the equipment monitoring Oscar's vitals. Her heart slammed in her chest as if trying to nail her to the door at her back, to keep her from having to face the boy she'd known who was now a man she didn't.

"Hi, Oscar," she said, approaching slowly and swallowing the lump of emotion threatening to choke off the rest of her words. He lay in a double bed raised at a slight angle, the sheets on the mattress a warm sunny yellow, the comforter a geometric pattern in navy and moss green. "It's me. Luna Meadows. We were in school together." She paused, letting that sink in if it was going to before adding, "I was best friends with Sierra." All of which he would know.

She stared down at his expressionless face, soft and peaceful, yet drawn and aged, remembering the boy from years ago who'd stolen more hearts than Sierra's with his lazy charm and smile that he never worked for. He'd been a pianist as well as a cellist, studying with Sierra but destined for even greater things. Sierra had never once resented his family's connections, or the fact that it was those connections, and not his artistic ability, that would take him places she would never be able to go.

His eyes were barely open, as if he were drifting off to sleep, or fighting against waking up. As if any moment he would open them and look at her, grin at her, welcome her into his room. Luna knew neither was the case. He was in a permanent vegetative state, breathing with the help of a ventilator, fed through a tube. How his family dealt with this, she couldn't imagine. She didn't want to imagine. Even now, tears brimmed in her eyes, blurring her vision, and her chest ached fiercely, but she took a deep breath and went on.

"I don't think you can hear me. But I wanted to come talk to you anyway, just in case. I want you to know what I'm doing, and why, and how sorry I am that I haven't come to see you in all this time. I should have come to see you before now. We really were good friends, weren't we? And good friends don't abandon each other the way I did you. Please forgive me."

Even if he could hear her, and did, she wasn't sure she'd ever be able to forgive herself, and, dropping into the chair at his side, she hated that she'd been so selfish, and so afraid. She reached out to hold his hand between hers. His skin was cool, his grip sadly lifeless, but she could feel his pulse in his wrist where it rested against her thumb. Sierra had loved his hands. She'd talked often of how he touched her, how gentle he'd been, how considerate, how sexy. And that had Luna thinking of Angel's hands, the scars he bore from his wood-working, how rough his fingertips, how calloused his palms.

"Do you remember the first day you walked Sierra to lunch? Well, I was there, too, so I guess you walked both of us. The genesis of my life as a third wheel," she said, and found herself smiling. "Sierra always said you were a *Teen People* god. A Gavin Rossdale or Nick Lachey god. She said your hair made her think of coffee, and she loved your smile. A surfer smile, she said, with dimples that went on forever.

"And she was right about the mossy color of your eyes. Once she told me that if boy bands had cellists, there would've been mobs of screaming girls waiting for you outside music hall every day. That's where we were when Sierra laughed and you heard her that first time. You'd just come through the door, and the girls were all over you, and she just thought it so ridiculous that society girls would act that way. I guess she thought they would have more restraint, but she was the one who did, and I think you liked that about her. She liked so many things about you."

She paused, bowed her head to rest it a moment on their hands, strangely wishing that she'd accepted Angelo's offer to come with her. She didn't need him to do anything, or say anything, but just knowing he was there for her to lean on—though why she was thinking his offer meant he'd let her . . .

"Do you remember the *Jennifers* who ruled the cafeteria? How every day they picked on poor Jill . . . What was her name? The tall girl. Thin. Always telling lies. But the *Jennifers* . . . They were such terrible bullies, the way they would pound her sandwich flat and steal her chips and cookies. Sierra couldn't stand it. And that day I crushed a bag of Cheetos and dumped the crumbs all over their heads? She told me you loved hearing that story. Of course, *I* didn't love having to mop the cafeteria the rest of the month, but it was worth it."

She stopped, took a deep breath, unsure why she was talking about things that he already knew and really didn't matter. That wasn't why she was here, and yet seeing him had her remembering those days. "I came to tell you that I'm building a school. Well, I'm not building it. And it's not a school as much as an arts center. Mostly for music. A conservatory, I guess, though if things go well, I'd like to see about our nonprofit applying for an academic charter. I know how important St. Thomas was for you and Sierra." Being able to provide the same resources through a public school would be such a dream. "I'm proposing we call it the Caffey-Gatlin Academy. I haven't said anything about it to your family yet. I will, but the time needs to be right. I did tell Angelo, Sierra's brother. He's here in town."

Her throat grew tight as she looked at Oscar's face, searching for a hint of the life he'd been so full of. A contagious life, a life everyone around him had fed off of and loved. It was gone. All of it. He was a living, breathing shell, and breaking her heart. Had she caused this? Could she have kept it from happening? Was there any way she could've talked her two friends into another solution? Had there been another solution?

If she'd come here as soon as she was able after the accident, would he have known it then? Would he have heard her voice over all the others? Would he have listened when she told him about Sierra, and then let go? She bowed her head and caught back a sob, squeezing his hand as she did. In what seemed like the distance, she heard the door opening, and looked up, expecting to see a nurse.

Standing on the other side of the bed was Merrilee Gatlin, looking thunderously angry. The older woman was dressed in a suit Luna was sure was Chanel, her long strands of pearls and handbag and low-heeled pumps perfectly accessorizing the outfit. Luna, her nerves fluttering, had the fleeting thought that all the woman needed was a Patchwork Moon scarf, but Coco would've said no, all she needed was a hat.

"What are you doing here?" Merrilee asked, wrapping the fingers of one hand around the gloves she held in her other. "You have no business being here."

Luna let Oscar's hand go and retrieved her brown leather hobo bag from the floor before standing. "I came to talk to Oscar."

Merrilee swallowed, looking from Luna to her son and back. "Oscar doesn't talk."

"I know that—"

"Oscar most likely doesn't hear either."

"I know that—"

"It's doubtful Oscar is even aware of his family visiting. He certainly wouldn't recognize a stranger," she said, and having regained her poise, she advanced.

Luna circled the foot of the bed before Merrilee blocked her in. "I know that. But I came anyway."

"Without his family's permission?" the older woman asked as they stood toe-to-toe.

Though Luna wore boots, Merrilee's pumps saw to her three-inch height advantage. But Luna would not be intimidated. "I wasn't aware my visiting required your permission."

"Common courtesy would dictate you ask us."

Merrilee wasn't worried about common courtesy. She was worried about controlling everything—and everyone—Oscar was exposed to. It was her nature. And Luna didn't meet whatever criteria Merrilee used. "I told him what I wanted to say. I don't imagine having any need to come back," she said, though it killed her to do so.

"See that you don't. I've been careful to keep him calm, to avoid any unnecessary stress."

And Luna had always been unnecessary to Oscar's life. Still, Merrilee was Oscar's mother, and no doubt still grieving; how could she not be? This wasn't the time or the place for bickering. "I came to tell him about the arts center—"

The other woman tossed up her hands in an expansive, exasperated gesture. "Why in the world do you think he would care about that? Even if he could hear you, he would have no interest in your little nonprofit."

Luna thought about keeping quiet, but . . . *oh why not?* "Our *little* nonprofit has decided to call the center the Caffey-Gatlin Academy—"

"Oh no. Oh no. You will not put my family's name on that, that . . . whatever it is."

"It's an education center. It will offer the sort of instruction Sierra Caffey needed a scholarship to St. Thomas to have. Not everyone has a tutor like Mr. Miyazawa in their corner pulling strings to see they can get into the right school."

"And not everyone should. It's a private school for a reason. To keep the public where it belongs."

Luna's hackles rose. "You know Sierra had Oscar's talent beat, and he knew it, too."

"He knew no such thing. And she certainly did not. She certainly did not," she repeated, as if the emphasis would negate Luna's words.

What was she doing here, trying to convince the mother of a very sick young man that he'd been less of a musician than she believed? And she'd thought Oliver Gatlin's antics cruel. She was no better. And she might very well be worse. At least Oliver only attacked those capable of standing up for themselves.

"I'm sorry. I shouldn't have come. Not today."

"See that you never do again."

Luna said nothing. It wasn't a promise she was willing to make. But it would be a long time before she returned.

~

Seeing Merrilee Gatlin left Luna rattled. The other woman had a reputation for often being rude, always being imposing, never being anything less than right. Luna hadn't found her impressive, or particularly elegant, and definitely not dignified. But then, Luna hadn't grown up in the societal circles where the Gatlins reigned.

She knew Dolly Breeze's elegance of spirit and loved that the older woman now worked for both Ten and Kaylie. She knew the impressive genius of Mo Dexter, whom everyone in Hope Springs turned to for technical help. Her definition of dignity was the way Mitch Pepper had dealt with what fate had handed him.

Then again, her mood could be tied directly into seeing Oscar, and the shame of not visiting him regularly. She should have; he'd been such a good friend. No, he wouldn't have known she was there. He certainly hadn't today. And yes, seeing him in his condition left her incredibly sad . . . for his family's loss, for her loss, for the loss of Sierra—something Oscar would never know. And oh, but she hoped he didn't know. That he wasn't trapped in an unresponsive body, but somehow still aware of that horror.

Whatever it was, she could not face Angelo until she had a better handle on her emotions. So why she'd driven back to the Caffey house instead of going home, she couldn't explain, except they did have a deal, and several hours still remained in day two, and she was going to see this *hashing out* thing through to the end. It had nothing to do with feeling vulnerable and wanting to see him.

She pulled her car past the house and parked between the woodshop and the barn. Then, before Angelo could realize she was here, she got out of her car to walk. She headed toward the far side of the two structures, wanting to do nothing but breathe in the fresh air, watch the treetops sway in the breeze, listen to the birds chirp and the squirrels chatter. She wanted to do nothing but be alive. To remember her friends alive and here with her. She didn't ever want to forget.

That, she knew, was why she'd never gone before now to see Oscar. She wanted to think of him thriving, the same way she always pictured Sierra. She'd seen her best friend's casket lowered into the ground, but she hadn't attended the wake, and had only viewed the graveside service from a distance, so she'd never seen Sierra's body. She didn't know what Sierra had been dressed in for her burial. She didn't know who had fixed her hair, or if they'd done it the way *she* liked, not the way her mother wished she would wear it.

Had anyone besides Luna known these things about Sierra? Had her face been left bare, or carefully made up with the cosmetics the two of them had pooled their allowances to buy? Would someone have taken the time to find out Sierra liked deep purple eye shadow with soft moss green highlights, the colors used sparingly to bring out her eyes? Would someone have cared to get her blush right? Her lip gloss?

The idea that Sierra had been put in the ground wearing the dress she'd made their sophomore year in home economics, the dress she'd hated with a passion, with its Peter Pan collar and cap sleeves and hideous paisley print fabric, the dress her mother was so proud of . . . Her chest aching, Luna caught back a sob, leaning against the barn near the door, then giving in and sliding down to a squat, burying her face in her hands to cry.

She cried for her friends, not for her own loss but for what had been taken away from the two of them, their future, their family, their dreams. Their daughter. Oh, their daughter. She had no doubt their Lily had been well cared for all this time, but it broke her heart to realize a piece of Sierra still existed. How much more hurt must Angelo have felt at learning the truth. And yet all she'd done was tell him to leave his sister's daughter alone. She hadn't once thought about what he must be feeling. She should go to him, apologize, ask if he wanted to talk.

The sound of a whimper kept her from doing anything. She stopped crying and swiped her fingers beneath her eyes and her nose. Having lived her whole life on a sheep farm, she knew more than she cared to about predators. They stalked and killed their prey as far away as they could from humans and their scents. If a coyote or wild dog had come this close to a barn, had come *inside*, it was most likely sick or injured. That made it a danger, and she didn't think her car keys would work as a weapon this time.

But the noise didn't sound like a big animal. It sounded small, and hurt, and afraid.

It wasn't a puppy she found peering at her from between the slats of a stall, but a full-grown dog. He just hadn't grown very big. His coarse, curly fur was short, except around his face, where it stood up like strands of crooked straw. His eyes were huge and black, and his ears flopped forward as he cocked his head and listened to her approach. She knelt in front of him, talking to him in a soft, calming voice, her words mostly nonsensical, but doing their job as the dog wagged its tail and started on a slow, forward army crawl toward her.

And then a shadow fell over him and he scurried away. Luna wanted to turn around and come out swinging.

"What are you doing in here?" Angelo asked.

"I heard a noise."

His boots scraped over the floor as he moved closer. "So you came inside without knowing what was here?"

"I knew it was an animal. I wanted to make sure it wasn't hurt."

"I repeat. So you came inside without knowing—"

"Shut up, would you?" she yelled, then more quietly, "Just shut up. I'm not stupid. I grew up on a farm, you know." But she was sad and angry and hurting about Oscar, and she was unable to keep the mixture from bubbling up into her voice. And the dog wouldn't think she was a horrible person, or tell her what to do, or berate her for the lies she'd told when all she'd been doing was keeping her promise to her friend.

"Okay, farm girl. Now what?"

She looked back at the dog. He'd cocked his head to the side, as if listening to the two of them argue. He didn't seem scared, but she still feared he might be hurt. If she had a snare . . . but she didn't. She could probably find a length of rope that would work. There were plenty of tools with handles she could use. But she needed food for bait.

"Go back to the house. In the fridge. Bring me the rest of my hamburger from the other night." When a guilty look pulled at the corners of his mouth, she sighed. "Is there anything there you haven't eaten that a dog might like?"

"If he's hungry, I doubt he'll be picky."

"Just go. Find me something to feed him. I'm going to see if I can rig up a snare pole. Just in case he's injured." But before she could do that, the dog dropped to his belly again and began crawling toward her, scooting through the dirt on the floor, his wagging tail sweeping through layers of detritus.

She patted a hand to her thigh and said, "Come."

The dog moved closer, stopping once he'd reached her feet and resting his chin on the toes of her boot. "Well, what a sweetie *you* are," she said, leaning down to scratch the top of his head.

"Be careful," Angelo said behind her, and she shooed him out the door, gaining her feet and walking out behind him, the dog following her, trusting her, and giving her the first reason she'd had to smile all day.

CHAPTER THIRTEEN

N ow what?" Angelo asked an hour later, as the dog, still damp from his bath but smelling a whole lot better, settled onto the same couch cushion as Luna, as close as he could get without being in her lap.

"Francisco."

"What?"

"That's his name. Every school needs a mascot."

He nearly hurt himself rolling his eyes. "And the Caffey-Gatlin Academy needs a fleabag named Francisco?"

But Luna ignored him. "I'll take him to see the vet tomorrow. See if he's chipped. Get him tested for the obvious things. Put up flyers."

Angelo didn't even want to know how much time and money she was going to spend on the mutt. "And tonight?"

"He can stay here."

"No, he can't."

"In the barn then."

"No, he can't."

"Angelo!"

"Neither one of us has time to dog-sit. You can take him to the farm."

"My parents are about to have a new baby in the house. I'm not going to bring a dog home until he's been treated for fleas and tested for heartworms—"

"Your call where he goes, but I'm not watching your dog."

"He's not my—" She stopped herself. And then she laughed. "He's not my dog yet. But he *is* my responsibility. I rescued him. I can't foist him off on someone else. Mitch Pepper taught me that when he convinced my father to let me keep Maya."

"Who's Mitch again?"

"Kaylie's father. Ten mentioned him this afternoon."

"And Maya . . . She was your dog, right?"

She nodded, smiling as if pleased he remembered. "A Chinese crested–Jack Russell mix. I found her in the ditch in front of the farm. We had two border collies and two Great Pyrs already, so Daddy made sure I understood she was my responsibility. Just like Francisco."

"Wait a minute. Are you calling me irresponsible?"

"Are you feeling irresponsible?"

"Have I ever told you that I don't like dogs?"

"Who doesn't like dogs?"

"I don't like dogs."

"Why?"

"I don't know."

She shook her head. "That's just crazy talk. Dogs are man's best friend."

"Not this man."

"As grumpy as you are, I'm surprised you have any friends at all," she said, leaving him to wonder what she'd think if she knew how few he had, how hard it had been to care about friendships when his family had cut him off. Hard enough to live with having failed as a brother and a son. No sense tempting fate and failing elsewhere.

Then he wondered whether his boss counted, his boss's wife, their two sons who were in and out of the shop as they handled the business side of the business. And . . . that was about it. He rented a small house in the town where he lived, and he supposed he was friends, or at least friendly, with the waitress at the diner where he ate breakfast every day. With the short-order cook whose biscuits were the best he'd ever had, and that included those at Malina's.

He worked long hours, never setting an alarm because he was an early riser, heading into the shop when it was still dark. And he stayed late because there was always work to keep him busy, and he had nowhere else to be. No one to go home to. No family to drop by on and catch up with his life.

"Angelo?"

"Sorry. Was trying to come up with a list of names I could count as friends." And wondering what it said that he was sitting with and drawn to the woman who'd caused his family to disown him.

"I don't have many either. Kaylie, Ten Keller's fiancée, is my best. She's actually the closest one I've had since Sierra. Seems I'm only capable of having one at a time," she said, grimacing.

"What about Ten? And Will? They don't count?"

"As casual friends, sure. That's not what Kaylie is. Or what Sierra was."

"Or what the mutt's supposed to be?"

"Sometimes a dog is a better listener than anyone."

"Yeah, but you can't take Frank here to Malina's."

That brought a smile to her mouth, a smile that faded too quickly and had him wondering whether she was thinking back to the morning they'd gone to breakfast. The morning she'd told him about getting so completely lost in her work she ended up needing bandages. The morning he'd been a jerk because he hadn't known what to do with that kiss and the lingering burn.

It haunted him still. He woke in the middle of the night with his heart pounding, feeling Luna's hands on his back, turning into her arms, only to find he was alone in the house where he'd always been alone, ignored, in the way, left to fend because he'd proved himself responsible. Looking forward to Luna's visits because she paid attention to him. And if that wasn't desperately pathetic . . .

So it surprised him when what she said was, "I guess it's too late for us."

Tread carefully, Caffey. Do not be dumb. "To be friends?"

She nodded. "Seems the least we could do. For Sierra."

"Hmm. I thought all the time you've been spending here was because you wanted to be something more." He didn't know why he'd said it. It was such a stupid thing to say, to even be considering. Especially when things between them had become less contentious.

He waited, thinking he must've gone too far, but finally, she looked up, her hand stilling on the mutt's head. The mutt on the cushion between them, keeping them apart. "We were too young, you know. Back then. You and me. Oscar and Sierra. All of us sneaking around."

"You three maybe. I was eighteen." He watched Luna stroke the dog, watched the dog shiver between them, thought back to her hands on his skin.

"And that made you old enough?"

"It made me horny enough."

"Were you ashamed of me? Being with the girl from the sheep farm when you could have had anyone?"

"No, Luna. I wanted the girl from the sheep farm."

The room, already dark, took on a new closeness, the light from the kitchen the only illumination on the first floor where they waited . . . for supper, for another box or two to be packed. For bed. Luna's eyes glowed, a deep brown of coffee and chocolate and caramel, her hair so rich and black, glossy even in the feeble light.

Her smile began slowly, just a tip at both corners of her mouth, then broader, reaching her eyes, shining there. "We fought a lot, you know. For two people who spent as much time as we did in bed."

"There's a fine line between love and hate." *Crap. That was not what he'd meant to say.* "Not that what either of us felt was love—"

"Oh, I know," she rushed to say, and he wasn't sure her letting him off the hook was what he'd wanted to hear. But it was the smart thing for both of them; until he learned the things he'd come here for, he had to keep his current involvement with her to this. Whatever *this* was. Friendship, he supposed.

Yeah. He could be friends with Luna Meadows. And with the admission came the strangest sense of lightness, of freedom, one he'd take time later to examine. Right now, he was hungry. He had boxes to pack. And he probably needed to make a run for dog food. Who would've thought?

Day Three

THURSDAY

It is better to spend one day contemplating the
birth and death of all things than a hundred years
never contemplating beginnings and endings.
—Buddha

CHAPTER FOURTEEN

W hat do you think?" Luna asked, raising the grate on the loft's freight elevator. Breathing deeply, she swore she could still smell the bales of cotton that had been stored here while awaiting shipment to East Coast textile mills more than a hundred and forty years ago.

"Are you kidding me? This is incredible. And it is so, *so* you," Kaylie said, stepping into the huge open space on the top level of the four-story warehouse. The floor was rough concrete, the room bare except for the six support beams that almost symmetrically divided the area into three sections.

"Because I'm vacant? And naked?"

"No, silly. Because you're an artist, and this place is a palette waiting for you to weave your magic."

"Very clever, you are, with the weaving instead of the painting."

But Kaylie was already halfway across the room, making her way to the long stretch of windows. She reached for the handle to one and rolled it open. The warm Hill Country breeze fluttered through, and she breathed it in, filling her lungs, smiling.

"If I didn't love my house so much, and hadn't just spent a ridiculous fortune putting it back together after the fire, I would be raising all kinds of money to buy this place." She closed her eyes, dropped her head back. "Open windows on both ends and you'll never need a fan. And the light is incredible. How can you stand not living here already? And there's even enough room if you decided you want to share the place. With a roommate. Or, you know, a man."

A blush stole up Luna's neck as she realized Angelo was the only man who came to mind. Not any of the men she'd dated casually over the years. Not any of those she'd dated seriously. Not even Will Bowman, whom she'd thought at one time she'd like to know better.

"Who is it?"

"What?" She glanced at Kaylie and frowned.

"The look on your face. What's his name?"

Luna sighed, walking the length of the loft as if she'd find a sensible answer along the way. She'd been living at home with her parents for twenty-eight years. She hadn't gone to college. She'd learned her trade while confined to her bed with a broken hip in high school. Once her scarf line had taken off with the first celebrity sighting, one from the Austin boutique draped artfully around Cameron Diaz's shoulders, she'd refused to give but just a handful of interviews, avoiding TV spots like the plague.

At heart, she was a small-town girl, and she'd lucked into a lucrative profession. And she'd done so without having to beat the streets and hawk her wares. But no matter how many men she'd dated, she'd had eyes for no one but Angelo Caffey since seeing him for the very first time.

How did she even function in the real world with so little real-world experience?

How could she possibly trust what she felt for him? How would she ever know if her feelings for him *were* for him, or if they were tied to the loss of his sister? She wanted desperately to believe that last night had been a turning point. That they had moved beyond the anger and reached a place where they could talk about the past, grieve what they'd lost. Explore what they'd both buried because the time had never been right.

"Luna? Is something wrong?"

"I think I'm in love," she said, swept away as a flood of emotions crashed over her, stunned her, left her struggling to breathe. "I think I have been for years."

"What?" Kaylie reached out, took hold of Luna's arm, and pulled her around. "What are you talking about? Who are you in love with?"

"Angelo Caffey."

"From the house, Angelo? Your friend's brother, Angelo?"

Luna nodded. "I met Sierra when we were both freshmen at the St. Thomas Preparatory School. Angelo went to Hope Springs High, but I actually met him the same day. He came to school to pick her up, and I came this close to punching his lights out."

With a shocked laugh, Kaylie let her go. "I need to hear this story. And as much as I'd love hearing it over a margarita, I need to hear it now."

"There's not a lot to it. Sierra and I were both waiting for our rides in front of the school. We were getting to know each other. I was telling her about a dog I'd had. We were fifteen and in private school. And not the cool *Gossip Girl* TV show kind of school. We were dorks," she said, rolling her eyes when Kaylie chuckled. "Anyway, Angelo drove up and honked. Sierra and I were talking, so she didn't move, staying to hear what I was saying. He honked again. I got up and walked to his car and, hypocrite that I am, yelled at him to stop yelling. He shoved the door open and got out, and was about to lay into me."

"But you didn't let him."

"I don't have siblings, so I'm the last person to understand the dynamics. But the way he was talking to Sierra just burned me up. I got close enough to jab my finger into his chest, and I kept yelling, until all of a sudden I realized he was breathing hard. And his chest was this solid wall of young football player muscle. And my chest was mush. I fell completely. Right there. Just like that."

"But you never dated?"

"I wouldn't call what we did dating," she said, and Kaylie *aahed* knowingly. "I spent a lot of time at Sierra's house. I loved all the noise. She had two sisters and three brothers. Angelo was the oldest. But we were never friends, he and I. And I always had to get in the last word."

"Sounds like you were meant to be together from day one."

"I don't know. How *can* I know?" She was so very frustrated with wanting to. "We were so young back then. But now that he's here—"

"He's not a boy any longer."

Luna nodded. "He came to clear out the house before we tear it down. Or that had been the plan. Now we may not tear it down. Will suggested building onto it, using the house for the staff, and I ran the idea by Ten . . . which I'm sure you already know."

"He mentioned it, yes. And I think it's a perfect idea. But then you know how I feel about renovating structures, especially ones full of history. It sounds like this one holds a lot for you."

"It does. Which makes it hard to know what to do. I don't want to spend time in those rooms and see Angelo, or relive memories of him being there, every time I turn a corner. I know how I feel, and I know he's not indifferent to me. But it's so hard to know where all the tension is coming from. We're in the house together, looking through all the things that are still there, and memories are everywhere, making me sad. But I try to hide it because I know he's got to be feeling even worse."

Kaylie reached out and took hold of Luna's hands with her own, squeezing. "You want to talk about it over an early lunch?"

Another nod. A reciprocal, desperate squeeze. "A long lunch. With a whole pitcher of margaritas."

Forty minutes later they were seated at the Gristmill Restaurant, where Luna had waited tables while in high school. Kaylie's father, Mitch, had worked in the kitchen at the time and helped Luna get the job. He worked here still, but he'd soon be splitting his time between Gruene, where the Gristmill was located, and Hope Springs, where he, along with Dolly Breeze, would be working magic in Kaylie's Two Owls Café.

Kaylie had waited so long to see her dream come true. Luna was thrilled it was finally happening. She was also thrilled her good friend had found such happiness with Ten. Kaylie deserved the life she was living more than anyone Luna knew. Not everyone left for twenty-three years believing she was alone in the world would've become the wonderfully selfless person Kaylie was. And now that Kaylie had found both her father and the love of her life, well, Luna couldn't deny her envy.

A happy envy. A good envy. But still. Envy. "So? When's the wedding?"

The huge diamond solitaire on Kaylie's ring finger sparkled in the light shining over the Guadalupe River and onto the Gristmill's patio, causing Luna to go still. White. Sunshine yellow. A bouquet of purple-cream calla lilies with golden tongues. The green of stems and leaves.

"Uh, hello? Earth to Luna."

"Sorry, I was just—"

"Designing a scarf. I know. I've been through this with you a dozen times now." Kaylie reached for her tea, held the straw for sipping. "Did you need to stop and type yourself a reminder?"

"You do know me well." Luna dug her phone from her pocket and added the details of the colors and design to her note-taking program. "I mean, I usually remember these things after I see them, but as the story develops, it's nice to have everything in one place."

"And what story is this?"

"I'm not quite sure, but you flashing that rock of yours is what inspired it."

"I do not flash my rock," Kaylie said, flashing it. "At least not often. And only in front of good friends who understand how happy I am. Rock or not. Because it's definitely not about the rock."

Luna grinned as she picked up her fork to dig into her salad. "Though the rock doesn't hurt."

"Ten is my true rock. The only one I care about." Kaylie looked down at her hand, splayed her fingers. Then laughed. "You're right. The rock doesn't hurt at all."

They spent the rest of the meal discussing the progress on Kaylie's café . . .

"I can't decide if opening before Thanksgiving is a good idea or not. People will be so busy with holiday planning."

"And that makes it the perfect time. They'll need a break from shopping. Or a place to sit and enjoy a meal and swap recipes with friends. Or have a cookie exchange. Or just do nothing for an hour but eat brownies."

"I hope you're right. Two Owls will definitely be ideal for any of that."

"Speaking of brownies, how did your recipe inspired by Ten turn out?" Luna asked. "The one with the coconut and *dulce de leche* and cayenne?"

"You never got to taste them? I'm going to have to bake you a batch. They are amazing."

. . . and the plans for Luna's arts center . . .

"We have a mascot, did I tell you? A dog named Francisco."

"A dog named Francisco. Because you weren't busy enough already?"

"Well, it wasn't planned. I found him in the barn. And if someone claims him, I'll of course give him up. But he's not chipped, and hadn't been cared for in a very long time, so he's mine, and the center's, until that happens. He's at the vet now. I'm picking him up after we leave here."

"What does Angelo think about that?"

"He says he doesn't like dogs."

"But he's putting up with this one for you."

Luna smiled. Said nothing.

. . . and Kaylie's very tentative wedding plans . . .

"We want to wait until we see what's going to happen with the café. I'm barely keeping my head above water as it is with those details. Can you imagine adding flowers and cakes and dresses, not to mention the venue and invitations . . ."

"They actually do have wedding planners for that, you know."

"Me? Use a wedding planner? Huh. I'm beginning to think you don't know me at all."

. . . and Luna's fear that she would never measure up as a sister.

"Why in the world would you think such a thing?" Kaylie asked, flabbergasted. "You're exactly who I would want for a sister. I think of you as a sister. You're caring and supportive and you make me laugh, and you let me know when I'm being stupid."

"You're never stupid."

"Only because you stop me in time."

Luna laughed. "Well, if that's all it takes to be a sister . . ."

"You'll be fine. Seriously. I lived in enough foster homes and had enough foster siblings to know." And then she frowned. "Weren't we supposed to order margaritas for some reason?"

The way the other woman asked made Luna wonder whether it was the offhand reference to her childhood that had Kaylie signaling for their server and placing the order.

Feeling they both needed a change of subject, Luna stabbed her fork into her salad and asked, "What do you have going on this evening?"

"Nothing that I know of. Dinner. Playing with Magoo. Playing with Ten when he finally gets home," she added, and waggled both brows.

"You want to come to Austin with me? I need someone to hold my hand."

"Hold your—" Kaylie stilled, her eyes widening. "Luna, what's wrong?"

"Oh, nothing. Sorry. I didn't mean to sound so dramatic." She looked down, smiled at the thought of what she'd decided to do, how right it felt, the anticipation. How Angelo's comments had played into her decision, though she probably shouldn't have let them. "I have an appointment with my hairstylist."

Grabbing for her drink before their server had even set the glass on the table, Kaylie asked, "The same one you see every month?"

"Yeah, but this time I'm having him do more than trim the ends."

Kaylie's eyes widened. "What?"

"I'm ready for something new."

"Uh-uh. You don't just decide you're ready for something new. Not with that hair."

"Why not?"

"It's . . . I don't know, iconic, I guess. I can't imagine you without it."

"You've only known me six months."

"And it feels like longer. But that's not the point. The point is—"

"It's just hair. It's the hair I've had all my life. It's been this long for the past ten years, and it's time for a fresh start," Luna said, and reached for her drink.

Kaylie sipped again, then put down the glass. "Does this have anything to do with Angelo?"

"No," she said, his question about her hair on her mind. "It has to do with everything in my life being new." And free of burdens. No more weight of any kind dragging her down. "A new baby sister, a new home of my own, a new career managing a nonprofit, though I'll have to keep the old career to make ends meet. I'm shedding my past. Adding a new hairstyle to the mix seems appropriate."

"And drastically insane, but if you're sure."

Luna nodded. "I am, but I have no idea what to do with it. I booked plenty of time with Caldwell and told him to start thinking, but I'm really not sure how short I want to go."

Kaylie's eyes were bright with ideas when she reached again for her drink. "We can come up with something, and on the drive, you can tell me more about Angelo."

"I'm not even sure I know where to begin."

"The beginning is always a good place. Especially since you wanted to punch his lights out the first time you met him."

CHAPTER FIFTEEN

Thursday afternoon, having picked up Francisco from the vet's groomer on her way back from Gruene, Luna turned onto Three Wishes Road, only to find a half dozen vehicles parked in front of her house. Vehicles belonging to volunteers who'd come to clean up the center's five-acre lot. There were riding mowers and weed eaters and tree trimmers and rakes.

The road was narrow, and she drove slowly, turning between two pickups into the driveway to park behind Angelo's rental. He stood on the front porch, talking to Will Bowman and Ten Keller, the three men deep in discussion and paying her arrival no mind.

She opened her door, and Francisco bolted before she could stop him, heading for the steps and jumping into Angelo's arms. The man who didn't like dogs had stolen this one's heart overnight, and had his heart captured in return. He tucked the wiry terrier beneath one arm as he continued to talk to Will, not even acknowledging Luna, still sitting in her car. She took advantage of his being distracted to appreciate him.

He wore his regular outfit of T-shirt and jeans, both worn and faded, both indecently clingy. Or maybe that was just how she saw him, his muscled thighs and tight rear end, his biceps stretching the shirt's cotton, as did his chest. He'd bound his hair at his nape with what looked like a leather shoelace, and his work boots showed years of abuse. Furniture oils and paints and scratches, the same sorts of scratches healed into scars on his hands.

She wondered whether he'd ever hurt himself badly enough to need stitches. She wondered if she'd ever find out on her own.

It amazed her how consumed she was with wanting to do that, wanting to touch him, learn him, share more with him than kisses. That kiss had been hungry, and needy, but she wasn't sure of the reasons behind the heat. Reasons beyond the physical, because that was obvious; she was a grown woman, after all. And the man Angelo Caffey had become left her breathless.

Filled with him, she stepped from her car, pressing her nails into her palms to remind herself of the present. Of *this* Angelo, but it was so hard to look across the yard and not see him climbing from his ride and trudging toward the house after football practice, or to see him jogging toward the street where a car of giggling girls idled. Oh, but the girls had giggled. And loved him. No doubt they still did, she mused, lifting her hand to return Wade Parker's greeting as he and his mower headed for the fence and the most unkempt section of the yard.

Across the street, taking it all in, was Hiram Glass, a table of honey from his bees for sale. Legs crossed, he sat in a webbed lawn chair with a hardcover book in his lap, something bulky, the size of *Moby-Dick* or *War and Peace*. Hiram was as much of a classic as the literature he loved. He wore a ball cap pulled low and tight, and tufts of white hair sprouted over his ears and up around the brim. He always needed a haircut. He'd needed one since the death of his wife five years ago. Since his hair had looked the same all that time, Luna supposed he chopped at it himself.

Her heart broke a bit, picturing him doing so, imagining him standing in his tiny house's tiny bathroom, staring into a silvered mirror above a pedestal sink, clipping away without really paying much attention to what he was doing. She'd seen him often at the Caffey house in the past. He'd been good friends with Mike, his wife, Dorie, good friends with Carlita. His honey had always been on the breakfast table, his tomatoes served with summer suppers.

He looked up then and she waved, wondering whether he remembered her, how he felt about her, whether he realized as he took her in that she was the girl who'd survived her own accident on the very tail of the one that had taken away the daughter of his friend. He seemed to frown, his gaze falling back to his book. Luna lowered her hand, wishing the snub hadn't crushed her, but just as she started to turn, his head came up and he waved. A big sweep of his arm, as if he *had* remembered and was glad.

If only everyone shared his delight at having placed her. Though, really, it had been a long time since she'd felt like a pariah. And it had been only the Caffey family's shunning that made her feel that way. Sierra's parents had treated her like one of their own, until they hadn't. She'd loved them, and they'd abandoned her, looked through her, refused her apologies, ignored her efforts to make things right.

She glanced toward the porch again. Angelo stood there still holding Francisco, Will and Ten having left him alone. He met her gaze, frowning as if asking her what she was doing, but she couldn't move, the hustle and bustle of so many volunteers rooting her to the spot. It took her breath away, the support for the arts center, the love for the Caffey family who would never know, the joy at being able to honor two young people who'd been stolen from the community too soon.

Just as she pocketed her keys, shaking off the moment's melancholy, another car arrived, one she easily recognized, having seen it too often lately. One whose driver wasn't here to lend a hand but to ruin the rest of her day. For no reason she understood, she hadn't destroyed Oliver Gatlin's check. She should have shredded it. Or torn it into pieces and thrown it back at him when he'd laid down his conditions.

She hadn't deposited it either, obviously, because she had no intention of agreeing to his terms. But the truth would come out soon enough, and then she would call him. But she didn't want to see him today. Shaking her head, she caught Angelo's gaze and headed that way, waiting for him to notice Oliver's presence. He did, his face going dark as he clambered down the porch and into the yard to cut the other man off at the pass.

～

Angelo stopped only long enough to hand off Frank to Luna. "Go on in. I'll get rid of him."

"It's my fight," she said, taking the dog. "You don't have to—"

"Yeah. I do," he said, and meant it. And then he raised a brow, watching her dip her head, watching her smile, watching her turn to do what he'd told her to. A primitive sense of possession puffed inside him, but he didn't have time to decide whether he liked it before he heard Oliver's car door slam.

He shut out all the activity around him. Nothing existed save for the man circling the end of his car as Angelo made for the driveway, beating Oliver to it, blocking the path beyond Luna's car, staking his claim. "What do you want?"

"I'm here to see Luna."

"I can pass along anything you think you need to say to her."

"If I were here about the center. But I'm not." He lifted his gaze beyond Angelo's shoulder, searching out Luna, no doubt. Then, without looking at Angelo again, he pushed forward, saying, "Excuse me—"

That was all he got out before Angelo stopped him, physically, his open hand making contact with the center of Oliver's chest. "You leave her the hell alone." And as the words hung between them, the fight went out of the battle between his head and his heart. Nothing mattered here but Luna.

Oliver's gaze crept back to his, but he didn't buck against Angelo's hand, or his threat. "Then you tell her to leave my family the hell alone."

Angelo figured he was talking about Luna's visit to Oscar, and let the other man go. "You're telling me Luna Meadows is bothering you?"

Oliver's jaw clenched hard. "She was in my brother's room when my mother went to visit. She has no business seeing my brother."

"I'm pretty sure she was your brother's friend."

"The same way she was your sister's friend? You saying you don't think it's strange that she's the only one of the three to walk away that day?"

"She didn't walk away," Angelo reminded the other man. "She was in her own car. And her car didn't go down the ravine."

"Damn lucky. Damn convenient, too."

Okay. This was getting out of hand. "You got something to say, Gatlin, then say it. Otherwise, get the hell off my property," he said, though it no longer was. "And leave Luna alone."

But Oliver only huffed. "So it's like that, is it? You're forgetting what she did to your sister because you like having her in your bed?"

"I'm not forgetting a damn thing," he said, flexing his hands at his sides, his anger boiling. "Including the fact that it was *your* brother driving. *Your* brother who couldn't control his car and didn't care enough for my sister, *my* sister, to make sure she was safe. That's what I think is strange. *That's* what you and your family should be worried about."

"Worried? I dunno." Oliver shrugged, as if responding was a bother. "Since your family was the one to leave town, they must be the ones with something to worry about."

"You mean more harassment from your mother? More undercutting and sabotaging their work? It wasn't enough to see them deplete their savings? To make sure they had no choice but to go?"

"Yeah. Choice. They're the ones who made it."

Angelo was fuming, afraid that if the other man didn't leave, his fury would turn physical. He'd tamped all of this down for so long, all this bitterness and blame for what was nothing but an accident. An accident that could so easily be laid at Oscar Gatlin's feet.

"You need to go," he said to Oliver, before he did something he would regret. He was that close to striking out, and this wasn't the time or the place, what with the audience of volunteers and Luna watching. "You need to go."

Oliver cast one last look over Angelo's shoulder, then backed a step away, another, another. He was shaking his head when he turned, frowning, as if he was more unsettled by what Angelo had said than being unable to talk to Luna.

Still holding Frank, she walked up beside Angelo. "Thank you for getting rid of him."

He would rather have used his fists. And his emotions running hot had him turning on Luna. "What did you think seeing Oscar Gatlin was going to accomplish?"

"I wasn't trying to *accomplish* anything," she said, flinching. "I wanted to talk to him."

"He can't hear you, Luna."

"You don't know that," she said, holding Frank tighter. "The doctors don't know that."

"He's in a permanent vegetative state. You told me that yourself."

"I don't care. I needed to talk to him. I needed to tell him . . ."

"What? What could you possibly have to tell him?"

"That I was sorry," she yelled, her eyes growing damp.

"Sorry for what?"

"That I hadn't been to see him before."

Angelo scrubbed both hands back through his hair. "Luna—" It was all he got out before stopping, because he had nothing else to say. He didn't know what she'd gone through the last ten years. What she'd suffered as a survivor. Blame, certainly, from the Gatlins, from herself. At least two years' worth from his parents.

Had his siblings pitched in? Giving her the cold shoulder? Or, since they'd just been kids when Sierra had died, calling Luna names, or egging her car?

"I'm sorry," was what he finally told her because it was the most honest thing he could say.

"What do you have to be sorry for?" she asked, swiping a finger beneath both of her eyes.

He'd hurt her again; what was wrong with him? "Everything you've gone through. The way my family treated you." He paused. "The way I treated you."

She shrugged as if it were nothing, when he knew better. "I don't blame you or your family for any of it. If the shoe had been on the other foot—"

"No. You wouldn't have done the same thing. You don't have it in you to be cruel."

She shook her head, gave a humorless laugh. "Oh, I can conjure up all sorts of cruelties, but you're probably right that I wouldn't be able to pull them off. Unlike Oliver."

Oliver Gatlin was a piece of work. "He accused me of forgetting about Sierra."

"What?"

"Said having you warm my bed had turned my mind to mush, or some such," he said, glancing over in time to see color bloom on her cheeks.

Her throat worked as if she was trying to swallow something she didn't like. "Did you tell him we're not sleeping together? Why would he think we were sleeping together?"

"I doubt he's the only one," he said, and when her eyes widened, he added, "Your car's been in the driveway every day since I showed up. Your very identifiable car with person-alized *PWMoon* plates. And by now, most of the town knows I'm staying here."

"That doesn't mean we're sleeping together."

"It's an easy jump to make."

"I don't know why. Until today, the only time we've been seen together is the night we ate at Malina's. And no one who saw us there would ever think we were intimate."

"Because lovers don't quarrel?" Did she really believe that? After their past?

"That was an argument. A real argument. Not a . . . lovers' spat." She stopped, as if realizing the ridiculousness of her logic. She also moved a long step away.

That made him laugh. "A little too late for that, don't you think?"

"I should probably go home. If you need me to take Frank home with me, I will, but I think he'd be a lot happier with you."

Well, crap. If he'd known she was going to run, he would've kept his mouth shut. "Considering he slept on my bed last night, yeah. I'd say so."

"You don't have to sound so smug. You're the one who doesn't like dogs, remember."

"I'm willing to have my mind changed. I just needed a reason to change it."

"And Frank's that reason?" she asked, even though they both knew they'd stopped talking about dogs.

"I've been too hard on you. About your keeping Sierra's secrets. And I've been thinking I'm as much to blame for everything that happened as anyone. If anyone is to blame," he hurried to add before she interrupted. "If it all wasn't just a big series of events gone wrong. It started with two kids who knew well enough what they were doing. Who should've used protection." His chest grew tight. His throat swelled. He rubbed at his eyes to keep them from watering. "Why couldn't they have just used protection?"

Before she could reach for him, he walked away and into the middle of the street to make sure Gatlin's car was gone. Then he headed across the road to see Hiram Glass. Because if a spoonful of honey could make the medicine go down, he figured a whole jar could do magic.

CHAPTER SIXTEEN

"Are you sure about this?" Kaylie asked Luna later that night, holding Luna's hand and squeezing as she met her reflected gaze in the salon station's mirror. Luna could only nod. She'd never thought of her hair as a penance, a weight she carried, a connection to the past. She and Sierra had been too close for her to need a physical reminder of the three years—was that really all?—they'd had.

But at separate times during the last six months, both Will Bowman and now Angelo had asked her what she was trying to prove, or hoping to accomplish, or what statement she was making by wearing it long. She'd certainly not done it for ease or convenience. It took forever to wash and even longer to dry, and managing the tangles and knots often felt like a full-time job.

Maybe there was something to their observations. She hadn't consciously made the decision to keep it long, to carry the weight, to bind herself to the past with the strands, but perhaps that was exactly what she'd done, keeping it the same length since the accident. And even the fact that she was hesitating seemed less an uncertainty about a new style than an attachment she was pretty sure couldn't be healthy.

"Because if you're not sure," Kaylie continued, "don't do it."

"Kaylie's right," Caldwell said, standing behind Luna and lifting her hair with both hands. He held it for a long moment, then let it go. All three of them watched in the mirror as the strands fell around Luna's shoulders like a long black cape. "But if you do cut it, I'd love to take it off in a tail to donate."

Luna thought about Skye, wondered whether her little sister would share her coloring, the black hair she'd inherited from both her parents, her mother's Hispanic ethnicity giving her skin its tone. Then she thought of another child somewhere, one who'd lost her hair to chemotherapy, or an illness, growing confident, feeling pretty again. Normal. Drawing compliments instead of stares.

Oh, good grief. It was only hair. She was tired of looking like her senior portrait. And it was getting in the way. "Yes. Cut it. I want it gone."

Caldwell studied her in the mirror, his hands on either side of her head, pulling her hair one way, then another, as if trying on different styles with the shape of her cheekbones and chin. "Do you have an idea of what you want?"

"Not a single one," she said, causing Kaylie to groan. "But I'm going to guess by that gleam in your eye that you do."

"Free rein?"

"Anything you want."

"Luna—" Kaylie said, groaning again.

"I trust him. But," she said, meeting Caldwell's gaze in the mirror, "I don't want to watch. I don't want to see anything till you're done."

He nodded. "I'll keep you turned away as much as I can. But it'll be up to you not to peek."

Kaylie groaned a third time, but she settled into the empty chair in the adjoining station for the show.

"No more groaning from you, miss," Luna said with a laugh. "Hold your commentary for the end."

"I'll just be over here with my phone taking pictures for your scrapbook," Kaylie said, raising said phone and taking one.

"As long as you're not over there posting them to Facebook before Luna can." Caldwell swiveled her chair, and Luna closed her eyes as he gathered her hair into a tail and bound it.

"No Facebook," Kaylie said. "But I was thinking if I had Angelo's cell number, I could send them to him."

Luna's eyes flew open. "Don't you dare."

Kaylie grinned. "Lucky for you, I don't have his number."

"Lucky for *you*, you mean. I would have to hurt you. Badly."

"Angelo?" Caldwell asked, lifting Luna's hair away from her neck. "Is this someone new?"

"No, he's not new. He's very, very old. Someone I knew years ago," she said, cringing at the sound of the scissors sawing through her hair. Cringing again as Kaylie's face paled. Then feeling as if she'd lost ten pounds when her head fell forward, freed of all that weight.

As Caldwell said, "Ta-da!" no doubt holding up the tail for all to see, gasps and cheers rising from the salon's other clients and stylists, she resisted reaching up to touch her nape and the newly shorn ends. "Wow. That's frightening. I wonder if I've done permanent damage to my neck."

"Nothing a massage won't fix," Caldwell said as he walked away, she assumed with her hair, and then he was back, saying, "So, this Angelo. Does he have good hands? Could he take care of your neck? Or should I book you a session with Wendy?"

Luna would've shaken her head if Caldwell wasn't holding it still. "Old friend. Very old friend. Not a masseur."

"When did a little thing like the lack of a license ever stop a man?" Kaylie put in, and this time it was Luna who wanted to groan.

"C'mon, Ms. Meadows," Caldwell said, urging her to her feet. She opened her eyes, staring at the floor as she got out of the chair, refusing to spare even a glance at Kaylie and risk catching sight of her reflection. "Let's get you washed so I can start in on my masterpiece."

She felt as if she could fly. That she could take off any moment and soar. And it took Caldwell what seemed like seconds to shampoo and condition her hair. There was no heavy towel wrapped around her head and threatening to fall down her back. There were only short, choppy ends dripping over the drape as she settled back into her chair.

Caldwell squeezed the water from her hair, then picked up a comb. "Let's do this."

Luna held Kaylie's gaze for a long moment, the other woman snapping another photo before Luna closed her eyes and stopped thinking about what was happening. She worried about it instead. Not that changing her mind was an option with her hair already gone, but would her parents like it? Would *she* like it? Would Angelo like it . . . ? And why did it matter what Angelo Caffey liked or did not?

More important, had he really changed his mind about her? Was he ready to listen to the whole story? To hear the truth of all Sierra had entrusted her with? He'd known about the pregnancy. Sierra had turned to him for help. She'd obviously expected support and guidance, but she had received such the opposite that Luna ached for her friend. To be discounted so thoroughly . . .

And Luna had thought Oliver Gatlin cruel. Then again, she doubted Oliver had the capacity to recognize the flaw in himself. Angelo saw it, regretted it. Had lived with such incredible guilt for a decade, while all she'd lived with was fear. Fear that her lies would be discovered. That she'd be unable to honor her friend's wishes. That she'd hate herself when all was said and done for failing everyone around her.

For failing herself. That most of all.

Ten years. She'd given ten years of her life to something that had passed in the blink of an eye. When she closed her eyes, and even now keeping them shut against the movement of Caldwell's snipping scissors, she could see only pieces of that night at the ravine. Flashes of blue sky and white clouds and the Kool-Aid sunset. Oak and mesquite and juniper in a spectrum of green. The red of the car. The red of her blood, darker, splattered. The red of the fire engine and the emergency lights spinning . . .

She wondered whether she could get all of that into a scarf, if she was ready to. If she could bear seeing it wrapped around the wearer's neck, or if she would unravel it thread by thread once done and let it go as she was doing with her hair.

"Luna?" Kaylie asked once Caldwell clicked off the blow-dryer and started in with his fingers, spraying the short strands and working product through. "Are you okay?"

She opened her eyes and looked at her friend, Caldwell brushing off her neck and shoulders before pulling her cape away. "I'm fine, why?"

"You're crying."

She was? Reaching up to swipe at her cheeks, she realized Kaylie was right. And that Caldwell was standing next to the other woman, both smiling. Both staring. Did that mean . . . ? Oh. He was finished? "That's it?"

They both nodded, both of their expressions expectant, Caldwell's smug with success, Kaylie's full of amazement. She laughed. Still crying, but this time with joy, Luna laughed. "I guess I should look now?"

Kaylie nodded fiercely, her eyes misting. "You should look now."

Caldwell stepped forward and swiveled her chair, and she looked at the woman in the mirror. At herself. At no one she recognized. Where once had flowed a waterfall, layers and angles and wedges fought over real estate, settling over her ears and her forehead, one extra long and pointed chunk sweeping against her chin. It was a mess. It was a gorgeous mess. It was art.

She covered her mouth with both hands and giggled, because she had never seen herself as this woman looking back at her. Did others see her this way? Confident? Playful? Ready for anything? Was this who she'd been all this time while frightened of the past and hiding?

Was this the woman Angelo saw when he'd kissed her? Or was she both women, the one beneath the dark veil of mourning, and the one finally free to cut away the past?

"Well? Say something," Kaylie demanded, getting to her feet, her phone now on video recording Luna's reaction.

Caldwell moved in behind her again, fluffing and tweaking and arranging what he'd already arranged. "If you're not happy with this, we're going to have to break up."

"I'm happy," she said, and laughed, her eyes brimming. "I'm absolutely giddy. I'm in love."

"With the new you? Or with this mysterious Angelo?" her stylist asked.

Both, she wanted to say, because it was true. The new her was . . . sensational. Absolutely stunning. And she'd loved Angelo Caffey since she was fifteen years old. "I'm in love with you," she said to Caldwell, "because you're a genius. And I'm in love with you," she said to Kaylie, "because you let me go through with it instead of talking me out of it, which I know you wanted to do."

Kaylie opened her mouth and feigned insult. "I never thought once about talking you out of it."

"I know," Luna said. "You thought about it ten thousand times."

"That's closer to the truth than you think."

"You know what I need now? New lipstick. And earrings. Pairs and pairs of earrings. I think they're going to be my new favorite accessory, now that they won't get lost in my hair."

"I told Ten not to expect me till late, so . . ."

"Just give me five minutes to settle up with Caldwell."

"Perfect. Five minutes is all I need to upload this video to Facebook."

"You do that, I won't invite you to my housewarming party."

"Ooh. Housewarming. I hope you're ready to shop for more than earrings, because I know *all* the best kitchen stores."

And she would. "You, Kaylie Flynn, are a woman after my own heart."

DAY FOUR

FRIDAY

Bear and endure: This sorrow will *one day* prove to
be for your good.
—Ovid

CHAPTER SEVENTEEN

When Angelo woke, he smelled coffee. Not Folgers. Starbucks. The rich, earthy aroma of espresso, and that of warm milk. There wasn't a Starbucks, or any coffee shop for that matter, in Hope Springs. The old coffeemaker in the kitchen had, amazingly, still worked, and since Luna had turned on the power and water his first day here, he'd been making do with drip, like he did at home. Though since he ate breakfast at the diner on the way to work, he paid for his coffee by the cup. But espresso . . .

He pulled on the same jeans he'd worn yesterday, tugged on a clean T-shirt and clean socks, shoved his feet into his boots and tied them. He'd showered before hitting the sack last night, and he couldn't be bothered with shaving this morning, or running more than his fingers though his overly long hair. Definitely a perk of the life he lived, looking like a bum and getting away with it.

On the other side of the bed, Frank stretched and yawned, then sat up and shook his head, his ears flapping, short white dog hair floating in the morning light before settling onto the navy comforter. "Nice one, Frank. I really love crawling into a bed covered in your mess."

Frank gave a quick couple of yappy barks, then ran out of the room, his nails clicking on the stairs as he made his way to the first floor. Angelo jogged down behind him, turning the corner into the kitchen and glancing at the countertop, where a new and pretty pricey-looking espresso machine gleamed in some sort of crowned stainless-steel majesty.

Then he looked down at Luna where she squatted in front of Frank, scratching his head. And looked again. And frowned. "What in the hell happened to your hair?"

"Nothing *happened* to my hair. I had it cut," she said as she stood.

Cut until there was nothing left of it. "I can see that. Why?"

Grabbing her mug from the counter, she crossed the room and opened the back door for Frank. "It was time."

"Because I asked you about it recently?"

"You don't have anything to do with my hair."

He wanted to believe her, but the evidence said otherwise. "If you say so."

"I do," she said, turning away from where she'd been watching the dog. "Now, can we get back to doing what we're here to do? There's almost nothing left," she said, and he swore he heard disappointment in her voice. "We should probably be able to finish today."

And then what? Was he going to leave? Go back to Vermont and build cabinets and porch rockers for the rest of his life? Leave her here to manage the Caffey-Gatlin Academy on her own? With Oliver Gatlin stopping by at every opportunity to harass her?

Get real, Caffey. Luna could handle Oliver Gatlin. The question was whether or not Angelo could handle walking away. A question that shouldn't have been so hard to answer. "Sure, but first . . . You going to show me how to use this machine?"

"It's idiot-proof," she said, lifting a lever that dropped the prepacked capsule of spent grounds into the drawer meant to catch it. Then she opened the cabinet door above, grabbed a new one, and popped it into the slot. "Push the lever down, wait for the flashing light to stop, choose a short or long pull. The other two buttons froth the milk. Or you can do the milk first, and the machine will add the espresso itself. Like I said—"

"Idiot-proof. And we needed this why?" Wait. Had he just said *we*?

"It's for the center. I have one at home. I wanted one here. I got tired of your idea of coffee."

He wasn't going to argue about that. He was tired of it, too. "You might need to run through that again."

That earned him an eye roll. "Too sleepy to pay attention?"

"Too busy watching your hair."

Her mouth pulled tight on one side. "And what was it doing?"

"Bouncing. Or not bouncing, but floating. Like feathers." Not that he knew a damn thing about women's hair, so feathers could be insulting, and insulting her was not at all what he'd wanted to do. He liked her hair. Liked how it fit her. Liked that it made her seem . . . all grown up. As if she'd shed the Luna who'd lived in his head all this time. As if, after ten years, she'd reached the end of her mourning.

She lifted a hand to her nape and fluffed at the sharp ends there falling seamlessly into place. "It's so strange, feeling air on my neck."

"I'll bet," he said, really liking her neck.

"And I didn't wake myself up even once last night pulling my own hair. That's a first." She set a new latte mug beneath the machine's spouts and went about brewing him a cup while he watched, while he thought about sleeping with her, getting wrapped up in her hair. "Thank you, by the way. For letting Francisco stay with you."

He leaned against the counter, his hands at his hips curled over the edge. "He doesn't snore. He doesn't take up much room. But that comforter's going to need an old-fashioned clothesline beating. He loses half his hair every time he shakes."

She handed him his coffee just as said dog scratched at the back door. "Depending on the reworked plans for the center, we'll have to find someplace for a doggie door. Letting this one in and out all the time is going to get old."

And now she'd said it. *We'll.* Not *I.* A slip, he was certain, because she couldn't really imagine he was going to stay. Though she *had* asked him about doing so. And he *had* let the idea of doing so linger. "Shirking your responsibility already?"

Pulling open the door, she stuck out her tongue. Frank scrambled into the kitchen to his food bowl. Angelo set down his mug and scooped out the dog's breakfast from the bag he'd picked up the other night and stored in the pantry. Luna brewed herself another coffee and carried it to the table, where a box from Butters Bakery sat.

He joined her, like they were some sort of couple, drinking their coffee together while watching their dog eat. He liked it. Too much, probably.

"Sierra would've loved having a dog," she said, breaking open a blueberry muffin.

His stomach rumbled. He chose apple cinnamon. "And you know that how?"

"Because she loved Maya. And Maya loved her. She'd curl up in her lap and stay there as long as Sierra would let her."

He popped a chunk of muffin into his mouth and watched Frank gobble his way through his kibbles. "Six kids, both parents self-employed, meaning no steady income. The maintenance on this house and the land. Affording a dog would've meant one of the kids going hungry. Most likely me."

She sputtered. "Why you?"

"Just the way things worked," he said, and shrugged. "The younger kids needed more help and attention. Sierra took up a lot of the family's time. I was pretty independent by the time I was twelve. Before that even. Not complaining. I had everything I needed. I just had to do more for myself than the others."

"You never said anything. Sierra never said anything—"

He shrugged it off. "She wouldn't have known. She was busy being . . . Sierra."

Luna cocked her head to one side, her hair grazing her chin. "Are we having a pity party?"

"Hardly." Though he'd feared she would think that. It was hard to explain. "She lived in her own world. You were her best friend. You had to see that."

"I suppose."

Was this Luna's selective memory, or a girl thing? He couldn't believe she wouldn't have noticed. Or had Sierra, with Luna, not been the same person she'd been at home? "You had to ask her a question twice or even three times before she heard, never mind getting an answer before she fell back into whatever she'd been thinking. She said she'd do something, like take out the trash for me when I was running late for practice, but never did, so I got in trouble, even though I'd cleaned the upstairs toilet for her."

"Did that bother you? The getting in trouble?"

No. That wasn't what had bothered him. "It got old, was all. I quit asking her to switch chores. Or asking her for much of anything. Hard to rely on someone whose head is always someplace else."

"Sounds like it did bother you." She looked down, picked at her muffin. "Or like you resented her."

"I don't know. I don't want to think so, but . . ." He leaned forward, elbows on his knees, coffee mug cradled in his palms. "It was more that I just wanted to get out of the house, be on my own. Not have to deal with the constant Sierra drama." He couldn't believe he was admitting this. He could *not* believe he was sharing his feelings with the girl who'd been his sister's best friend.

Especially the things he was ashamed to have ever felt. He hadn't been ashamed at the time, and he wasn't even sure he'd been ashamed after leaving. And that was as bad as accepting that he hadn't thought about his family much once he'd left home.

"She relied on you." When he didn't respond, she went on, pushing. "You know that, right?"

"She shouldn't have," he said, then lifted his mug to drink.

"You were her brother. You *are* her brother. Of course she should—"

"She needed me to come home. I didn't come home."

"Angelo—"

"No, Luna. I let her down. *God*—" It was a prayer for forgiveness, his use of the Lord's name, even though he would never be able to forgive himself. He left his mug on the table, walked to the back door, pushed it open when Frank came up and asked to go out again, and watched the dog snuffle his way through the yard.

"It wasn't just that I wouldn't come home. It was what I said to her. The words. How I said them. I kept cutting her off. Yelling at her." He turned to look at Luna, her eyes wide and filled with so much sadness he wanted to slam his fist through the wall for putting it there. "She was trying to tell me something, but I wouldn't let her."

"Why are you being like this?"

"Like what?"

"A jerk."

"Because I like my life now without having five kids in my business all the time?"

"That's not nice. Or fair. None of us asked for this family. You and I got stuck. We're the oldest. It happens."

"I'm done with it happening."

"Angelo, listen to me—"

"No. You listen to me. I'm going to Rome. That's the only trip I'm taking this year. I'm not even sure I'll make it home at Christmas."

"Please, listen—"

"Sorry, sis. No can do."

"I'm sure it wasn't that bad," she said, her throat working as she swallowed.

"I hung up on her, Luna. How is that not bad?"

She flinched. A quick jerk of her shoulders and head. "She never told me. She told me everything that summer. But she never told me that."

"And what does that say, huh? She obviously didn't want you to know."

"Why wouldn't she want me to know?"

"Because the last thing I told my sister was that she needed to grow up. That she needed to stop expecting everyone else to do her dirty work. That if she was old enough to spread her legs, then she was old enough to deal with being so irresponsible that she didn't make the Gatlin kid use a condom. And if she was old enough to get pregnant, then she was old enough to tell our parents without me holding her hand while she did."

"She didn't need you to hold her hand."

"You don't think I don't know that? What she needed or didn't need doesn't matter. The last words I said to my sister were, 'Grow up.' Then I hung up. I didn't say good-bye." He slammed his palm against the screen door. It flew open and bounced against the wall. "I didn't say good-bye."

He carried the fact that he hadn't out the door and into the morning sun. It shone down brightly to warm him, when he didn't deserve warmth anymore than he deserved light. He didn't deserve anything more than what guilt handed him.

He could have saved his sister's life.

CHAPTER EIGHTEEN

Luna spent most of the morning second-guessing everything she did around the house. Mostly because she didn't remember what she'd been doing and had to retrace her steps. Her mind was not on any of her tasks—not on emptying the living room's shelves and drawers, which she'd finally finished, not on climbing into the attic a half dozen times to bring down stored boxes, which she'd also done. Not on tossing out the complete waste of fabric stored in Carlita Caffey's sewing room, fabrics that had been shredded into nests for squirrels and rats.

Her mind was on Angelo's pain.

Of course he and his family had suffered. They'd lost their family's heart. But not realizing that Sierra had called him, what she'd asked from him—and worse, what he'd said to her—Luna had no idea the weight of the burden he'd carried. A weight thick with guilt and regrets even more debilitating than those that had bound her to the past for so long. She couldn't imagine having lived with those words echoing in his head all this time. Even now, her chest was so tight she had to stop at the bottom of the stairs to catch her breath.

She didn't know where Angelo was. She hadn't seen him since he'd walked out of the kitchen earlier. She'd wanted to follow, but she was still reeling from what he'd told her. Those words . . . She couldn't even imagine them coming out of his mouth, and he'd said them to his sister? His then seventeen-year-old pregnant sister? His sister who'd needed him to help her through the hardest thing she'd ever done in her life?

It was so not like the Angelo Luna had known during her high school years. Granted, they'd had very little time together before Sierra's death, a year and a half at the most. But not once during those months, or the two years following the funeral, had he been anything but kind when he spoke of Sierra. Even now, Luna didn't doubt his affection for his sister had been anything but real. She only wished she understood what would've caused him to lash out.

She moved to the door of Sierra's room. Neither she nor Angelo had yet crossed the threshold, as if this room were where all of his sister's secrets were kept. As if entering would break some sort of imaginary seal that had kept her memory alive. As if doing so were a sin, a sacrilege. And yet here he was, sitting at her vanity table, her mirror giving Luna two Angelos to look at as she stood in the door.

She studied the one who lived and breathed. "I wondered where you'd gone."

He looked up at her, his eyes bleary, appearing drunk when she knew that wasn't the case at all. "Everything is still here. Nothing's been touched since that weekend." He reached behind him, picked up a bowl and a spoon from the vanity. "This is her cereal bowl. This would've been the last meal she ate in this house. You came by that morning to pick her up for school. After school, the two of you were supposedly headed to art camp in San Marcos. The next time she was in this house, she was dead."

179

Luna closed her eyes against the rising rush of tears, opened them again, and walked in to be assailed by memories. How many nights had she slept in this room, either bunking on the floor or crammed with Sierra into her twin bed? They hadn't cared how crowded they were, how little sleep they got. They'd talked and laughed, tried out makeup, painted each other's nails. Sierra had put braids in Luna's hair and looped them all over her head. Luna had done the same for Sierra, and they'd danced like the best of Bollywood.

She walked to the vanity, picked up the plain black frame holding a five-by-seven photo of Oscar. It was the official St. Thomas Preparatory School portrait taken at the end of their junior year. Luna's own portrait sat on the mantel in her parents' den. She'd packed away Sierra's when cleaning the living room shelves just yesterday.

"They . . . got married," she heard herself saying before she could stop the flow of the words, and she mentally begged Sierra's forgiveness. In her peripheral vision, she saw Angelo lift his head. "Friday morning before the baby was delivered that afternoon."

"What do you mean, married?" he asked, breathing heavily, his nostrils flaring.

"I mean married. Man and wife. Mr. and Mrs. Oscar Gatlin."

"You were there?" he asked, and she nodded.

"They were very, very much in love, Angel." She returned the frame to the table and looked at him. "You know they were."

"What I know is that she should never have gone to St. Thomas." He stopped, flung the spoon and bowl across the room. The bowl shattered, the shards scattering, the spoon clattered, and Luna flinched. "That school ruined her life."

She backed up to sit on the foot of the bed. "How can you say that?"

"Easy. It's the truth."

"She had an amazing talent. You can't deny that."

"I'm not denying her talent, but she could've continued to study with Mr. Miyazawa. She didn't need any of what St. Thomas offered. She sure as hell didn't need Oscar Gatlin."

"Without St. Thomas, she never would've met Oscar. And I would never have met her." *I wouldn't have met you either.* "I don't even want to think what high school would've been like without her."

"You'd have survived. You've survived since."

"Sometimes I'm not so sure," she said, wanting to take back the words. What she'd gone through didn't matter when compared to this man's loss.

"What's that supposed to mean?"

"Nothing."

"Luna? What do you mean?"

She tore off the rest of the bandage. "Look at me, Angel. I'm twenty-eight years old and only just now moving out of my parents' home. When I was confined to bed after the accident, my mother brought me a loom. I've done nothing else with my life. Nothing. It's like if I take a step out of that world, I'll lose Sierra forever."

"Sierra's been gone for ten years, Luna. You lost her . . . *we* lost her a long time ago."

He was right, but even knowing that, she couldn't bring herself to make the break. "My head knows that. My heart can't let her go."

"You don't have to let her go. I think about her daily, yet I've moved on with my life."

"Have you?" she asked, before she could stop the words from spilling.

"What's that supposed to mean?" he asked, his frown deep.

"You're hiding away in Vermont. Out of touch with your family—"

"Hey, that's on them, not me."

"Have you tried to contact them? Have you made any effort at all to make amends?"

"Because I'm the one who needs to?" His eyes were wide and wild. "You were there that day. You know what happened."

"No, Angelo," she said. "You would've had to talk to me for me to know."

His jaw tightened. His gaze grew hard before he dropped it to the floor, staring down, flexing his hands, his elbows on his knees. "Teenagers." He bit off a rush of sharp words beneath his breath. "Married."

He wanted to change the subject? Fine. "Their bond was stronger than I've seen in some longtime married couples. They knew what they were facing."

"How could they know what they were facing?" He barked the question at her. "Who knows anything at eighteen? Sierra was all about her cello. And Oscar . . . you know the Gatlins wrapped him in swaddling. He probably never had to deal with so much as a hangnail."

She bristled. He hadn't known Oscar at all. "You weren't here to see them. I'm not even sure your parents realized what those two had as a couple—"

"They were eighteen. What did they even know about being a couple?"

Her heart clutched as she thought back to the things she'd felt for Angelo at that age. "You think eighteen-year-olds can't fall in love?"

"Not those two. They didn't even live in the real world. All they knew was music."

The way all she knew was weaving. "They lived music. It's all they needed to know."

"I build furniture for a living, Luna. You think I don't know a little bit about what it's like to be an artist? Or a crafts-man, at least? I've never worked a nine-to-five, or left my work at the office, or known what to expect any particular day. I understand immersion. But I also got my degree. Sierra left public school at fifteen, and for three or four years before that, she spent her afternoons and weekends with Mr. Miyazawa. She never even bothered with her driver's license. How was she in any way equipped to be a wife, much less a mother? And to balance that with any sort of music career? Uh-uh. I can't see it."

"She couldn't see it either. Nor could Oscar. That's why they made the decision they did. As much as they both wanted to be a family with their child, the timing was all wrong."

"So you say."

Oh, he was frustrating. "They were my best friends. I knew them as well as I knew your family."

"You only know what you saw."

"What's that supposed to mean?"

"Did you ever hear my parents fight? Did you ever see my father swing his guitar, *his guitar*, at Felix and Emilio when they were arguing over who had to take out the trash? Were you ever there for dinner when my mother set a loaf of bread and a jar of peanut butter on the table? No jelly. No milk. No plates or napkins or knives. And that when there was hamburger in the fridge, even tuna and noodles in the pantry. But she wasn't in the mood to cook."

She swallowed against the burning sensation rising up her throat. "I never saw any of that."

"Well, it happened. You get a whole house full of creatives or artists or whatever together, everyone living in their own heads, there's a whole lot of crazy in the air. And most of the time, you don't even know anyone's breathing it in until the yelling starts."

Yelling. Crazy and loud and unexpected. "Is that why moving day got so ugly?"

"You want to talk about moving day?" he asked, surging to his feet to hover over her. "Fine. We'll talk about moving day."

～

For eight years now, the number-one rule of moving day had been the same as that of *Fight Club*. So why in the world he was breaking it to talk about what had happened . . . He took a deep breath. Blew it out. Took another. She did this to him, this woman. Made him nuts. Made him angry. Made him weak. He couldn't tell her no, but telling her yes was just as bad. Nothing in his life had been the same since the first day he'd seen her, when she'd whipped around the hood of his car after he'd honked at Sierra.

"I don't even know what you want me to say." A good place to start, he guessed. "Or what you want to hear."

"I want to hear what was going on in your head. Why you wanted me there." She pulled her knees to her chest, wrapped her arms around them. "Why you picked that day to tell them we were together. Without talking to me. When you knew they hated me for lying about driving Sierra to art camp. When you knew they blamed me for her being in Oscar's car, never mind that she was eighteen and capable of thinking for herself."

Seeing Luna there, sitting on his sister's bed like so many times in the past . . . He shook off the memories that were strangling him and looked down at his scarred hands. "I thought . . . I don't know what I thought. I knew they weren't happy about me calling my mother's family for help. I guess they expected things to continue as they had been, but after Sierra died, every time I talked to them things were worse than the last. I had to do something, and it was the only thing I could think to do."

"But what does that have to do with me?" she asked, her impatience causing him no small amount of grief, though his avoidance was causing him the greatest.

"Sierra was gone. I hadn't lived at home in three years. I was the outsider, and I wanted someone in my corner." He stopped, shook his head. "No. I wanted *you* in my corner. I wanted *your* support. Being with you was the only thing that got me through those years. I thought if you were there, you'd get me through that day."

"Then why didn't you tell me that when I picked you up at the airport?" she asked, leaving the bed, coming to kneel in front of him, to take his hands in hers and squeeze. "I hadn't seen your family since the funeral. I had no idea what I was walking into." She bowed her head, pressed it to their joined hands. "All that time we were together, and you never told me how it was for you at home. For all of you."

He huffed beneath his breath, pulled his hands free, and got to his feet. He couldn't do this with her touching him. "When did we ever talk about anything that mattered?"

She was slow to respond, pushing up to sit on Sierra's vanity bench, as if moving that far was all the strength she had. "Everything we talked about mattered, Angel. I learned more about you those weekends we spent together away from Hope Springs than I did the whole time I was in high school."

"What I was doing at school, sure. What I wanted to do with my life. Hopes and dreams and all that crap—"

"It was not crap. It was important. It was what I wanted to hear. It was what made you *you*." She paused, and he leaned back against the doorframe, his hands stacked behind him, his gaze on Luna's bowed head. "That's what hurt so bad when you walked away at the airport without saying a word. And then you vanished. No calls. No letters. It wasn't that you didn't choose me over your family. It was that you didn't choose anyone. You just . . . checked out."

"I chose myself," he sniped back, then more calmly, "I chose myself. Selfish? Maybe. But I had to get away. My father standing there, looking at me, telling me I was no longer his son . . ."

Even now, the power of those words spoken in that voice, the same voice that had cheered at his football games, praised his craftsmanship as they'd built the family's table and chairs . . .

"He said that to me? After I had been the one to pick up all the slack he couldn't be bothered with because he was *called* to play his guitar. Funny how he was never *called* to fix the washing machine so his kids could have clean clothes. Or *called* to make sure there was enough gas in the car to get us to school. And that was high school. College was even worse," he said, and pushed off the door to pace. "I was the one who kept my brothers and sisters from going hungry, from having to live in the dark. Did you know my junior year at Cornell I ate one meal a day? It was a good meal, granted, usually something a customer in the restaurant where I worked sent back to the kitchen. Sometimes leftovers that would've gone into the trash.

"And you want to know why I ate one meal a day? Because I had no money. I waited tables. I bussed tables. I mopped floors. Anything I could to get more hours because I needed the money to send home. Sierra couldn't work because her music took up all the time she wasn't in school. Isidora wasn't old enough, though she did wash dishes at Butters Bakery on weekends. Emilio and Felix and Teresa? Yeah, they helped out around the house, but they were kids, and they never got to *be* kids. I hated my parents for that."

She looked up at him, tears rolling down her cheeks, silent tears, desperate tears. "Why didn't you tell me any of this then? We were together for three years. More than three. Almost four."

He stopped, scrubbed both hands down his face, and sighed. "Because you were my escape. My time with you was the only time I didn't have to think about the real world."

"So what we had wasn't real. I wasn't real."

"No, Luna. You were the only thing that was. And that's why I wanted you with me when I came home that last time. I wanted my parents to know how important you were to me. I thought if they saw us together, something might click. I don't know. Like they would wake up and realize that you'd done what you'd thought best to help Sierra. I never thought . . ." He took a deep breath, gathered his words. "I never thought they'd pretend you weren't even there. At least until they yelled at you to go. I thought they'd see how happy you made me. How you meant as much to me as you'd ever meant to Sierra."

She swiped at her face, swiped again, finally gave up and just stared at him. "Why couldn't you trust me to tell me what it was like for you?"

"I didn't want you to know. I didn't want anyone to know. My home life couldn't have been more dysfunctional, yet on the outside we looked like one big happy family. I was the football star. Sierra the musical prodigy. The Caffeys were so lucky. Just look at all that talent under one roof," he said, and then he was done, dropping to squat on the balls of his feet, banging his head against the doorframe behind him.

"You didn't have to walk away," was what she finally said, her voice tiny and hurt in this room full of more pain than any family should know.

"Yeah. I did. I'd failed my sister. I'd failed my parents and siblings. If we'd stayed together, I would've failed you, too. I couldn't ruin your life." But he'd been unable to get over her either. Unable to believe what he'd lost. It had been easier to disappear, to not exist. "I screwed up. You were the best thing that ever happened in my life, and I couldn't see it because of the worst."

CHAPTER NINETEEN

Luna's suite of rooms in her parents' home was the size of a small apartment, which meant she'd hoarded an apartment's worth of junk over the years. As daunting and unappealing as the task was, she was going to sort through it all as she packed. No way was she going to haul boxes filled with grade-school artwork, and gossipy middle school notes from friends, and all the photos and autographs she'd collected in high school to her new place. Mementos, yes, but only the most valuable. She had so few, and almost all were connected to Sierra.

Sierra. Angelo. Moving day.

Cleaning out Sierra's bedroom after the girl's brother had stormed out of the room had given her too much time to think—about the things he'd said, about the things she'd found, about how she hadn't known the Caffeys at all. They'd been her favorite family in the world, next to her own, of course, yet it seemed she'd been seeing a façade. It broke her heart to realize that. But it broke her heart even more to learn the true atmosphere Sierra and Angelo had grown up in—especially when her home life had been the stuff of dreams.

Luna's own bedroom was the same one her parents had brought her to from the hospital, the four-poster iron frame of her queen-size bed the same glossy white as her crib had been, or so she'd learned from pictures. She'd painted the walls a couple of times over the years, almost coming full circle. The original sunny yellow she'd seen in the photos with the crib was now a deep autumn maize, with one accent wall colored like red West Texas clay, and the hardwood floor a buffed buttery brown.

In the interim years, her father had added onto her room, turning it into a full wing. She had her own bath and dressing room, her own study and sitting room, her own entrance. Except for sharing the house's kitchen, her living quarters were fully self-contained. Skye was going to love this room. She'd be the envy of her friends, the go-to girl for sleepovers. And their poor parents, dealing with all those giggling girly girls, then all those squealing, drama queen tweens, and then all those moody, broody teenagers.

Laughing, she taped the bottom of a box, tossing it up against her shelving unit. She taped a second for trash and a third for anything she might want to donate. She had way too many clothes. And her shoes would almost require a separate moving van. An exaggeration, of course, but she really needed to curb her shopping habits. Her money would be much better spent pulling the arts center together. There was so much to arrange for, so much to buy . . . and that had her laughing, too, as it struck her how happy she was with, as her mother had called it, her new vocation as the director of the Caffey-Gatlin Academy.

Was this another part of the break from her past? Giving up extravagance for austerity? Not that she'd truly been the former, or would ever be the latter, but this tectonic shift in her priorities was leaving no part of her life alone. That was one thing she and Sierra had never shared. Her best friend had loved to go shopping with her, but she'd never wanted to buy anything.

Except once, Luna remembered, when Sierra had fallen in love with a pair of earrings that had to be two inches long. Feathers and beads and distressed metal charms . . . a tiny key, an even tinier book, the tiniest heart Luna had ever seen. Luna had returned to the store the next day and bought them, gifting them to Sierra two months later for her birthday. Strangely, Sierra had seemed less excited to receive them than she had the day she'd found them on the store shelves.

Luna had always wondered about that, if something about the earrings made her friend sad, or if it was Luna having money she didn't that bothered the other girl, or if Sierra had felt out of touch with her peers because none of the girls at St. Thomas would have been caught dead wearing the colorful peacock feathers she'd loved. Looking back now, and with all she'd learned from Angelo about the family's hopes for Sierra, she couldn't help but wonder if the earrings had reminded her friend that her talent was as much burden as blessing.

Sierra couldn't concern herself with fashion, or with fitting in. She couldn't spend money frivolously when there were camps and workshops not covered by her scholarship. She couldn't run off for an impromptu movie or concert; she barely had time for TV.

Maybe that was why being with Oscar had consumed her. He'd become her world while understanding her world. It was the land he'd come from, too. A land few understood. Luna certainly hadn't. She loved listening to the music they played, but that was all it was for her. For Oscar, for Sierra, it was everything.

Luna had never seen Sierra wear the earrings. In fact, the last time she'd seen them, they'd been stashed away in the tree trunk that served to support the Caffeys' tree house. How many times had they sat inside it the summer of Sierra's pregnancy, talking about the decision Sierra and Oscar had made to give the baby away? Who knew how many things of Sierra's might still be hidden there? Most likely, time and the elements had ruined anything that remained, but Luna didn't care. She wanted to find any pieces of Sierra she could.

And since she was so not in the mood to start packing, she saw no reason she couldn't go looking for them now.

CHAPTER TWENTY

She reached for the ladder rung hammered into the trunk of the tree, pulled at it, tugged, testing its give. It shifted, a corner broke free, but it held. The one beneath her foot remained stable, too, and she made her way slowly up the tree, holding her breath the entire way and praying she wouldn't crash to the ground. Breaking a bone would be bad enough. Having to explain to Angelo she'd done so for a pair of peacock earrings was worse.

After boosting herself up and onto the floor, she swung her legs around and crawled to the corner where the tree trunk served to support the asymmetrical room. She'd never been able to stand up while inside, but on her knees she could reach deep into the knothole Sierra had carved away in the trunk, creating a niche where she'd hidden anything she didn't want to fall into her parents' hands—much the same way she'd hidden things from her siblings in the tallest of the kitchen cabinets.

Instead of the earrings, Luna found a small leather case shaped like a jeweler's necklace packaging box, and except for the embossed initials on top, it was identical to one Luna had in her room. Identical to those given to all St. Thomas Preparatory School freshmen the first day of class, along with a fountain pen and a leather-bound journal. The three items made up one of the least practical school supply bundles Luna had ever seen, but it was a tradition she imagined this year's incoming students had seen continued.

The box was wrapped in a sealed plastic bag, that one shoved in a second bag, and those shoved in a third. Sierra had taken great care to keep whatever was inside clean and dry and from becoming bug fodder. Her heart racing, Luna took the same great care removing it from its coffin of protective layers, peeling away the plastic as she would the tissue paper from one of her Patchwork Moon scarves.

And then the box was free, and her hands were shaking around it. Sierra had hidden this out here for a reason. Wrapped it and wrapped it and wrapped it for a reason. Whatever was inside, she hadn't wanted it found, or destroyed before she could get back to it. Luna swallowed hard, murmured a rough, "Wow," wondering what had been going on with her friend, and if Luna had a right, all these years later, to know.

The case sat in her lap, and it weighed almost nothing. She could lift it with one hand, hold it like a serving tray, bounce it back and forth like a hot potato, but she didn't. It was too important, and splitting open the outside bag had felt like a total disregard for something that couldn't possibly be more precious. This was Sierra. This was a secret even Luna hadn't known. One she doubted Angelo had known either.

She ran the tip of one finger over Sierra's embossed initials, thinking of other things he didn't know. He didn't know that Luna loved him. That her love for him had been alive longer than Sierra had been dead. That she'd thought of him every day since meeting him, even the years he was away, even with the distance between them. He was everything to her, and she didn't know why, but wasn't that the way of love? Knowing? Accepting? Trusting the emotion unconditionally?

Maybe she was romanticizing instead of being practical. But love wasn't practical. It rarely made sense. What she did know was that she wanted Angelo with her when she opened the box, and yet she wanted him far, far away. She wanted to rush through, get it over with, glance through the contents, and then return the box to the trunk of the tree. She wanted to open the box slowly, give everything she'd find inside its proper due.

She closed her eyes, squeezed them, felt the sting of hot tears on her hands before she realized she was crying. She wiped them off on her jeans and made sure the box was dry. Then she flipped the latch, happy to find it unlocked, and lifted the lid. She waited, counting to ten, then to ten a second time, before finding the strength to open her eyes. It took another count before she was able to look down at what she held.

Sierra had knitted the booties inside. She'd labored over the needles and pattern while the two of them had sat in this very tree house and talked about school and clothes and how much they hated wearing uniforms, but how doing so had made the pregnancy easier; Sierra had never had to explain why she was wearing the same baggy outfits over and over again.

Luna had shown her friend her mother's selection of yarn, and Sierra had chosen orange. She didn't yet know the sex of the baby, and orange would be perfect for the little one's first Halloween. The booties were flawed and the stitches uneven, one bootie slightly longer than the other, and Luna was caught between laughing over the memory of Sierra's frustration, and crying at the realization that the booties had never been worn.

Beneath the booties was a Polaroid of Sierra's first sonogram. It had still been too early to determine the baby's sex, but one tiny hand was obvious, as was the baby's head, and bulges that that would one day be eyes. Sierra had been as anxious to find out the baby's eye and hair color as anything. And then when they'd learned they were having a girl, she'd sobbed. By then they'd made the decision to give Lily a new home and family, and her friend's anguish had left Luna wrecked.

Underneath the Polaroid she found the two gold wedding bands her friends had never got to wear. Sierra's fingers had been too swollen, and Oscar had told her he'd save wearing his, too. They'd planned to make a big deal of slipping them on. More plans that never saw fruition.

Near the bottom of the box was a photo of Sierra and Oscar together, Sierra's smile crooked, their heads touching, Oscar's hand over Sierra's belly, her hand on top of his. They'd taken it on the front steps of the St. Thomas School before Sierra had chopped off her hair after the ride in Oscar's convertible that had tangled it beyond saving. Their cello cases were beside them in this, the place where they'd met.

It had been spring, Sierra probably four months along and over the worst of her morning sickness. Still, her face was paler than normal, and though dark crescents smiled beneath her eyes, those close to her should've been able to see she wasn't well. She was losing weight when she shouldn't have been. Her hair, that first trimester, had been lifeless and lank.

Why hadn't anyone seen that? Why had no one picked up on the signs? Why had Luna, at seventeen, been the only support the other girl had? Why had any of this had to turn out the way it had? Why wasn't Sierra here with her now, her ten-year-old daughter running with Francisco through the yard while the two older women—yes, older, Luna and Sierra both—revisited that crazy year?

The sound of the first step Angelo took on the tree house's ladder brought Luna's head up. The second had her scrambling to grab everything and shove it all back in the box. The third caused her to stop, and by the fourth she'd given up. She didn't have time to hide what she'd found, and why bother now, when Sierra's secrets were no longer at risk? Luna had already spilled them.

At risk were the raw emotions Luna had no time to quell. When Angelo's upper body came through the open trapdoor, he stopped, his sweeping gaze taking in the box, the folded sheets of paper Luna hadn't yet looked at, the CD case containing, she was certain, a copy of the music Sierra and Oscar had played at their wedding as well as during Lily's birth, and the photos. And then his gaze met hers. That was where it stayed as he finished his climb, rolling to the side to let the door slam into place, then crossing his legs to better fit in the tree house's limited space.

"Been a long time since I've been up here," he said, picking up the CD case from the stack of the contents, but not looking at what he held, at what he turned over and over in his hands, sharp corner to sharp corner, as if keeping the black-backed case in motion would prevent him from seeing it. But he couldn't keep up the motion forever, and finally he stopped, his throat working as he glanced down.

Luna's gaze fell to the label. Sierra and Oscar had designed it together, and Oscar had printed it at home. The artwork depicted both a bass and treble clef, and a series of musical notes on a staff. The recording was that of a small-scale piano and cello concerto they'd written.

A part of Luna wanted to listen, and to do so with Angelo. Another part of her wanted to break the CD into dozens of pieces so no one would know the full extent of what the young couple had lost. But they deserved better than denial. She owed them this audience, as did Angelo, and his family, and Oscar's, too.

Still . . . "We don't have to look at this now."

"Yeah," he said, his voice gruff. "We do."

"We can take it back to the house," she said, feeling this need to put things off.

But he shook his head. "No. Here. The house is empty. But I can still sense her here."

"Okay," she said, watching as a frown passed over his face.

He reached for the stack of papers, each addressed to its intended recipient, and shuffled through them, then handed her the one with her name, along with a long gold chain.

∽

"This is my mother's." Luna pulled the delicate necklace from the folded sheet, as if fearing it too fragile to be moved, and draped it over her hand, the cross coming to rest in her palm. "I'll bet Sierra meant to give this back to me. She just never had the chance."

Angelo looked down, giving her a moment, the big loops of Sierra's handwriting staring back at him from the papers he held. Sierra's handwriting. God, he missed his sister.

Missed waiting for her to get her butt in the car after school. Missed tripping over her cello case in the downstairs hall. Missed her giggles coming through her bedroom ceiling. Missed having to go to her concerts wearing his father's frayed sport coat and extra tie, and sit in the St. Thomas auditorium with kids his age wearing Hugo Boss.

He missed the way she was slow to look up from whatever she was doing, always so intent, so focused, her lids and lashes like a curtain rising to reveal the brightest eyes of anyone he knew. He wasn't sure he could take this, but he nodded toward Luna's note.

"You want to read it?"

Luna shook her head. "I can't. I just can't."

"You want me—"

She nodded. "Out loud."

If he could keep his voice steady . . .

Luna, I found this in my room the day Oscar and I put all these things together for Lily. Or not really for Lily, since we won't ever know her as more than the greatest gift we could have given away, but to use to tell our parents about her, and how she brought us even closer than we already were. Because of that, she'll always be part of our lives.

And their lives.

And even your life.

I think I'm as happy about that as anything. You've been there with us since the beginning, and I know you would've been the most wonderful auntie ever. Auntie Luna. You get the extra ie. I took the letters out of the word friend.

You're the best friend I've ever had. You're what being a friend means. I hope I'm handing this note to you, along with your necklace, but if you're reading it without me, it's because it was easier for me this way. I want so badly to tell you Oscar and I are leaving Hope Springs after we give Lily away, not later, after graduation, like I'd told you, but it's for the best. It really is. We'll be able to be together the way we want, no parents mucking up our lives, telling us we're too young to be in a relationship, or we don't have time to be in a relationship, or I'm not good enough for Oscar and he's out of my league.

Without you to see me through the crazy that was St. Thomas, I never would've made it. But the thought of going away and being without you saddens me so deeply, even while I'm thrilled my husband and I will be starting our new life together. It's going to be weird, I know, being high school seniors, married and on our own, and Oscar's trust fund keeping us from begging for scraps on the street. New York, Luna. NEW YORK. You know what else is in New York? JUILLIARD! Keep your fingers crossed Oscar and I both get accepted. I'll call and write. And I hope I end up telling you in person about this latest adventure in the theme park of my life. Maybe we'll sit in the tree house and cry together about being apart.

But in case I don't find the courage, these are the things I need you to know.

He stopped reading, needing to clear his eyes, and his throat, and he looked up at Luna, who he was certain couldn't see anything at all through the wash of tears that had to be blinding her. "Did you know they were leaving?"

"After graduation, yes," she said, shaking her head. "But not then. Not after the baby. Did you?" He said nothing, and Luna went on. "Why wouldn't she have told one of us? Just because it was too hard?"

"I don't know. Maybe they were afraid one of the parents would find out somehow," he said, because he had no other words, and then he lifted the letter. "You want me to go on? Would you rather read this later? When I'm not around?"

"No. You read it," she said, and a shudder ran through her. "It's almost like hearing her voice when you do."

The tree house was small, the space close, the warmth nearly suffocating. He wasn't sure he could breathe to keep reading. He wasn't sure he wanted to. He feared he'd be listening for Sierra's voice to echo back at him. He'd never thought they sounded the same . . .

No one has ever understood me the way you do. I love my family dearly. I love Oscar with so much of my heart I want to burst. But if two people could be made into one, I think maybe two people could be made from one, and that's what happened with you and me. We used to be the same, and something happened, and we found each other again by luck or by fate.

You know what I'm thinking. You know what's best for me. You don't finish my sentences because that's just creepy, but sometimes I don't even have to say anything because you've said it first. And usually better. Because you're braver than I could possibly be. You know yourself, when I knew nothing until I found music, and Oscar, but I still learned most of everything from you.

So you're the better half of our whole. But I think you need me, too.

"Stop." Luna didn't say the word; she sobbed it. "How can she say I was braver? She was going away with Oscar, and ten years later, I'm still living at home. And I wasn't better. I've never been better. Look what I've done since she died. I've hurt the people I love. The people *she* loved." Another sob. "I haven't told anyone the truth—"

"Luna—"

"No," she wailed, and doubled over, the chunks of her hair falling forward, but too short to cover her face. He wondered if she regretted cutting it, if she missed the shield. She had nowhere to hide. And he had nothing to keep him from seeing the extent of her suffering.

Scooting across the floor, he sidled up to her, stretching out his legs and lifting her onto his lap. She curled against him like a broken doll, limp and damaged. Her face was wet where she rubbed her cheek against his chest, and the dampness was chilling here in this room above ground, the two of them alone, suspended as if in a bubble. As if on a cloud.

"I'll let you finish reading this later," he said, but she was already shaking her head.

"No. Please. I need to hear it. I need to know. Please," she said, melting into him as if she needed his strength.

He didn't even bother trying to clear his throat.

Without me, you would think too much. Worry too much. Which you probably don't believe, but I see it. You're going to have a permanent frown if you're not careful. Those ugly wrinkles like road humps on your forehead I saw them in the cafeteria when you Cheeto-ed the Jennifers. And that first day, when Angelo drove up and honked and your eyes went all angry, insulted, don't-even-think-about-it LUNA because he was being disrespectful. That was Angelo. Shrug. I'm used to it and love him. That sibling thing. But I love you, too.

you're the best champion any underdog could ever have. I'm happy you're my friend. I would never have made it through being pregnant if not for you. Thank you for the crackers. Morning sickness. Gah. If I didn't want so badly to have a family with Oscar, I wouldn't mind if this was the only baby we had, because I don't ever want to go through months of puking up my guts again. I know labor will be worse, but a day or two of pain? Okay. Ninety days of wanting to die? No, thanks. (Remember this later, when you think about having kids.)

"I can't—" he said, and she took the letter from his hand, smearing the moisture from her eyes on the back of her wrist, then blinking to focus, and pushing out of his lap to sit beside him while she read the rest out loud.

He likes you, you know. Angelo. He likes you a lot, even if he won't say it. When I told him I knew you two were together, he clammed up. I think the two of you would make an even better couple than Oscar and I do. Can you imagine being my sister for real? Please never forget me. And when Oscar and I come to Austin on tour (because you know that will happen . . . me and Oscar and Yo-Yo Ma), make Angelo bring you to hear us. I want to look out in the audience and see your beautiful face, and all that long hair, and play something just for you. Something that will be our secret, our song. We'll have to decide on one now, so later, when you're in the crowd and I'm up onstage, we'll know that I never would've made it without you.

I love you, Luna Meadows. Best friends forever.

She finished, and she folded the letter, then smoothed it, her shaking hands causing the paper to crackle. She said nothing as she placed it back in the box, as through her tears, she said, "Here," handing him the folded sheet addressed to him. "I shouldn't have cut my hair. She wanted to see my hair."

He took the letter with one hand, threaded the fingers of his other into her short, choppy locks. "Your hair is gorgeous. She would've loved it. I love it. It was time and you know it." And then it was his turn to share his sister's words for him.

You were right not to come when I called. If you'd come, and I'd told them, I would never be able to go to New York. I would be staying home, raising Lily, loving Lily, missing Oscar while he's away at school, and eventually hating my life because such a big part of it is missing. I want it all. Oscar. Lily. AND music. I know Momma and Daddy are counting on me to make something of myself, and the thought of disappointing them is too hard to take. Going to New York with my husband will give me that chance. Oscar and I can study without having to worry about working our way through school AND without having our parents trying to keep us apart. I know it's weird, doing this as seniors, but it's what we want for us. And Lily will have such a good life with her new family. I had the attorney make sure they are NOT musicians.

I'm sorry my music has taken so much away from you. And from Isi and 'Milio and Teresa and Felix. I owe all of you such a big apology. I don't have it in me to make right now (mostly because there's no room with all this baby, ha), but soon I will. Somehow. I'll make it up to all of you. Please don't beat yourself up, because I know that's what you're doing. Let Luna convince you. She may not know it, but she loves you, too.

And that was it. His sister's last words meant to be read once she was living the life she wanted. But she'd never made it back to Hope Springs, and her words had been stored away for ten years, no one knowing of her plans, the sacrifice *she* had made to see her dreams come true. He leaned against the tree house wall, broken, hollow. Gutted.

"What now?" he asked, because he had no idea.

Luna looked over at him, her damp eyes solemn, the gears in her mind obviously whirring to an inevitable conclusion. "Now I show these things to Oscar's family. And then we should show them to yours."

I show them to Oscar's family, she'd said. Then *we* show them to yours. He wondered if she realized she'd made the distinction. "Why? What good will it do now?"

"They have to know. They deserve to know. We can't . . ." She paused, shivering where she still sat close, then reaching for one of his hands and bringing it to her cheek. "This is bigger than my vow to keep Sierra's secrets. And I know how you feel about what you said to her when she called—"

"You're right," he said, shaking his head. "It's time."

CHAPTER TWENTY-ONE

O rville and Merrilee Gatlin lived on the far east side of Hope Springs, where the neighborhoods were gated, the lots professionally landscaped, the houses the size of small mansions. And then there were the cars. The cars always got to Luna. Oscar's high school ride had cost as much as the sporty number she drove now, courtesy of Patchwork Moon. In high school, she'd had a ten-year-old Toyota Corolla, and that only because she'd saved four years of babysitting money and her father had gone in halves.

Still, her nonprofit would not be where it was today without the donations and support of the area's inhabitants. These were the homes of doctors and lawyers and technology moguls, many whose offices were in Austin, an hour away. They had the best of both worlds, really. The small-town peace and quiet offered a respite from the hustle and bustle of the state capital, while Austin's proximity provided Hope Springs's residents easy access to good food, good drink, top-notch entertainment, and college football.

Orville Gatlin was one of the few on the east side who wasn't a doctor or a lawyer or a mogul. He was a renowned metal sculptor, his work shown in galleries nationwide. He worked in a warehouse in Hope Springs's old textile district, the same area where Luna had bought her loft. He didn't try to hide his celebrity as Luna did hers, but then, having Jay Z, Kate Hudson, and Robert Downey Jr. wear her scarves meant she didn't have to be the face of her art.

Today the three doors to the Gatlins' garage were closed, only Oliver's BMW parked in the driveway. Of course, he *would* have to be here when dealing with his mother was going to tax every bit of Luna's nerves. She pulled her Audi far enough forward to reach the paved walkway to the front door. With her hands gripping the steering wheel and her forehead pressed against it, she gathered her thoughts and tried to remember to breathe.

This day had been a decade coming. Now that it was here, she ached for it to be over, her whole body trembling, regrets tumbling down and piling at her feet like anchors to moor her. She'd promised to keep Sierra and Oscar's secrets until they were ready to tell all. She'd just never thought those truths would be told posthumously, or that she'd be the one to reveal them. And even then, she hadn't known all of what they'd kept to themselves.

What would've happened had she found the letters sooner? If, once her hip had healed, she'd climbed the tree to cry for Sierra? If she'd braved facing the Caffeys to feel the spirit of her friend? If she'd done that, returned to the place where they'd hoped and imagined and dreamed, and not lost herself in Angelo instead, how much heartache might she have saved?

Wishes aren't horses, Luna. They're really, really not. Exiting her car, she pressed Sierra's box to her chest, the weight of it growing with each step she took toward the Gatlins' front door. Once there, she lifted her chin and reached for the big brass knocker. The door opened two minutes later. Luna spoke to the well-dressed young man who answered it with a polite, "May I help you?"

"I'd like to see Mrs. Gatlin, please."

"Is she expecting you?"

"No, she's not. But if you'd tell her Luna Meadows is here—"

"I'm surprised you'd think giving me your name would get you an audience, Ms. Meadows," Merrilee Gatlin said, stepping from her sitting room into the foyer, her heels striking the marble sharply. With a wave of her hand, she dismissed the man who had responded to Luna's knock. "We'll finish going over my calendar this afternoon, Tod."

"Yes, ma'am," he said, and he very nearly bowed. "I'll be in my office."

Luna watched Tod retreat down the hallway, wondering whether it was part of his job to keep the riffraff away. "I'm surprised you'd think I'd try to see you under false pretenses."

"The way you got in to see my son?" The older woman's arched brow lifted almost into her hairline. "Without so much as a courtesy call to let me know of your intention to visit?"

This was where Luna wanted to point out the lack of courtesy she was being given here on the front porch, but on that she kept her silence. "What I had to say to Oscar was for his ears alone. And I understand that he most likely didn't hear me. That doesn't mean I didn't need to say it to him."

Oscar's mother considered her for a long moment, her gaze dropping to the box Luna held. No doubt it was curiosity over the worn leather case embossed with the St. Thomas Preparatory School logo that finally gained her entrance into the Gatlin home. She stepped inside. Mrs. Gatlin closed the door, gesturing for her to move into the sitting room. It was the closest room to the front of the house. And that was fine. Luna wasn't here for a tour.

Oliver was sitting in one of the two wingback chairs, legs crossed, a tablet PC on his lap. As if he'd been reading the news or a book, or checking his stocks, and just happened to be doing so in what was surely the most uncomfortable room in the house. Chilly while at the same time cloying, all white floral chintz, the furniture, the walls, the paintings, with navy and green the only accents.

Luna promised herself never to weave anything in just those three colors.

Oliver swiped a finger over the gadget's screen, minimizing whatever he'd been viewing before setting it on the table at his side. He got to his feet when his mother entered. "Miss Meadows. Are you here about our last conversation?"

"In a manner of speaking, yes," she said, and couldn't deny the sense of satisfaction she felt when Oliver frowned and fell speechless, dropping back to his chair once his mother had arranged her skirt to sit.

Merrilee looked from her son to Luna, indicating she should use the settee. It was stiff and uncomfortable, and very likely stuffed with horsehair. Luna didn't care. She didn't plan to stay long, and she would never be comfortable here. "I've been going through the things the Caffeys left when they moved, and earlier today I found this box. The things inside will answer a lot of your questions."

"And what questions would those be?" Merrilee asked.

"About the weekend of the accident. Why Oscar was where he was when it happened. Why he and Sierra were together when they shouldn't have been." Luna dropped her gaze from Merrilee's to the box with Sierra's initials, squeezing her hands into fists before flipping the latch to open it. She set the music CD on the table, along with the letter Oscar had addressed to his parents.

Then, just as she heard Merrilee's sharp intake of breath, she added the sonogram photo and the orange booties. "Sierra was almost nine months pregnant at the beginning of our senior year. The weekend of the accident, she delivered the baby."

Beneath two bright circles of rouge, Merrilee's face blanched to the color of bone. "What do you mean, she delivered the baby?"

"Oscar and Sierra had a child. Together. They gave it up for adoption."

"Just a moment." Merrilee pressed her fingertips to her throat as she swallowed. "Are you telling me I have a grandchild? A Gatlin child, who is living with someone else?"

Oh, the arrogance. "She's not a Gatlin child any longer. She has a family of her own. A life of her own. She's ten years old." Luna faltered, then stumbled beneath the building waves of emotion as they swept over her. "And if you hadn't been more insistent on Oscar doing things the Gatlin way instead of allowing him to live the life he wanted, your granddaughter might be here with you now."

"If I have a granddaughter," Merrilee said, anger like ice shards in her voice, "she will be with me. I'll have my attorney—"

"Mother, no," Oliver said, rubbing at his forehead, as if the puzzle pieces he'd found in the ravine were clicking into place. "This isn't a matter for attorneys."

"What are you saying, Oliver? Of course it is." She turned in her chair, her hands gripping the arms. "This child needs us. She's your niece. Your father's granddaughter. *My* granddaughter. Your only brother's little girl."

"No." He shook his head, his expression pained and sorrowful, and nearly breaking Luna's heart. "She belongs to, belongs *with* the family who adopted her."

"She's a Gatlin," Merrilee said, nearly spitting out the name.

"She's a Smith. Or a Jones. Or maybe even a Caffey. And we'll never know," Oliver said, clearing his throat, blinking the moisture from his eyes.

Merrilee turned on Luna then. "Why? Why would you do this to me?"

Why, indeed. Did giving this woman such devastating news make her happy? Did it make up for all the pain she and her husband had caused the Caffey family? "Because it's the truth. You've painted Sierra as a slut and ruined both Mike's and Carlita's reputations. You ran the Caffey family out of town, and why? Because you didn't know the truth. You couldn't bring yourself to believe that your son was in this relationship because it was where he wanted to be. He loved Sierra. She was his life. Not you. Not whatever you think it means to be a Gatlin."

"How dare you—"

"Mother, enough," Oliver said, rising. "I think Ms. Meadows deserves the floor."

But his mother was shaking her head. "I refuse to believe any of what she says."

"You don't have to believe it," Luna reminded her. "You have Oscar's letter, which I'm certain will tell you the same thing."

"I'm sure these were a joke," Merrilee said, waving a dismissive hand over the items Oscar and Sierra had so carefully, so lovingly put away. "A prank. I know Oscar wasn't always happy with the restrictions we placed on him, and on you, Oliver. I'm sure he did this to strike back."

Luna could not believe the woman's gall. "He did this to show you what he couldn't tell you with words. He was a musician. An artist. This is as much a part of him as his child. As much a part of him as he is a part of you."

She got to her feet. "I want you to leave."

"Mother—"

"No, Oliver. I want her to go."

"That's fine," Luna said, carefully repacking the box.

"You leave all of that," Merrilee ordered.

There wasn't enough money in the world. "The letter is yours. The rest of these things belong to me. I bought the property as well as the buildings and their contents."

"I'm sure Luna wouldn't mind making copies," Oliver said, and Luna nodded, silently thanking Oliver for being so unexpectedly kind.

"I want the originals," Merrilee said, demanded. "They are mine," she added, then collapsed into her chair, and while Oliver tended to her, ringing for tea, lifting her legs onto an ottoman and sitting beside her, holding her hand, Luna quietly made her escape.

∼

Angelo wanted to kick himself. He should've gone with Luna to begin with. He should've ignored her when she told him she needed to see the Gatlins alone. He shouldn't have let that happen. He didn't know who was inside, if it was just Oliver and his mother, or if Luna was having to tell their son's story to Orville Gatlin, too. Or if Merrilee had an entourage, a half circle of pinched faces disapproving behind her, shoring her up, damning Luna for being alive.

Sierra had been right about one thing: Angelo had never known a braver woman in his life than Luna Meadows. He couldn't say with any certainty that in her shoes, he would've made this decision—to pull into the open this festering wound that desperately needed to heal. He'd had ten years to come clean, but he'd been eaten up with guilt, and feared his parents learning about Sierra's pregnancy would hurt them more than living with her death. What good could come of their knowing?

Luna had made him see things differently. His family not knowing the whole story wasn't fair to her. She'd taken the brunt of so much anger . . . from his parents, from the Gatlins. And he hadn't been innocent, the way he'd treated her, the things he'd thought—and all because he hadn't known the truth. Telling his family was no guarantee of forgiveness, and not for a minute did he think he could ever get back what he'd lost, but Luna was right: the air had to be cleared for the healing to begin.

He'd kept the secret of the pregnancy, but this had blossomed into so much more. Sierra and Oscar were leaving Hope Springs. Sierra and Oscar had gotten married. Sierra and Oscar had given their baby away. Without being able to see the entire picture, how could anyone know what to feel, or begin to understand?

Movement in front of him had him pushing off the car where he'd been leaning. The box of Sierra's things clutched to her chest, Luna walked down the sidewalk from the Gatlins' front porch to the driveway where he waited, parked on the far side of her car, out of sight. He couldn't even imagine how close to the edge Luna's anxiety had driven her. Her head was down, her steps hurried. Then behind her, the Gatlins' front door opened. Oliver hurried out and down the walk toward her, calling, "Luna, wait, please."

She stopped. Angelo pushed off his car, took two steps toward the sidewalk before Luna looked up and saw him. He stayed where he was when she held up one hand before turning to Oliver. Stayed and sweated and spewed a hateful tirade in his mind. If these people had hurt Luna, so help him . . .

But Oliver was hanging his head, his hands at his hips, repentant. His voice was low, leaving Angelo to imagine what he was saying, what he wanted, what wool he was trying to pull over her eyes. But then the other man lifted his head, and Luna reached out with one hand, placing it on his arm and rubbing as if comforting him. They both nodded, an awkward departure, before Oliver returned to the house and Luna continued to her car.

He met her there, asking, "What did he want?"

"Nothing. I'll tell you later. I need to . . . go somewhere. Can you come with me? Follow me?"

"Sure. Where are we going?"

"Don't ask me anything right now, please. I just . . ." She waved him off, her eyes hidden behind large sunglasses. "I'll tell you everything, but I need to get out of here. And I need you with me."

"Sure," he said, something full and possessive lodged in his chest. "I'll be right behind you."

CHAPTER TWENTY-TWO

L *osing Oscar killed me, but knowing what he felt for Sierra . . .*
It doesn't make the loss any easier, but I had no idea of any of
what they'd planned. How she felt about him. That she wasn't using
him. I can't believe they had a child. I just can't. . . . I'm sorry. I've
been an ass.

Oliver Gatlin's words played over and over in Luna's mind
on the drive from his home to the far side of Hope Springs.
There the old textile warehouses had stood solid for over a
century not far from the Guadalupe River. Oscar had been
her friend, but not once had she sensed any of his endearing
humanity in his brother. Until today. Today it was as if the
pin of her truth had poked through the skin of his loathing
and popped it.

I want to help with the academy. Anything I can do. Money.
Connections. Cash the check I gave you. If you got rid of it, I'll write
you another. I'll double the amount. Just tell me what you need. It's
yours, and without my mother getting in the way.

What she needed was to have all of this put behind her:
the lies, the waiting for the other shoe to drop. To reach
the end of a decade of deception without everyone writing
her off, hating her. What she needed Oliver Gatlin couldn't
give her. But Angelo Caffey could. Even if it was just in this

moment, just for today, just this one time. Even if she was the only one in love.

Glancing in her rearview mirror, she saw his rental car close behind, saw one of his hands gripping his wheel, saw the aviator sunglasses he wore hiding his eyes. Saw, too, the hard set of his jaw as he bore down on her. Her stomach began to tingle. The tingles rose, breathing grew difficult, and her chest ached. And then the tiny tickling sensation became bolder, traveling lower in her body to make itself known.

This wasn't part of her plan for today, but everything inside of her was stirred into a froth and she had to let it out, and she needed Angelo. Oh, she needed him, her Angel, her love. Whether or not he shared the things she felt . . . she didn't care. It didn't matter. Losing herself in him, with him, was the only cure for this anxiety, this alarming sense of consuming disquiet. This debilitating fear that he'd leave her again. She couldn't bear the thought of that happening.

Once at her loft, she unlocked the freight elevator and lifted the grate, waiting for him to join her before closing it and punching the panel for the fourth floor. He stood silently leaning against one wall. She stood silently leaning against the opposite. The only sound was that of the ancient car grinding through the torturous climb.

All too soon they'd reached their destination, and she knew there was no going back. She stepped into her new home and crossed the big room, leaving Angelo to follow while she caught her breath. While she thought about having him here with her, not just now but permanently. Did he have any idea how she felt about him? How could he, when she'd only recently admitted it to herself? Unless somehow he'd been aware of what she'd tucked soundly away . . .

"Is this your new place?" he asked from behind her.

His voice echoed, but she placed him near the long wall between two of the big front windows. "It is. I just got the key on Wednesday."

"When do you move in?"

"As soon as I find the time." They were exchanging banalities, nothing more. She owned the loft outright. Her possessions were where they'd always been, in the only home she'd ever known. She could move anytime she wanted to. But she would never have this time with Angelo again. This time filled with deep reds and deeper purples and the deepest of blues. Swirls of passion, ribbons floating and wrapping her up, a dancer's skirts swishing.

She couldn't stop herself, turning, walking, then running into his arms, hers going around his neck, bringing his head down, his mouth to hers. She was desperate and she didn't care, because she needed this, needed him, needed to lose herself for a little while.

He kissed her back, a frantic press of lips and teeth, of tongues seeking and finding and sliding to mate. He was greedy, his hands, his hips, but just as quickly as he started he set her away, his eyes dark and fiery. "Luna, what are you doing?"

Please, please don't let this go wrong . . . "If you have to ask, then I'm obviously doing it wrong."

"No, baby. You're not." He reached up, tugged on the point of hair brushing her chin. "I just need to know why. And that you're sure."

"I'm sure," she said, and then she was finished talking. She held his face, kissing his jaw, his chin, his neck, nipping at the skin of his throat, bruising him. Marking him as hers. She didn't want to let him go, couldn't let him go, and reached for the hem of his shirt, pulling it up his chest, over his head, and off.

Then she buried her face against him and breathed, feeling his heartbeat, feeling her own, her cheeks damp, his skin damp, too, her tears salty on her tongue. Raising her head, she brought her hands to his chest, spreading out her fingers and flexing them. His skin was resilient, the muscles beneath firm. The hair dusting his chest a wedge of soft black.

He reached for her wrists and shackled them. "I need you to be sure."

"I've never been more sure." It was a promise to him, to herself. "Not of anything. I want this. I want you."

Desperate mouths found heated skin, and hands reached and touched and grabbed tight. Clothing tore and fell, but only the bits and pieces necessary for flesh to find flesh. Belts and zippers, boots, denim jeans and a pair of rayon-and-wool-blend pants that had cost too much for how they were being discarded on the floor.

Silk panties and cotton briefs, and then skin and a slick condom. Her smooth legs and his roughly haired, and firm muscles—hers—sculpted muscles—his—until her softest parts opened for his hardest and he pushed deep, taking her, claiming her, and stilled. They both stilled, Luna pinned to the wall at her back, her legs around his waist, his feet spread.

He braced his weight against the bricks with one hand, used the other arm beneath her bottom to hold her. She couldn't move, impaled, filled with him, anchored by him. Breached. Against her neck, his breath was damp, and hot, and ragged. His hair lay against her cheek, glossy strands the same color as hers, and now almost longer than hers, and so very thick and soft.

He was thick elsewhere, and not soft at all, and he began to move, his thighs and his hips in motion as he rocked into her, pushed against her, held her still as he rubbed and ground and married his body to hers. Her thighs burned, and her back stung from the bite of the bricks through her blouse, and she didn't care about any of the pain. All she knew was the pleasure. Angelo deep inside her, wrapped around her, holding her, loving her. Loving her. *Loving her.*

All too quickly they finished, caught up in the moment's fierceness and their need. Angelo pushed hard, shoving her tight to the wall. She swallowed the gasp of pain as her shoulders met brick, and gave in to the sensation sweeping her away, crying out his name, gripping his neck for fear of falling. He slipped from her soon after, and lowered her slowly to the floor, standing with his forehead on hers until his legs started to shake, too.

They sat side by side after that, leaning against the wall, Luna in the crook of Angelo's arm as she curled into his body, her knees bent and braced on his thigh. She spread her fingers over his belly, feeling the cord of muscles there, feeling the crisp hair, the smooth skin. She wanted him naked, not to make love with, but to touch, to feel, to learn. She wasn't looking for his reaction; she knew how to elicit that.

What she didn't know was how sharp to the touch his hip bones would be, how rough the soles of his feet. Silly, maybe, but she wanted to know these things as well as the more obvious . . . the pressure of his lips, the texture of his beard, the curve of his ear and the lobe. They needed a bed, and more time, and no clothing. They needed aeons to discover each other, and she feared even now the blocks between them were being mortared back into place.

She couldn't let that happen. She refused to let that happen. Not when she had within her grasp exactly what she wanted. Angelo. Her Angel. Her love. "How long can we stay here?"

"You've got the keys. I'd say that's up to you."

"I don't have food." Or dishes or blankets or more than water from the faucet to drink.

"It's still up to you."

He was warm and solid, and she didn't want to move. "Forever? Until we wither up from dehydration and start looking like those little dolls made of dried apples?"

He let his head roll toward her. "There are little dolls made of dried apples?"

She reached for his hand and aligned their palms. "I take it you never wandered through the booths at your mother's craft shows?"

He snorted at that. "I helped her cart her things to her booth. Then I took off for the river with a six-pack. Nothing better than floatin' down the Guadalupe half numb."

"I can't even remember the last time I was on the river."

"I can't believe you ever were," he said, pulling away to look down at her.

Just because she hadn't been there with him . . . ? "Why not?"

"You never seemed like a party girl."

"I wasn't. That didn't mean I couldn't have a good time."

"Did you? Just now?" he asked, clearing his throat and closing his fingers over hers.

He was worried. "It's been so long you couldn't tell?"

"I was kinda caught up and hoping I wasn't leaving you behind."

"I had fun," she said, her blush seeming out of place after what they'd done. "Trust me."

"You gonna tell me what that was all about?"

"Does it have to be about anything?" She bounced their joined hands on her bare thigh. "Besides the obvious?"

"The obvious being . . ."

Why was she having so much trouble saying it? "Sex."

"Yeah," he said, his chuckle coarse. "That part I got."

"There's more?"

"Not always. Not all women. But you. Yeah. There's more."

"Everything. All of it. Today. The last few. It's been . . . stressful," she said because no other word came to mind.

"So I'm stress relief."

"That's not what I meant," she said, and he laughed.

"It's okay, Luna. I don't mind."

"You don't mind being used? Even though that's not really what that was?"

"I don't mind, no. Not by you. But when you do figure out what that was, I want to know."

"Because you can't just let it go?"

He waited one heartbeat, two, then asked, "Do you want me to let it go?"

She wanted to get dressed. Right now, strangely, unaccountably embarrassed, that was all she could deal with, and she got to her feet, Angelo following, adjusting himself into his shorts and his jeans. Her things were a bit more tangled. She scooped them up and headed for the bathroom, so glad she'd worn a tunic today and wasn't having to walk away with her bottom bare.

~

While Luna freshened up in the loft's bathroom, Angelo stood in front of the windows at the far end of the cavernous space, staring through the gap between two louvers across the treetops of Hope Springs. Luna's new home was on the fourth floor, giving her a pretty much unobstructed view of the town. From here he could see Second Baptist's bell tower, and realized he hadn't heard it ring once since he'd been back. A funny thing to notice, but he'd grown up with it chiming at noon every day.

The police department tested their emergency broadcast sirens at the same time. Those he'd heard, and yet there was a boy-who-cried-wolf vibe to the whole thing as he, no doubt along with others, pushed the noise to the back of his mind. Familiarity breeding . . . not contempt, but apathy, maybe? Or indifference? Hard not to become inured to a warning when the event never came to pass. Or easy to ignore, which was exactly what his whole family had done when it came to Sierra and Oscar.

All the signs were there. He'd heard his sister's bedroom window slide open late at night, looked out his own window to see her rushing across the yard, or getting into Oscar's car at the property's edge, or running with him into the woods. Sometimes he'd heard the window below him close after her, knowing it was Luna shutting it, Luna keeping his sister from getting in trouble. Luna sleeping alone in the room beneath him, and keeping him awake. Awake and thinking about tiptoeing downstairs and testing the door.

She'd been the one to finally tiptoe up to his. To knock softly. To come in when he'd called. To stand at the foot of his bed where he was already hard and pull off her T-shirt. She hadn't been wearing a bra, and her breasts had been firm and high, and she'd been sixteen. He'd been eighteen, and scrambling out of his drawers like a kid given the keys to the candy store. He'd had a condom beneath his mattress because he'd wanted to be ready if he was ever lucky enough to talk her into his room. He hadn't even asked, and there she was, her pajama shorts coming off, then her panties . . .

What he didn't understand was how his parents had missed Sierra being pregnant. Luna had packed crackers to help her through morning sickness, but how had she made it through the family's breakfast? The girls at St. Thomas wore white blouses tucked into green-and-black plaid skirts. Unless Sierra had covered hers with a sweater, he couldn't imagine the outfit doing a very good job of hiding a baby bump. Then again, by the time her bump would've been noticeable, the school year was over, and Sierra was no doubt spending her summer hours behind her cello or in the tree house.

Luna had been there for his sister every step of the way. And except for Oscar, she'd been the only one. Angelo sure hadn't been dependable, or aware, but then, neither had his parents nor the youngest of his siblings. That year had been a perfect storm of his being self-involved, his parents wrangling two teens and three soon-to-be, and Sierra in her own world and in love.

If not for Luna . . .

A sudden breeze through the window brought him back, and he looked off into the distance. Somewhere on the horizon the Edwards Plateau fell away toward West Texas, juniper and cedar and scraggly mesquite giving the ragged land the personality of a stubborn mule. And yet it was a mule with a kick—in Sierra's case, a deadly kick—demanding that those who lived here and traveled here respect the cantankerous nature of the hilly, winding roads.

If only he had come home . . .

Funny word, home. He hadn't thought of Hope Springs as more than the place he'd grown up for a very long time. It was the house, not the town, that he pictured when anyone used the word. He also pictured Luna. He'd always pictured Luna. He'd been sixteen when he'd met her, eighteen when she'd come to his room, but she was as much a part of his time here as his family, or football, had ever been.

This was the only home she'd ever known, but she was hardly a country girl, even if she lived on a farm. She did her work here, but she sold her scarves in Austin and saw them worn by celebrities worldwide. She drove a fancy import and dressed the part of designer. That intrigued him, the juxtaposition, how she'd brought the big city to the small town, and enjoyed the best of both worlds.

She should be able to take her life anywhere, work from anywhere. And yet she was still here. In Hope Springs. Where she'd lost Sierra and Oscar. Where her own injuries had confined her to bed. Where the secrets she'd kept had originated, and where they still belonged. It was as if she'd been frozen in time. As if because of his family, and the Gatlins, she'd never been able to leave. Why that bothered him so, the idea that he'd been a part of her possibly never reaching her full potential . . .

He knew exactly why. He loved her and wanted her with him. He'd loved her since high school and had fought it for years. But now, after this . . . intimacy, he needed to tell her. It was long past time. He should've told her ages ago, but he wasn't brave enough. Man enough. Both reasons keeping him from telling his parents about Sierra's phone call.

He needed to tell his parents about Sierra's baby. They deserved to know the truth. It would hurt; he knew that, but keeping them in the dark was hurting them in other ways. They were placing blame where they shouldn't. They believed things that were untrue when the reality was, he'd been the one to keep the truth from them all this time.

Luna's hand on his back brought him back to the present. He turned from the window and took her in his arms, holding her to him, his eyes closed as he stroked a hand over her head, feathering her hair with his fingers. "Do you have a passport?"

"Yes, why?"

"Can you get Kaylie or someone to watch Frank for a few days?" he asked, finally steady enough to open his eyes.

"Probably, why?"

"Can you afford a few days away from the center?"

"Yes, Angelo." Her eyes were bright, but worried. "What's going on?"

"Then pack a bag."

"Where are we going?"

"Mexico."

"To see your parents?"

"I want to take them Sierra's box. I want them to know about the baby, and the wedding. About Sierra and Oscar leaving Hope Springs."

She frowned as she held his gaze, as she studied him, searching. "Are you sure?"

"I want them to quit hating Oscar," he said, nodding. "To stop blaming you for what wasn't your fault."

"I tried to understand that. I really did," she said, her cheek pressed to his chest. "All the blame for what was an accident. What good did it do anyone?"

"You lived. You're the only one who did. Blaming Oscar gives them no satisfaction, because they want someone else to hurt as much as they do."

"Even though if Oscar *and* Sierra had made the choice to use a condom, none of this would have happened. Sierra wouldn't have died. Oscar wouldn't be in a permanent vegetative state. There wouldn't have been an adoption."

"And you and I wouldn't be here now. Together. In love."

"Is that what we are?" she asked, her voice breathless and taut. "In love."

He answered her with his eyes, which were damp with emotion, with his hands holding her face, with his mouth on hers, a tender brush of lips and encouragement.

"Do you think we would've stayed together if Sierra hadn't died?"

"Yeah. We would have," he said, and kissed her again, threading his fingers into her short, choppy hair.

"Will you come to the farm with me while I pack? I want to tell my parents where we're going, and that I'll explain it all when we get back. I don't want them to worry."

"Of course, but are you sure you want them to know?"

She nodded. "I should've told them ten years ago. I should've told everyone."

"Even knowing the trouble the Gatlins would've tried to cause with the adoption?"

"I can't think about what might've happened. I only know what I should've done."

CHAPTER TWENTY-THREE

Luna was still finding it hard to believe that Angelo's parents had remained in Mexico. She could easily picture Carlita Caffey living there, having grown up there, and assimilating with no trouble at all. It was different with Mike. She'd thought him so similar to her father, and she couldn't imagine Harry giving up his life in Texas. His high school football. His friends and his farm. His pan sausage and sauerkraut kolaches. And then there were Angelo's siblings. At the time of the move, their ages had ranged from ten to sixteen.

The four had been in school, involved in extracurricular activities there and at church, busy with all the things that kept kids in Hope Springs going from morning to night, and Isidora only just dating. To leave all of that behind when they were learning themselves, growing into their skin, starting down the road of who they would one day be . . . That had to have been as hard on the kids as on their parents, who took the brunt of their anger and blame. Then again, Mike and Carlita hadn't had any trouble laying all of that at Angelo's feet.

Leaning back in the passenger seat of her car, the wind ruffling the layers of her hair like feathers, she marveled again at how Sierra's and Oscar's choices had impacted so many. How her choices and Angelo's had done the same. She'd kept her friend's secrets as she'd promised, when revealing them might have provided closure. And Angelo had refused those two years after the accident to push her for answers, loving her, trusting her—his choice costing him his family, his life in Hope Springs, and eventually what he'd had with her.

Yet here they were now, his right hand resting comfortably on her thigh while he held her car to the road with his left, while he braked and shifted and accelerated, the muscles beneath his jeans drawing her gaze, her memory, her imagination. Oh, how hungry he made her . . .

They'd lost eight years. They would never get them back. But they were together in a way they couldn't have been when they were younger. Yes, they had much—so, so much—to work out. She had no illusion that the journey ahead wouldn't have plenty of bumps. Maybe even a few bruises. But with all they'd endured to get here, she couldn't imagine a wedge existed capable of driving them apart.

The wind and the sun and the distant horizon reminded her of a movie, some postcollege, road-trip escape drama, the characters in the story needing a last hurrah before enduring the "*the jaws that bite, the claws that catch*" of adulthood. Thinking of "Jabberwocky" brought to mind her friendship with Kaylie Flynn, who loved the poem as much as she did. Theirs was a friendship she hadn't once compared to the one she'd shared with Sierra, but a friendship just as vital to her life. The two women were such individuals, her relationship with one incomparable to the other. And, yes. At eighteen, in love and pregnant, then married, Sierra had no longer been a girl.

For miles and miles the terrain had been barren, corn shriveled and gone to husk and dried cotton fields and pastures too yellowed to graze and the highway cracked from years of being baked by the sun, then patched in black ribbons of tar. Life was there, she knew, beneath what the heat of summer had killed. Come late winter, the stirring would begin, the living things biding their time, and yet those that would never return fulfilling their own purpose, ashes to ashes, dust to dust.

A part of her wondered if bringing Angelo into her life had been his sister's purpose. She hated the thought. Hated the idea of her friend losing her life so her own would be grand. And she knew logically that accidents happened, coincidences occurred, events transpired—all of it a big series of cause and effect as the world went around. But logic was hard to draw on when her emotions were stripped raw.

If she'd moved on and left Sierra behind, this Angelo might not exist, and wouldn't be a part of her life now. A very important, essential part. The thought of not having him, the thought of losing him . . . It was as devastating as what she'd suffered losing her life's dearest friend. Yet if Sierra hadn't died, if Angelo hadn't suffered his guilt over ignoring his sister's cry for help, if Luna hadn't suffered hers over all the lies she'd told, the secrets she'd kept, she and Angelo wouldn't be on their way to fill in the blanks of his sister's story for his parents.

Holding on to her best friend all this time had brought Luna her Angel. And that she would never regret.

"I can hear you thinking from over here," he said, squeezing her thigh. "The wheels turning, dredging up more old secrets I'll have to get out of you."

She smiled, but she didn't look over, her head lolling to the right, her eyes drifting shut. "How do you know I'm thinking anything? Maybe my mind is blank. Like a canvas.

Waiting for inspiration I can turn into a scarf. Besides. I'm finished with secrets."

"That's just about the best news I've had in a while."

"What's the best?"

"I think you know," he said, his voice deep and raw.

She placed her hand atop his and squeezed. He spread his fingers, his palm still on her leg, and she threaded hers between, weaving them together. "Did you expect this to happen?"

"When I came here? Or . . . ever?"

She gripped harder, holding his hand. She was never letting him go. "It took so long to get here. There's been so much sadness. I just hate it. Not that we're together, but . . . all the rest."

"Ten years ago? Eight years ago?" He shook his head. "We weren't really ready. I wasn't, anyway."

"For this?"

"This. You." He paused, his laugh gritty. "Eighteen-year-old me didn't have a clue what to do with you. Beyond the obvious."

"I can't believe I was only sixteen."

"Sixteen going on thirty. You were so smart, so sharp."

"That's not what I was going for," she said, laughing as she wondered which of them had been the most clueless. He slid his hand farther up her thigh. She left it there, needing him. "I'm nervous about seeing your parents. Do they even know we're coming?"

He shook his head. "No reason to risk them meeting us at the gate with shotguns."

"You thought it best not to tell them I was with you, you mean. And that we're together." Because his parents had made it more than clear they never wanted to see her again.

He took a deep breath, squeezed her knee, and then let her go, leaning against his door and away from her. He wasn't rejecting her—she knew that—but it was hard not to take the distance personally. "It's okay, you know, to not want to talk about it. Just don't forget I'm here, okay?" And then she added, "For you," because she didn't want him to think she was looking for sympathy. "If you do want to talk. Or if you just need a shoulder."

"I need you," he said, and he reached for her then, cupping her nape, bringing her close, one eye on the road—she hoped—as he kissed her.

His lips were soft even as he pushed against her, the kiss firm and possessive and urgent. She fell into him, body and soul, giving him the assurance he seemed to be searching for, that she was here, and she wasn't going anywhere, and to ask because she wanted to give.

He lingered at the edge of her lips, finally moving back to his seat, but his hand stayed on her shoulder, then her arm, and finally he opened his palm. Asking. "I'm sorry. I didn't mean to pull away. I'm probably as nervous as you are. And I'm trying not to think about the reason we're making this trip."

She leaned an elbow on the console and nuzzled her face to his shoulder. "They're not going to want to see me. Or have anything to do with me. I don't know why I agreed to come—"

"You came because I asked you to—"

"—and I don't know why you asked me to."

"You're as much a part of what's in Sierra's box as I am. We're the only two she told about it. You told the Gatlins because Oscar can't. We'll tell my parents, and then we'll tell yours."

"Oliver may turn out to be less of a dick than he's been acting like all this time."

"Don't let his big check fool you."

"It's not just the check. He really was apologetic."

"He should've done his own thinking instead of letting that piece of work Merrilee think for him."

"He wants to help with the center—"

"He wants to get in your pants—"

"Angelo!"

"What, you don't think it's true? Because, trust me. Guys know these things."

That had her thinking back to what Will Bowman had said about him. "I don't care if it's true. It doesn't matter if it's true. The center needs volunteers *and* money. And if Oliver wants to offer both as an olive branch, he's welcome."

But Angelo had stopped listening, his focus snagged by the near distance. She followed the direction of his gaze, and a yawning pit opened up in her stomach.

"There's the turnoff to their place," he said, pointing at an approaching road sign and slowing the car. "Are you ready?"

"To go back eight years and have them hate me again?" What was she saying? "Not that I'd have to go back eight years for that."

He made the turn and then rolled to a stop, the long road ribboning ahead of them, an open pasture on one side, a fence on the other, a cluster of buildings huddled tight in the distance. "I want you with me while I share all of this with them. But if it's too uncomfortable, I'll understand."

But she was shaking her head before he finished. "It's not about me. It's about them. I'll stay by your side through anything, but if they don't want me there, I'll wait outside or in the car or wherever. I'm not going to add to the pain this is going to cause them. I can't do that to them. I love them too much."

His eyes softened, his dark hair and dark lashes and the dark stubble on his face giving him the look of a pirate. And yet his eyes were so kind, the same eyes that had seemed to shoot fire at her so often in the past. He reached up to cup her face in his hand, and she rubbed against him, a cat, hungry, selfishly so.

"Do you know how much I love you, Luna Meadows?"

"Do you know how happy I am that you didn't let another woman snatch you up?"

"No other woman ever got that close. You were always in the way." This time when he kissed her there was a deep desperation mixed with his desire, as if his finding her after all this time wasn't enough. As if the future they faced was too harsh, and their connection too fragile.

It wasn't fragile at all. She knew that, and she did her best to tell him so, to tell him to trust her, using her hands and her mouth, holding him, tasting him, breathing him in. Learning again the sharp edge of his cheekbones, the ridge of his brow. The hollow of his throat where his rumbled groan vibrated against her fingertips. Showing him how strong they were together, because of all they had overcome.

When she finally pulled away, his eyes were shining with so much emotion she was convinced she'd reached him. And for the things ahead awaiting them, that was enough.

"Are you ready?" he asked again.

She nodded. "With you? For anything."

CHAPTER TWENTY-FOUR

The house his parents lived in was small, the yard clean and well-kept, with beds of flowering succulents, but still resembling a desert. The size would suit having only their youngest still with them, maybe their youngest two, if Teresa hadn't left home, though he wondered what it had been like when they'd moved here eight years ago with the four children they'd claimed. Two now underfoot where there had once been six. Sierra's passing had reduced the number to five. His ostracism had made it four.

Isidora and Emilio, if they'd gone to college, would have their degrees by now. Teresa, at twenty, would be in her third year. Felix, at eighteen, a high school senior. But Angelo knew nothing of what had gone on in his parents' or his siblings' lives. Felix's notes had been little more than his saying hello. Eight years ago he'd brought Luna with him to the house on Three Wishes Road. Eight years ago he'd been told to leave and to never come back.

He'd thrust the girl he'd loved into the madness that the Caffey home had become, hoping to force his parents to stop blaming her for something that wasn't her fault. Sierra's death had been a horrible accident. She had not died at Luna's hands. But his parents looked at Luna, who'd spent hours and days, weeks in their home, and seen only what they no longer had.

Luna reached for his hand and squeezed it. "I always imagined your parents living in a house the size of the one in Hope Springs. I don't know why. I guess it's how I knew them, and it's what seemed to fit."

"Yeah." His throat was tight, his nape sweating. He couldn't think of anything else to say. All he could think of was the day he'd last seen them. His father telling him he was dead to them. His mother chastising him for his disrespect, bringing *that whore* to the house after what she'd done, when all Luna had done was survive. His mother had spit on the ground in front of him. She'd actually spit.

He couldn't imagine the next few minutes were going to go well, but he opened his door, and Luna, because she was as much a part of this moment as he was, opened hers. The smells of fried meat and fried onions reached him, as did the sounds of clattering pans, the strains of his father's flamenco guitar. And a voice—his mother's?—singing plaintively in Spanish. Dinner hour at the Caffeys. Except there was no cello. Ten years now, and there had been no cello, but the fact that there was music again gave him hope.

They slammed their doors, one, two, and the guitar stopped. The singing ceased. Moments later, as Angelo and Luna were halfway to the porch, the front door opened. His father stepped out, his expression blank, as if he hadn't yet recognized his son, or hadn't yet processed the reality that his son, after eight years and being banished, was standing in his yard. Angelo couldn't imagine he looked that much different, and yet his father . . .

Mike Caffey appeared not to have aged a day. He was still trim, his dark hair full, his boots and the tan knit slacks he'd favored so similar to what Angelo had last seen him wearing, the moment felt like déjà vu. And then his mother walked out, a dish towel in her hands, a colorful skirt of turquoise and red swishing around her knees. She wore the last eight years less favorably. Her hair had gone gray, and her cheekbones stood out sharply where the knot at her nape pulled it away from her temples.

"Mom. Dad." The two simple words nearly choked him. He squeezed his hand around Luna's, then let her go and moved forward. She fell behind him, giving him this time, waiting, respectful. "It's good to see you."

"Angelo," his father said, and his mother nodded, twisting the towel around her hands.

He wished he'd held on to Luna a bit longer, but knowing she was there . . . What had he expected? For his parents to jump from the porch in a stage dive and wrestle him joyfully to the ground? At least they hadn't turned and walked away. "I've brought you something."

They both looked at the box he held, and a stillness settled over them. They would recognize the box from St. Thomas, of course. They would know he was here about Sierra.

He waited on the porch for Luna to join him. She was hesitant, at first, her smile, when he turned to look at her, honest and true but filled with trepidation. Her hand was trembling, her fingers cold when he squeezed them with his. They followed his parents into the front room . . . hardwood flooring, a braided earth-colored throw rug, squat pottery lamps, furniture he'd never seen. His father's flamenco guitar in the seat of a leather recliner, as if waiting for him to return.

"She can stay in here," his father said, gesturing toward a cushy corduroy sofa facing a big-screen TV before walking into the next room.

His mother started to follow, then paused, and asked without looking at Luna, "Would you like something to drink? Tea or coffee? A soft drink?"

"No, thank you, Mrs. Caffey," Luna said, her voice catching. "I'll be fine."

Carlita Caffey nodded with what Angelo swore was relief and left them alone.

He went to Luna as she sat on the couch, knelt in front of her, feeling as lost as she looked, as helpless. As hopeless, too. "I didn't think this would be easy. But I did think, being Mexico and all, it wouldn't be quite so cold."

Tears welled in her eyes as she smiled, as she lifted a hand to brush his hair from his face. He reached for it, bringing her fingers to his mouth for a kiss.

"It'll be fine," she said. "We're here. We're inside."

"Yeah, but you're in here. I need you in there."

"And I'll be with you," she said, leaning her forehead against his, then kissing him the way he needed in that moment to be kissed, a desperately powerful clinging of lips and shared breath. "Now go."

He swallowed hard and pushed to his feet, carrying the box into the kitchen where his parents waited. He set it on the table. It was a table he didn't recognize. One everyone in his family—except for him, except for Sierra—had sat around to eat dinner after their move from Hope Springs. The table he'd grown up knowing was in the house on Three Wishes Road. Soon it would be part of the Caffey-Gatlin Academy, maybe in the teachers' lounge, maybe in the conference room.

The old table was solid, one his father had built, one with eight chairs Angelo had helped him construct. That had been one of their first projects together. To this day that time with his father was one of his favorites, holding memories no others did, his father sharing his knowledge of the wood they'd used, explaining the best use of his copious collection of tools, setting Angelo on the path to his own career. He was glad the table would still see years of good use. He would've hated to see it destroyed. He had Luna to thank for that, and he was happy about that, too.

His father sat at the table's head. His mother sat to the right. He pulled out the chair across from her, scraping it forward, wishing for more elbow room because he felt as if he were being crushed by expectations. He flipped the lock on Sierra's box with his thumb, then cradled it unopened between his hands.

"Luna bought the house on Three Wishes Road out of foreclosure." He didn't ask how they'd let things get to that point. That conversation could wait. "She's been . . . *we've* been going through everything that was left there, and she found this in the tree house," he said, hearing his mother's sharp intake of breath, his father's slower, deeper, shaky inhalation. On the drive down he'd worried they wouldn't be strong enough to look through the contents. Even thinking about what he and Luna had found inside still left him gutted.

It also left him to realize that as close as he and Sierra had been, allies growing up, he had no clue as to the rich life that had thrived in his sister. The letter she'd written to Luna . . . How could anyone at eighteen know another person that well?

"What is it?" his mother asked, bringing him back to the present. She reached a tentative hand toward the box lid, placed the tips of her fingers there, and then curled them into her palm as if she'd been burned. When she raised her gaze to his, tears swam in her eyes. "Angelo?"

He nodded while he gathered his thoughts, found his voice, cleared the choking emotion from his throat. "Sierra left letters inside. One for Luna. One for me. One to both of you, and one from Oscar to the Gatlins. There's also a music CD. Songs Sierra and Oscar played together. Some that they wrote." He braced his elbows on the table, rubbed at his temples to push away the pain throbbing there. "There's also a photo from a sonogram."

His mother gasped. His father's head came up, and then he stood, shoving away from the table, knocking his chair to the floor. He left it there as he walked to the kitchen sink and slammed his hands down on the countertop, slammed them again and again. "I knew it. That son of a bitch. I knew it."

"No, Dad. It's not like that." Angelo opened the box, reached into the bottom beneath the papers there for the narrow gold bands buried at the bottom of the box. Wedding rings the couple had never worn. Had Sierra left hers because her fingers were swollen? Had they intended to stop at the house for the box on their way out of Hope Springs? He set them on the table, watched them spin to a stop. "They were married."

"Married?" This from his mother. "Angelo, what are you saying?"

"Oscar and Sierra got married the Friday before the accident. Luna was their witness." He nodded toward the box. "The CD contains the music they played at the ceremony." *And in the hospital during Sierra's delivery,* though he kept that thought to himself.

"And the sonogram picture? Was Sierra pregnant when she died?" His mother pulled the box closer, shuffled the letter and CD aside to find the photo. She lifted it out with shaking hands. "Why wouldn't the authorities have told us? Did they not know?"

"I'm not sure what they knew or didn't know. But, no. She wasn't pregnant when she died." He closed his eyes, swallowed. "She'd already given birth."

"What?" his mother asked, gasping, the photo fluttering to the floor as she covered her mouth with both hands.

His father returned to the table, planted both palms on the surface, and leaned forward, an angry bull bellowing. "Where's the baby? Does that damn Merrilee Gatlin have our grandchild?"

"Angelo," his mother pleaded. "Tell me what happened. Where's my baby's child?"

"Listen to me, please," he said, reaching for the photo where it had fallen and dusting it off. "Don't jump to conclusions. Don't think you know what you can't. I get that this is hard to hear, but the Gatlins didn't know about any of this until recently. Only one person knew."

"One person?" his father asked, slowly straightening. "One person? The person you brought here with you? Luna Meadows knew all this time, and you brought her here with you? How dare—"

Angelo pushed to his feet, steaming, holding his father's gaze. "No. This isn't on Luna."

"Of course it's on Luna," the older man said, and gestured wildly. "She saw the accident. She spent that weekend with Sierra. Is that when she had her baby? That weekend?"

He nodded. "They arranged the adoption through an attorney. All of Sierra's medical bills were paid. She was well cared for."

"How did we not know she was pregnant?" This from his father. "How did she hide that from us?"

And this—"No one knew? But you? And Luna? And Oscar? She told no one else?"—from his mother.

"Why didn't you tell us?" His father again. "Why didn't you say anything?"

"I didn't know about the adoption until recently. Until Luna told me," he said, feeling battered by their questions because the answers they wanted had gone to the grave with his sister.

"Did you know she was pregnant?"

He scrubbed both hands back over his head, holding his hair from his face, listening to his father's words echo. "Sierra called me near the end of her junior year. She asked me to come home and be with her while she told you."

"You didn't. You wouldn't."

He answered his father with a shake of his head, shame and guilt both weighty.

"Please, Angelo. You're the only one who gets me. And you know what this will do to them."

"You should've thought about that sooner."

"I should have. You're right. But I can't go back, and I need you now."

"I can't. Not this weekend. I have plans."

"Next weekend then? Can you come next weekend?"

"No. I've got plans then, too."

"Plans not to come home at all?"

"Something like that."

"I was selfish. And stupid. I was getting ready to go to Rome. I was wrapped up in my own life." He'd been a jerk, and worse, not much of a brother.

"We could've taken the baby," his mother said, her voice rising, her fingers knotted together, her knuckles chapped and red. "We could've helped her while she finished high school. She didn't have to give away our grandchild! Now we have nothing left of her. Nothing! Do you understand?"

He understood more than they could know. "I thought she would tell you. I never thought otherwise."

But his mother was crying now, hearing nothing he said. "Oh, my baby. My Sierra. Why didn't she tell us?"

His father walked around the table to where Angelo was standing. "Do you know why she changed her mind?"

"Yes, sir," he said, his hands going to his hips. "I think so, only I just found out."

"From Luna."

"From Sierra. From the letter she wrote to Luna. She and Oscar were going to New York for their senior year"— though he didn't tell them the part they'd played in Sierra's decision—"and then to study music. She wanted her baby to have a full-time mother, not a nanny, or a series of sitters, or to grow up in day care. And she knew how important it was to the family that she succeed. But she also knew how much of a struggle you had with your four still at home. She and Oscar decided the baby would have a better life with parents who could give her what they couldn't."

"Or that damn Oscar Gatlin decided that."

"No, Dad. They decided it together. It's in the letters Sierra wrote."

"Her?" his mother said, looking up. "Our grandbaby . . . She's a girl?"

"Lily. They named her Lily," he said, and that was when his mother broke.

Her sobs rent through him, tightening his chest, a boa constrictor choking him. He turned to his father, who was shaking his head, grief wet on his cheeks, but silent. "Dad—"

It was all he managed to say before his father was pointing toward the door. "Get out. Just go. Leave the box."

"I'll leave your letter. And I'll make you a copy of the CD and the photo. But I'll be back for the box." He hadn't talked about this to Luna, but the box belonged to the Caffey-Gatlin Academy, locked inside a glass display case, the contents hidden, the lid closed.

"Fine. But come alone. I don't want that woman in my house."

"Luna is with me."

"I don't care—"

But Angelo damn well did. "I love her."

"After what she did—"

Enough. He returned the rings and the photo to the box with the CD before closing it with the booties still inside. "Nothing Luna did would've changed what happened. Sierra chose to marry Oscar. She chose to study music. She and Oscar chose to give their child to a family desperate for one of their own. Luna knew about the baby, yes, and thank God she did, because she helped Sierra through all of it. The morning sickness, everything. But she's not to blame for any of this. And you know that."

Angelo exited the house the way he'd come in, but found the living room empty. His heart jumped as he pushed through the front door. Luna stood in the yard, behind the car, facing away.

He couldn't get to her fast enough. "What are you doing out here?"

"Thinking. Breathing. Nothing." She crossed her arms as if hugging herself. "Giving you time with your parents. Trying to pretend I didn't hear them yelling about me."

Ignoring the latter, he wrapped an arm around her shoulders and hugged her, bringing her close to his body and letting her settle there, letting her stay. How had he ever thought he hated her? How had he ever thought she hadn't been his whole life since the first time he'd seen her?

"Those are all good things. Especially the breathing part. I'd hate for you not to do that."

She leaned her head against him, rubbing so that her short, spiky hair scratched his shirt. He missed her long hair. He loved her short hair, but he missed threading his fingers through the waist-length strands and watching them flow. He'd done it so often years ago. He hadn't done it enough since being back.

"How're you doing?" she asked, nuzzling again.

"Your head's on my heart. I can't imagine being better than this."

"I mean with your parents," she said, though he felt her smile where her cheek rested on his chest. "I can't even imagine having to deal with such news after all this time."

"It's going to be rough for a while. And not just on them," he said, letting that sink in before he looked down.

She looked up, searching his gaze. "On me, you mean. Because of the secrets I kept."

"Yeah."

"And even more on you."

"That too."

She nodded, swallowed. Tears welled, and she blinked them away. "Do we need to leave now? Do you want to put me on a plane so you can stay a few more days? I know they don't want me here."

This woman. "No. I'm not going to put you on a plane. If we need to leave now, we'll do it together."

"Angel, this is your family. You haven't seen them in ages. They haven't seen you. I'm not going to get in the way of that, especially with the news you brought. They need time to process that. I need to go. At least find me a room somewhere. A motel. A hostel. I'll be fine."

She might, but he wouldn't. He needed her with him. Her mind. Her body. All of her. "We'll drive into town, give them some time. We'll test the waters when we get back."

"I'm so sorry about all of this," she said, catching back a sob. "About everything."

His own chest tightened, and he had to force out the words. "Luna, I love you. You're my life now. Even if my parents never come to understand what you did, I do—"

"But you wouldn't have done the same thing."

"I don't know what I would've done. But I did enough. Or I didn't do enough, not coming home when Sierra asked me to." The knife of his guilt sliced impenetrably deep.

"It helps, you know. Knowing you love me."

"I'll always love you," he said and pulled her to him, wrapping her in his arms. "I'll forever love you."

"That helps most of all."

"C'mon," he said, guiding her toward her car. "Let's go find a bed."

"Angelo!"

"Uh-uh. Tonight you call me Angel."

DAY FIVE

SATURDAY

The best thing about the future is
that it comes one day at a time.
—Abraham Lincoln

CHAPTER TWENTY-FIVE

This morning's arrival at the Caffey house a mirror of last night's, Luna and Angelo slammed their doors in quick succession, then walked toward the house. Luna, however, stopped at the front of the car to lean against the hood. Angelo, reaching the porch steps alone, frowned and came back to where she waited. "You're not coming in?"

She shook her head, crossing her arms to keep from pulling him to her, holding him, rubbing her cheek to his that was bristled with the whiskers he hadn't had a razor to shave. She'd loved his parents dearly, but she was an outsider now, unwelcome, unwanted. Unwilling to put herself through their rejection again. "I came in last night."

"That was last night," he said, but the smile he gave her was sadly knowing.

"I can't imagine if I come in now things will be any different. Any . . . better." She shrugged as she added the latter, her chest tight as she did.

He lifted a hand, tucked the short strands of her hair behind her ear. "I won't be long."

"I know."

But he didn't go right away. He stood in front of her, his fingers trailing from her ear to her jaw, his gaze following his hand as if creating a visual as well as a tactile memory. Or maybe she had it all wrong. Maybe he didn't want to go in either, but wanted to stay with her. Maybe he needed her with him.

Maybe she was being selfish, when what she'd wanted to do was give him this time.

Before she could move, however, the door opened, and the screen followed, squeaking on its hinges as all screens seemed to do. Angelo dropped his hand and hung his head, shaking it while breathing deep.

"I love you," she whispered, and he gave a nod before turning, his long stride carrying him to where his father waited. He shook the other man's hand, and the two talked quietly, Mike Caffey's fists shoved in his pockets, Angelo's shoved in his, too.

Angelo was shaking his head, his gaze cast down, while his father seemed intent on holding his attention, and being three inches shorter, ducked his head to get in his son's face, as if making demands, as if lecturing. As if making sure Angelo understood what he had to say.

Moments later, his mother came out, hugging Sierra's box to her chest. Then, as if he were in her way, she stepped in front of her husband to get to her son. She wrapped one arm around Angelo's neck and kissed his cheek, tears like tattoos of her sorrow marking her face. It broke Luna's heart to see Carlita Caffey so tormented, and her own tears burned like black tar.

But Angelo insisted on taking a stand. He understood the why of what Luna had done—understood, too, his parents' feelings about Luna keeping Sierra's secrets for so long. But he needed them to know he'd forgiven her, and that he wasn't blameless in all that had come to pass.

Sierra had chosen her path. No one knew what had caused Oscar to lose control of the car. It had been an accident. A tragic, senseless accident. But that was all. Luna had suffered enough at their hands, and the ostracism had to stop. Angelo had chosen to be with her, and she hoped they accepted that she was a very important part of his life.

That, more than anything, was why Luna knew they would weather this particular storm. She and Angelo had both made questionable choices, and recognized doing so. But neither blamed the other anymore, and slowly they were coming to forgive themselves for their lapses in judgment, their terrible mistakes.

They were coming, too, to understand what the other had done, and why. The reasons meant everything. Whether good or bad, those motives could not be ignored. They came from the root of who she was, what she believed about friendship and loyalty, and from the core of what had made her fall in love with Angelo so many years ago.

And what had her loving him more than she'd thought possible today, especially after last night . . .

They'd spent the night in a tiny little motel, their bungalow so small it would've fit in her loft a half dozen times with, she was pretty sure, room to spare. There'd been a wonderfully plush full mattress, the perfect size to ensure they touched while they slept. Angelo had wrapped his arm around her waist and pulled her into his body. At some point he'd turned over, and she'd spooned the same way against his back, her nose to his nape, breathing him in, her fingers threading through his chest hair, tugging, toying with his nipples until he groaned.

They hadn't lasted long like that, need rising between them until neither could breathe without spilling ragged sounds into the room. She'd pulled him toward her, or he'd rolled over her, she couldn't be sure, and it hadn't mattered because they wanted the same thing at the same time, and the act transcended what she'd known in the past, even what she and Angel had shared in the hours before.

He was rough in his gentleness, demanding as he asked, thorough while skimming over her body with his fingertips and his mouth. The night had been all about learning, and longing, the physical desperation of a relationship that had endured the emotional wringer's fierce battering. Neither of them had slept much at all. They'd dozed, drifted, talked in shorthand snippets, questioned, shared.

She knew so much more now about what it had been like for him growing up the oldest of six siblings. She'd seen only what she, an outsider, an only child, had wanted to see: the laughter, the beehive buzz of activity, the fun and games. What she hadn't seen were the creative personalities clashing, the artistic moodiness that bordered on depression. How his parents had already been coming apart before losing Sierra. How more and more responsibility had fallen onto Angelo's shoulders. She was surprised he hadn't cracked, though he'd laughed when she'd said that, swearing football had kept him sane.

She was also surprised how well he'd hidden all of that when they were together halfway between their two worlds, but those times neither one of them had wanted to talk about home. He'd wanted to talk about school, what he was learning, how much he loved what he was learning, how much he'd looked forward to his trip to Rome, what he'd seen while there, what he'd studied, and she'd wanted to listen to every word.

The Angelo she'd known who attended Cornell had been neither the Angelo who'd quarterbacked the Hope Springs

Bulldogs, nor the man in the car beside her now. That Angelo had been less boy than man, though not yet with this one's presence. Fitting, she supposed, since the two years between Sierra's death and his family's move hadn't seemed to belong to either of her lives—the one where Sierra was, the one where she wasn't. They'd been magic years, drifting years, years spent trying to escape their shared loss by not talking about it at all.

A part of her wanted to go back there, to float down that river, eyes closed, knowing nothing but freedom and bliss. But there was a reason it was called *real* life, and she'd much rather go through this current heartache with this Angelo, because these were feelings she could trust. Feelings she would always remember. Feelings that would mold her and shape him and make them into something true.

Three hours after leaving the Caffeys' home, and the solemn good-bye Angelo had shared with his parents, Luna took her passport from Angelo's hand. After the border patrol agent waved them through, she watched in the passenger-side mirror as the crossing disappeared behind them. Once it was nothing but a speck, swallowed up by the shimmer of heat rising from the road, she turned in her seat, tucking her feet beneath her.

"What are you going to do when we get back to Hope Springs?"

Angelo shrugged without looking over. "I'm driving your car, so I figure I'll go to the house. You can stay, or you can head home. Up to you."

That wasn't what she'd meant, but he was so typically practical male that his response didn't surprise her. "Let me try that again. Tomorrow. The day after. What are your plans?"

He waited several long seconds, then glanced in the rear-view mirror and slowed the car, pulling to the side of the road. There was nothing around for miles. No houses. No gas stations. No billboards. Not so much as an intersection with another road to take them someplace else. No car but hers traveled the long, straight highway that would return them to the civilization she called home. The sky reached miles to the horizon, leaving her with a sense of insignificance, and yet with Angelo for company she felt more vital than she ever had in her life.

Dear God, she loved this man.

Pulling the keys from the ignition, he opened his door and climbed from the car. She watched through the windshield as he came around to her side, and reached for her own door as he approached. Once she was out, he took her hand, leading her away from the road and into the scrub brush and dirt. She held tight and followed, apprehension creeping down her spine like a scorpion—a thought that had her watching carefully where she stepped, and then her nerves had her laughing.

"I'm guessing you've got a destination in mind here? Because I'd hate to think you decided this would be the perfect place for the buzzards to pick my bones clean."

He let her go but kept walking, throwing his arms out wide before lacing his hands atop his head, turning in a circle, and howling as if driven by demons. In the distance she saw a shimmer of light, a reflection, a mirage. The sound of Angelo's call echoed, and then he came back to her, a great purpose in his hurried steps, and she heard him muttering beneath his breath.

"I don't know where I'm going. I don't know what I'm doing. I don't know how to say this. I just don't—"

"Angel, stop. What's wrong?" she asked, her heart burrowing deep in her chest to keep from getting broken. *Please don't let something have gone this terribly wrong!*

Hands on his knees, he leaned forward, his shaking head bowed. "I never thought I'd do this in my life. I've never wanted to, never felt I needed to . . ."

"Angel, tell me what's going on," she said, her voice a painful whisper in her throat. What in the world was going on?

"Luna Meadows," he said as he straightened, his cheeks wet, his eyes bright, his expression hopefully solemn. "Will you marry me?"

Her heart. Where was her heart? It wasn't beating. She was going to die. Had he really just *proposed*? "You want me to marry you."

"I don't know why you would want to," he said, but she knew exactly, and she smiled. "It's not fair for me to think you would when I can't manage to get my head screwed on straight. And the road with my family won't be easy—"

"The road with mine will be," she said, walking toward him, moving his hands away from his waist and pressing their palms together, then lacing their fingers, folding hers down to hold him tight and waiting for him to do the same. He did, and she smiled. Joy found where her heart was hiding and yanked hard, throwing it into the sky to burst and rain down confetti.

She'd never known happiness could feel like this. "I love you, Angelo Caffey. You're in my blood, beneath my skin. You fill my thoughts with only good things and my days with so much beauty and my life with hope. Those are the reasons

I want to marry you. But only some. There are many, many more."

He pulled their joined hands around his back, bringing their bodies close. "Like the way I fill your body?"

"That would be one," she said, lifting high on her toes for his kiss. "And this would be another."

She pressed her lips to his, then parted them, taking his tongue into her mouth and loving it with hers, loving him with her hands against his back, loving him with her heart that fluttered around them in tiny bright pieces. Being happier than this . . . She couldn't imagine any moment of her life being better than this. Except one.

Holding his biceps, she pulled back to look at him, getting a frown for her troubles. "When?"

"When?" he asked, obviously confused.

"How soon can we get married?"

"Well, we've got a car," he said, looking over her head to where he'd parked. And then he grinned. A wicked flash of teeth and dimples cut deep in the scruff covering his chin and his cheeks. "As long as we've got money for gas, we can head back to Hope Springs by way of Las Vegas, if you'd like."

"I absolutely, positively, one hundred percent like." This was their time, so long in coming. Later they would celebrate with family and friends, a reception on the farm perhaps, or a party at Two Owls. But becoming Angelo's wife . . . It was a moment too intimate to share. She wanted it with him. Just him.

And then she turned and ran as fast as she could for the car, giggling at the sound of Angel's steps pounding behind her, giggling even louder at the sound of her future falling perfectly into place.

CHAPTER TWENTY-SIX

Six weeks later . . .

Luna stood behind the island in the loft's sectioned-off kitchen, adding more wineglasses to those already in use. When she and her mother had worked up the guest list for tonight's reception, she'd never expected a one-hundred-percent affirmative response. And looking out at the crowd in the loft now, she was pretty sure there were more people here than had been invited.

She didn't mind. Except for the fear they would run out of food and drink. But having this large a turnout—yes, there were definitely more people here than invitations had gone out—thrilled her. Not for her sake but for Angelo's. He'd been gone from Hope Springs a long time. His return would no doubt raise questions, as would his marrying Luna after being back less than a week.

Tonight, she hoped, would answer the biggest: Was their marriage some kind of stunt, meant to draw attention to the Caffey-Gatlin Academy, or were they truly in love? She couldn't imagine that anyone seeing them together could doubt the veracity of the emotions binding them, emotions that were true and pure and too strong to doubt. Emotions that left her weak in the knees with their power.

"What are you doing back here?" Kaylie asked, joining her in the kitchen and taking the glasses from her hands. "You're the guest of honor. You're supposed to be mingling. Go mingle," she added, having slipped behind Luna to nudge her with her hip.

"I can't mingle. I'm the hostess," Luna said, but she mostly didn't want to mingle because she was enjoying watching everyone else do it. She thought back to the day so many volunteers had come to clean the yard at the arts center, to the love the people of Hope Springs still had for the Caffeys, how even Merrilee Gatlin's machinations hadn't been able to destroy it. How she herself was so very proud to be part of the family, even while saddened by the refusal of Angelo's parents to forgive and accept. She hoped someday soon . . .

"You can and you will," Kaylie was insisting. "Having the reception here does not make you the hostess. It was just a matter of logistics. If not for the construction, I would've insisted we use my house. And if not for the smell of sheep, we could've used the farm. Now go. Mingle. Show off that rock that puts mine to shame."

"It does not," Luna said, looking again at the ring Angelo had surprised her with in Vegas. It was an amazing ring for a Vermont cabinetmaker who couldn't afford decent T-shirts—though she was quite the fan of his indecent ones . . . "You're right. It does," she said, just as her mother arrived.

"Julietta." Kaylie set down the glasses to give Luna's mother a hug. "You look amazing. How're you feeling?"

"About ten thousand times better than I was a month ago," Luna's mother said, her dark hair pulled back in an elegant braid, color high on her cheekbones. "When they say the first trimester is the worst? Believe them," she said, and

Luna smiled at the thought of the crackers she'd brought to school for Sierra.

Kaylie looked from mother to daughter. "I'm threatening your girl here with bodily harm if she doesn't get out there and enjoy her night."

Luna tried to object, but her mother interrupted. "I saw her back here and came to see what she was doing. So, what *are* you doing?"

"I was just getting more wineglasses—"

Her mother took her by the shoulders and turned her toward the main room. "You let me and Kaylie do that. Your job is to enjoy your guests. And your new husband."

Luna tried not to blush. Her parents had been ecstatic to get her call from Las Vegas telling them she and Angelo were now man and wife. And by the time they'd returned to Hope Springs, her mother and Kaylie had already cooked up this get-together to celebrate.

But it was still strange to think of herself as her mother's married daughter. "Fine. I'm going. But you might want to start washing what glasses you can. I'm not sure we'll have enough to get through the night otherwise."

The first person she ran into as she circled the kitchen island into the loft's main room surprised her. She'd sent him and his parents an invitation, but doubted any of the three would come.

"Luna. Congratulations. I wish nothing but the best for you and Angelo."

"Thank you, Oliver," she said, offering her cheek when he leaned to kiss it. "I'm so glad you came. And I'm so, *so* glad you're going to be part of the arts center." His doing so was the best way she could think of to honor Oscar. "That makes me happy."

"Good," he said. "And I appreciate you sending the invitation for tonight. I would've hated to miss the party of the year." His smile was teasing, but genuine, no malice in sight. "This is some place. I knew the warehouses had been gutted for residential use, but I had no idea so much finishing work had been done. The brick walls, they're original?"

"They are. It's one of my favorite things. I'm just sorry I won't get to enjoy them as much as I'd thought."

"Why's that?" he asked as he lifted his drink.

"We're converting the barn on the Caffey property into a house, so I'll use the loft just for weaving." She glanced around the cavernous room, still mostly empty save for two lamps, two lamp tables, the sofa, TV, and the bed from her room at the farm. And the strands of tiny white lights dangling from the beams overhead. "We're staying here temporarily. But since Angel's at the center most of the time, and I don't need anything but my loom when I'm working, we decided to rough it instead of decorating here, then decorating there."

"Makes sense," he said, then glanced around the room. "Where is your husband? I wanted to say hello, but I haven't seen him since I got here."

"Last I knew he was with my father, over near my loom." She looked that way, catching a glimpse of Angelo's black hair. It hung loose to his shoulders, and he'd given in to her wishes when she'd begged him this morning not to shave. The breeze through the open windows stirred the strands, and the light from the full moon, and that of the street lamps shining in, cast his profile in dangerous shadow.

She thought back to what her mother had said, and wished everyone gone. She was through celebrating. She wanted to enjoy her husband.

"There he is," Oliver was saying. "Good to see you again. And I mean that," he said, adding an, "Excuse me," to the woman arriving as he left.

Luna pulled Tennessee Keller's sister into a big hug. "Indiana. I haven't seen you in ages."

"Who cares about that?" the other woman said. "Tell me everything you know about that man."

Luna laughed. "That was Oliver Gatlin. Merrilee and Orville's oldest son."

"He's tall, and dark, and handsome . . . and I hope single?"

"As far as I know," Luna said, her attention snagged this time by movement at her side, and she smiled as her gaze connected with that of the boy who'd been raised by wolves.

Will Bowman lifted his empty wineglass in greeting, his slash of dark hair falling over his brow and obscuring one of his eyes. "Ms. Keller. Mrs. Caffey. And how strange does that sound? Mrs. Caffey."

"I happen to think it sounds lovely," Indy said, the pulse at the base of her throat thumping visibly when Will turned his gaze on her—where it stayed while he handed Luna his glass, saying, "Point me to a bottle."

"Kaylie just kicked me out of the kitchen, but c'mon. I'll find you a corkscrew."

Indy and Will followed her back that way, where she grabbed a bottle and a corkscrew from the island before her mother or Kaylie could object. Then, at the sound of the elevator engaging again, Luna looked over to see who else had arrived, because she couldn't imagine who it might be.

She swore everyone who lived in Hope Springs had already crowded into her loft. Thank goodness she hadn't moved all of her things into the space before she and Angelo had taken off for Mexico—then Las Vegas. And if that week in Las Vegas hadn't been the best she'd ever known . . .

Luna Meadows Caffey.

Who knew Angelo had it in him to be so spontaneous? Who knew she had it in her to abandon everything for the love of her life?

The couple who exited the elevator were young, and no one Luna recognized. The man couldn't have been more than twenty, and perhaps still even a teen. The woman wasn't much older. Both had dark hair. Both were beautiful, with a touch of Latin heritage evident in their cheekbones. Both had eyes that reminded her of Angelo . . .

"Oh. Oh. Oh," she said, shoving the wine bottle and corkscrew she held into Will's hands, then hurrying into the main room and signaling frantically for her husband. He was still near her loom talking to her father and Oliver Gatlin, but, as if sensing her anxiousness, looked up and caught her gaze.

She motioned toward the elevator, and he glanced that way, going completely still before shoving his wineglass into her father's hand and taking off for the front of the room, dodging clusters of milling guests in his haste to reach the door. He beat her there, and she heard him call, "Felix! Teresa!" seconds before he wrapped his arms around both of his siblings at once.

He buried his head and his shoulders shook, and Felix and Teresa cried with him, the three creating a picture that left no one, even those who hadn't known the family, unmoved. They stood in a group hug for what seemed like ages, but couldn't have been more than a minute or two at most. Finally he stepped back and lifted his head, looking for Luna and waving her over.

"I'm sure you both remember Luna."

"Of course," Teresa said, leaning close to kiss Luna's cheek. "You always made cleaning the kitchen so much easier, since I had less to do with you there helping."

Luna laughed. "It was so quiet at home that hanging out with all of you felt like a day at Six Flags," she said to Teresa, then turned to Felix. "And you. It's like looking at Angelo all over again. I can't believe you've grown up."

"You cut your hair," Felix said. "I've always pictured you with it long."

"It was long until a couple of months ago," Angelo said, looking from Luna to his brother, then his sister, his voice hopeful as he asked, "'Milio and Isi? Did they come with you? Or Mom and Dad?"

"It's just us," Teresa said, and Felix shook his head. "We don't see them much. Isi and 'Milio. And Mom and Dad, well. You know. You were there."

Angelo nodded, swallowed. "Yeah. It's okay. I'm so glad to see both of you. I'd hoped to see you in September, but we didn't stay long."

"Mom told us. About Sierra. The baby. Her and Oscar getting married," Teresa said, her voice catching on the last word. "The music you're playing . . ."

Angelo nodded, his throat working. "It's Sierra and Oscar. A piece they wrote. We found the CD in the tree house," he said, and that's when Felix broke, too, tears welling and threatening to fall.

Luna stepped in, wrapped an arm around his shoulders. "Listen. Why don't you go back to the bedroom area behind the kitchen? Angelo knows where. Y'all can talk. I'll get my mom and Kaylie to start winding things down."

Teresa nodded. Felix did, too. Angelo threaded his fingers into Luna's hair and pulled her to him, kissing her cheek and whispering, "I love you, wife," against her ear. She watched him walk away, an arm slung around the shoulders of both siblings, hugging close one, then the other as they made their way through the crowd.

She joined them twenty minutes later, having left her parents along with Kaylie and Ten to finish up in the main room. All three of the Caffey siblings sat on the bed, Felix cross-legged and hunched over, Teresa's legs tucked to her side as she leaned against one of the footboard's tall posts. Angelo sat propped against the headboard, and Luna crawled up to join him. He wrapped an arm around her shoulders and pulled her close.

She rested a hand on his thigh. "So I'm guessing this is what you did with the invitation you asked me for?"

Angelo nodded. "Felix and I have stayed in touch. The day the family moved, he asked if he could write. I gave him my address, and he used that of one of his friends so our parents never knew."

"When I heard Mom and Dad talking about the property being foreclosed on, I wrote and told Angelo," Felix said, toying with the laces on his shoe. "Angelo never got a chance to get out anything he might've wanted the day we moved."

A mystery solved, Luna mused, glancing from younger brother up to older. "I always wondered how you knew I'd bought the property. You never said."

"I can keep secrets, too, you know," he told her, then dropped a kiss to the tip of her nose.

She looked back to his brother and sister. "I'm so glad you came. And you'll stay, yes? A few days, at least? I'd love for you both to see what we've done with the house, and what we're doing with the barn. We want you to stay as long as you can. You will, won't you?"

By the time she finished, both of Angelo's siblings were looking at her and smiling, Angelo chuckling deep in his chest. She glanced from one to the other to the other, her mouth pulling into an answering grin. "What's so funny?"

"I was just telling these two how you're like a dog with a bone once you get an idea in your head," her husband said, gesturing toward the others with one hand.

"I'm pretty sure I learned that trick from you," she told him, leaning against him, loving him, knowing that whatever happened with the rest of her life, she would have this man with her—which made every epic thing they'd gone through to get here seem like nothing at all.

ABOUT THE AUTHOR

Alison Kent is the author of more than fifty published works, including her debut novel, *Call Me*, which she sold live on CBS's *48 Hours*, in an episode called "Isn't It Romantic?" Her novels *A Long, Hard Ride* and *Striptease* were both finalists for the *Romantic Times* Reviewer's Choice Award, while *The Beach Alibi* was honored by the national Quill Awards, and *No Limits* was elected by *Cosmopolitan* as a Red Hot Read. The author of *The Complete Idiot's Guide to Writing Erotic Romance* and a veteran blogger, Alison decided long ago that if there's a better career than writing, she doesn't want to know about it. She lives in her native Texas with her geologist husband and a passel of pets.

Read on for a sneak peek of Alison Kent's next
Hope Springs novel.

The Sweetness of Honey

Available Fall 2014 on Amazon.com

CHAPTER ONE

The bees were what had sold her. The bees and Hiram Glass. The lovely octogenarian had tended the hives for years, selling the honey at the same farmer's market where she sold root vegetables, and vine vegetables, and leafy greens, and the years the weather cooperated, strawberries the size of her fist.

She would leave the back of the plot where their busy hives thrived untouched; these days, honeybees faced so many obstacles as it was. That would allow more than enough room for the expansion of IJK Gardens—though the Hope Springs, Texas, property would be more of an annex since the greenhouse in Buda that served as her bread and butter was forty miles away. It was a nice bit of separation. Business from pleasure from play.

The annex would be her baby, her indulgence, the heirloom vegetables she'd grow here her specialty. They would cost more to cultivate, requiring higher prices, but the demand was equally high. Consumers determined to avoid genetically modified foods would pay for quality produce. And pay for the honey from her bees.

Her bees. The words made Indiana Keller smile. Even now, standing across Three Wishes Road, in the Caffey-Gatlin

271

Academy driveway, she could hear them. She had to close her eyes, and be very still, and hold her breath, and bow the muscles of her imagination, but the hum was there, a soft busy vibration of work being done.

Work had been her life for years now. Work kept her sane. Work left her no time for a personal life. Work was her savior and most of the time her friend. An easy one to keep. Demanding yet constantly loyal, and in the end, she was the boss. That was the part she liked best. Calling the shots. Taking charge had helped her through some very dark days.

Those days were long gone. And with this new venture calling her name . . . She couldn't believe the gorgeously overgrown and scruffy acreage across the street was hers, all hers, and there was absolutely no rush to get done all the things she wanted to do. As long as her impatience didn't get in the way, she could take her time with the tilling and the planting and the cottage, and all the things she needed to learn about the bees.

Just as the thought entertained her, a new sort of buzzing set up along her spine. Not one she heard, but felt. An awareness. A clear breach of her private communion. What she heard were footsteps crunching the driveway's gravel, and she flexed her fingers, then rubbed at her palms where her nails had dug deep. The steps drew closer, and they were firm, heavy, most likely belonging to a man. Possibly Angelo Caffey. Or a member of her brother's construction crew.

But neither was who came to a stop beside her.

"Can I help you with something?" the man asked, smelling earthy, salty. Privileged.

"No. I'm fine," she said without looking over. She knew who he was, but doubted he remembered her.

"Are you a friend of Hiram's?"

"I am, yes. Why?"

"Because friends of Hiram know he's not one for trespassing. He says it's bad for the bees. Strangers disturb them."

No doubt he knew as well as she that Hiram had moved before the property sold. And that the bees deterred most strangers. And yet she'd parked in the driveway across the street. As bold as she pleased. "And you are?"

"Not a stranger," he said, that privilege again.

"Then that makes two of us."

He waited a moment, his weight shifting from one hip to the other. "Does he know you're here?"

"Hard for him to know when he moved to Boerne to be near his son."

He smiled. She felt it in the way he relaxed his stance, in the pull drawing her to face him. It was hard to resist, that pull, because she knew what she would see. But it was so *so* easy for the very same reason. Looking up at his face gave her a very great and particular sort of enjoyment. "Have we met?"

He was shaking his head when he said, "I was about to ask you the same."

She held out her hand. "Indiana Keller."

"Keller," he said, taking it, holding it, his shake firm and lasting. "As in Tennessee? Though if you're Indiana, that's a really dumb question to ask, the state thing and all."

She thought of Dakota and her smile faltered. "And you are?" she repeated, even though she knew.

"Oliver Gatlin."

"As in the Caffey-Gatlin Academy? Though since you're standing on the center's property . . ."

"Sounds like we're both full of dumb today."

"It's nice to meet you, Oliver." Officially. Since they hadn't been introduced the night she'd first seen him.

"And you, Indiana," he said, then released her. "Though . . . weren't you at Luna and Angelo's wedding reception?"

"I was," she said, inordinately pleased that she hadn't been invisible after all. She never knew, actually, if what little effort she took with her appearance made her stand out, or blend in, or any difference at all. "And you were."

His expression darkened, but in a searching, curious way. It was nothing nefarious. Nothing strange. "And you didn't introduce yourself?"

"Then?" She shook her head. "You were too busy with Angelo."

"I'm never too busy to meet a new friend."

Friends. Was that what they were going to be? Because what she was feeling . . . "And now you have. It's always nice to be friends with the people you see regularly."

"Will we? See each other regularly?" he asked, and this time the look in his eyes did give her pause.

It was an interesting look, one that had her pulse blipping a bit as she made him wait. "I imagine we will, since I bought Hiram's place."

"Ah," he said, nodding. "So not a trespasser after all."

She looked over her shoulder at the buildings making up the Caffey-Gatlin Academy, then down at the driveway before lifting her gaze to his. "Not on Hiram's property anyway."

"And not here," he said, returning her smile, his simply devastating, with dimples and deep lines like a starburst at the corner of his eyes.

That was good to know, though her friendship with Luna Caffey kept that from being a worry. But Oliver extending such an invitation, when they had no history and had only just met, tickled her. Warmly. "Are you working with the center now?"

While she waited for him to answer, a truck slowed in front of them on Three Wishes Road, before turning into the driveway Hiram had rarely used to park behind her Camaro. The tire tracks were more ruts than anything, and visible, though the strip between was green with weeds gone wild. It was just like Will Bowman, however, not to care about the state of things beneath his wheels. Like Indiana, he let very little get in the way of what he wanted.

And that had her wondering about Oliver Gatlin. Did he share the same trait? And did it matter? It wasn't like she'd be working with Oliver as she would be with Will—though having her IJK annex across the road from the Caffey-Gatlin Academy might put them into contact more often than otherwise.

A silly thought. Luna and Angelo's reception had been a fluke encounter. She and Oliver Gatlin belonged to completely different worlds. She wasn't quite sure how she felt about the possibility of seeing him regularly.

Working with Will Bowman was going to cause her plenty of grief as it was. The man drove all who knew him to drink with the way he had of dodging questions, changing subjects, digging for truths those under his scrutiny preferred not to reveal. Revealing nothing of himself in the process.

It occurred to her then she had no idea what, besides enjoy his family's money, Oliver had done with his life. Then again, she knew nothing of Will Bowman's before he'd started working for Ten.

But when Oliver spoke, it wasn't in response to her question. "I'd ask if you had a trespasser, but since there's a Keller Construction sign on the side of that truck, I guess he's expected."

Will Bowman was never expected. A strange thought, but there it was. "Yes. I was early to meet him, so thought I'd enjoy the view from here."

He was quiet for a long moment, finally shoving his hands in his pockets and saying, "Then I'll leave you to it."

And that was it. He turned with only the slightest nod and walked back into the house, vanishing as if the last few minutes had been conjured by her imagination. Such a dismissal was probably the norm for Oliver Gatlin, but she knew so little about men, and even less about his silver spoon variety.

That lack of knowledge was likely the culprit behind the difficulty in her closing the gap time had left between her and Ten. She was trying. Oh, but she was trying, putting herself in Hope Springs, in his path, hoping to get back what she could of what they'd lost. Ten just seemed . . . unreachable, as if keeping her at arm's length was the best he could do. As if he wasn't ready for anything more.

"Too bad for you, big brother," she muttered, taking a deep breath before heading across the street. Because if all went according to plan, she was not the only family member who'd be coming back into his life.